"Don't you dare try to take advantage of me, Callahan. I don't kiss men."

Sims softened his hold. "You don't kiss them, or you don't know how to kiss them?"

"Does it matter?" Josie whispered.

"It does to me. I've never taken advantage of a woman in my life and I apologize if you thought I intended to now."

"Apology accepted," she said. "Now, if you'll just release me."

He rubbed her arms gently. "Why are you so frightened, Josie?"

"I'm not frightened."

"I was only kissing you. There's nothing wrong with kissing. Just relax. Let me thank you for all you've done for me. Let me show you how I feel."

His hands slid down to her waist, pulling her closer. "You don't know how, do you?"

"Of course I know how," she snapped.

But she didn't. She was a shy, hesitant girl, not the in-charge doctor or confident lawyer she appeared to be.

"You've been driving me crazy for the last few days. Now it's my turn. You owe me at least one kiss . . ."

SANDRA CHASTAIN

—

THE OUTLAW BRIDE

BANTAM BOOKS

New York   Toronto   London   Sydney   Auckland

THE OUTLAW BRIDE

ISBN 0-7394-1305-8

Published simultaneously in the United States and Canada

Bantam Books are published by Bantam Books, a division of Random House, Inc. Its trademark, consisting of the words "Bantam Books" and the portrayal of a rooster, is Registered in U.S. Patent and Trademark Office and in other countries. Marca Registrada. Bantam Books, 1540 Broadway, New York, New York 10036.

PRINTED IN THE UNITED STATES OF AMERICA

THIS BOOK IS FOR ELLEN TABOR
AND THE SISTERS OF CATHEDRAL SCHOOL
OF SAVANNAH, GEORGIA,
WHOSE DIVINE INSPIRATION HELPED
MAKE THIS BOOK POSSIBLE.

AND FOR ANNE BOHNER AND KARA CESARE,
EDITORS EXTRAORDINAIRE

THE OUTLAW BRIDE

PROLOGUE

Hell couldn't hurt this bad.

He awoke to white-hot pain that pierced his body. The unbearable agony radiated down his arm and across his chest into his groin, pinning him to the heat-baked earth. The dry burn of the sun overhead sucked the very air from his lungs.

Sims Callahan felt as if he were being branded with fire. He thought that he had died and gone to hell. But dying would be too easy.

Clenching his teeth, he tried to still the pounding in his head so he could think. There was something he needed to remember. Something . . .

Ben! He had to find Ben. Callahan was afraid that his brother was wounded, lying in the hot sun. His brother was too young to die.

Callahan didn't know where he was or what had happened, but he knew that if he didn't get out of the sun, he would die too. A new wave of pain racked his lower body. Then, just for a moment, there was nothing except the realization that now, when his life was about to mean something, it was slipping away. "No!" he whispered, reaching out to find something to grab onto. There was nothing except flat earth and hard rock. He was the only living thing in this hell.

Hours passed—days, maybe—and he lay, unable to move, fighting black-robed Death hovering just at the edge of his awareness. The heat turned to cold. The light to dark and back to light again. He was growing weaker.

"Are you alive, white man?"

Callahan tried to blink open his eyes to see who was talking to him, but they were sealed shut.

"Who . . ." he whispered, in a voice so hoarse that he wouldn't have recognized himself. "Who's there?"

All he heard was a grunt, then nothing but silence and the feeling of pain. The sun continued to beat down and then a shadow moved over him.

He was being lifted. "No . . ." he cried out, but felt his voice stick in his throat. His mouth was too dry to speak. Mercifully, Callahan passed out, but not before looking down and seeing an Indian's moccasins.

A feeling of doom had rushed through the Sioux Indian when he'd seen the black-and-white horse on the mountain ridge—the death horse, his people believed. He'd followed the horse to the wounded man. There was a time he wouldn't have helped a white man, but that was before a white woman saved the life of his father.

He glanced back at the ridge. The horse was gone. Bear Claw lifted the man and draped him over his horse, mounted, and rode away.

By the time the sun reached the rim of the Laramie

mountains, the Indian's destination was in sight. The man was still alive, but just barely. Bear Claw would deliver him to the valley his people shared with the white medicine woman and her family.

It was up to the medicine woman to save his life.

1

Josie Miller faced the meanest judge in the Wyoming Territory with a stolen watch in her pocket and a teary-eyed prostitute beside her.

Josie swore silently, then faced the makeshift witness stand and Judge Carl McSparren. She tried not to compare him to the polished, educated men she'd read law for back in New York City. After all, there was a time when she, too, had been just as rough around the edges as the man she now faced.

Truth was, even though she was an attorney, she hadn't changed a whole lot. She still had to prove herself in a territory where law was more often associated with gunfights than trials. Like her adoptive mother, Dr. Annie, Josie was determined to demonstrate that even a woman with a past could succeed, and she would start right here in this courtroom.

The "courtroom" was actually a saloon, and today it

was filled with townspeople who had gathered to see what the lady lawyer would do next.

Until now, that hadn't been much. Josie had helped Dr. Annie in her medical clinic more than she'd practiced law. But that was changing. She finally had a case that enabled her to help someone who needed it most in the wild west—a woman. Her client was Ellie Allgood, a bar girl accused of stealing a customer's gold watch. According to Ellie, Virgil Wayne had given it to her in payment of her "services." Since Mr. Wayne was drunk at the time, she'd hidden the watch before he decided to reclaim it. And she'd done a pretty good job. Even the sheriff, Will Spencer, couldn't find it when he searched her room. But that didn't keep him from arresting the girl. In fact, if Ellie hadn't told Josie where to look, the *alleged* stolen watch would not now be burning a hole in Josie's pocket.

Though Josie never talked about it, even to Dr. Annie, she had seen just what Ellie's line of work could do to a woman—her own mother had been a prostitute. Alone and desperate, there'd been no one to help her. That kind of life took away a woman's humanity and made her give up all hope. Now Josie was determined to find a way to help Ellie make something of herself.

Ellie could return the watch to the stranger, but in Josie's mind there was a bigger grievance at hand. The girl had performed a service, and she deserved to be paid. More importantly, Josie wasn't about to let an innocent girl be found guilty. But unless she came up with a miracle, Ellie was going to be branded a thief.

Trying desperately to think up a plan, Josie approached her client's accuser. "Now, Mr. Wayne, you say you came into this bar, the one in which we are presently located, for dinner and whiskey. What were you doing in Laramie?"

"Caught the Cold Springs Spur down here to ride the train over to Cheyenne." He gave a broad grin and announced, "Getting married on Sunday."

Josie gave the man a long, serious look. "I suppose that's why you're so dressed up?"

Wayne smiled and tugged proudly at the collar of his new black wool suit. "Yep. Marriage is a serious thing. My future pa-in-law is an important man, and I want him to know that I'm good enough to take care of his little girl."

"And you say the gold pocket watch you were carrying was sent to you by your fiancée as a betrothal gift?"

"Yes, ma'am."

"Generous gift. You're pretty excited about getting married, are you?"

"I sure am."

"Ever met the bride?" someone in the make-shift courtroom called out.

The onlookers laughed. The judge banged a shot glass he was using as a gavel on the bar and called for order. When the laughter stopped, he said, "Answer the question, Wayne."

Mr. Wayne frowned. "Well, no, but I met her pa. They have a big cattle spread south of Cheyenne that I'll have me a piece of, when we get hitched."

Josie glanced over at her client. Ellie's pale face had a defeated look that said she was ready to be found guilty. Josie shared her desperation, so she chose her words as carefully as if they were her last. "Mr. Wayne, if you were in such a hurry to get married, why didn't you take the afternoon train to Cheyenne? Why stay over?"

"Well, I just thought I might have me a little private bachelor party before I took a wife. A man's entitled, ain't he?"

Josie sighed. When it came to prostitutes, men had all the rights.

"You bet!" an observer called out. "Once you wed Azzilee Gunther you won't never have another party."

Sounds of agreement filled the room. Azzilee Gunther's far-from-attractive looks and terrible demeanor were well-known throughout the territory.

"Silence in the court!" the judge said, then turned to Wayne. "You do know she's pug ugly, don't you, son?"

He gulped. "I know, but I figure it won't matter none in the dark."

"Judge McSparren, I object!" Josie said sharply.

"So will Wayne when the lights come on," one of the men shouted.

The courtroom rippled with laughter.

Josie bit her lip in frustration. "Mr. Wayne, according to Ellie, after your . . . 'private bachelor party' you had no money and so you offered her the watch in payment for her services."

"I wouldn't never have done that. It's engraved special. Miss Azzilee would have my hide if anything happened to that watch. It . . . it belonged to her granddaddy."

Josie knew that she'd bitten off a bitter chew. The word of a dance-hall girl against a man about to marry into a wealthy family would be hard to defend. And now that Wayne had revealed that the watch belonged to the bride's granddaddy, the onlookers were beginning to grumble. The judge and the jury might tease Wayne, but they were solidly on his side. Even if she offered to return the watch, Ellie would be found guilty.

She took Ellie's hand and gave it a sympathetic squeeze. If Dr. Annie and Dan hadn't saved her from jail by taking her in and making her a member of the Miller family, Josie could have *been* Ellie. Suddenly, Josie felt a renewed determination. The Wyoming Territory had legally given women freedom, granting them the right to vote and hold office, but that wasn't enough. She had to make these men recognize this freedom.

The judge filled his whiskey glass and tapped it on the bar. "You boys quiet down back there."

The grumbling stopped when the judge addressed Josie. "Well, now, little lady, you ready to give up? The way I see it, unless you got more proof there ain't no use wasting my time."

"Wait just a second, Judge," she said. "We believe we can offer proof that will contradict Mr. Wayne's claim."

Josie was beginning to see a way out. It meant reaching back into her past, a past she'd thought she'd left behind. Proving Ellie's innocence wouldn't come from upholding the law, but from breaking it. If Josie failed, she'd be ruined. If her ruse worked, Ellie would be free.

"Mr. Wayne, how long would you say you occupied my client's bed?"

"I don't know. Maybe five, ten minutes, all tol'."

"And did you remove your clothing?"

There was a gasp. Josie could tell from his expression that Wayne didn't want to describe his actions.

"Uh, no, ma'am. I didn't. I just unbuttoned my pants and she kinda laid herself on the bed."

"And where was your watch?"

"In my coat pocket."

"Is that the same coat you're wearing now?"

"Yes, ma'am."

"And were you wearing it when . . . when you unbuttoned your trousers?"

"No, ma'am. I wasn't wearing it. Didn't want to wrinkle it none. Hung it on the back of the chair."

Josie turned to Ellie and whispered, "You sure you never saw the watch until you asked for your money?"

"Sure as can be, ma'am."

Josie turned back to Wayne. "And how much did Ellie charge you for this five minutes?"

"Ah . . . I don't rightly remember. I'd had me a few drinks by then."

"But you do remember taking precautions against losing your gold watch, don't you?"

He looked startled. "Of course."

"Mr. Wayne, if the watch was safely in your jacket pocket, then how did Ellie get it?"

"Well . . . it must have happened when—when—when she hugged me after."

Ellie blanched and shook her head.

"She hugged you?"

A ripple of laughter broke out from the crowd.

Wayne grinned. "Yeah, reckon she was grateful."

"Why don't you show me how she hugged you, Mr. Wayne," Josie said, walking toward the witness in the chair by the bar.

"Show you?"

"Show me. Just stand up and pretend that I'm Ellie."

"But I couldn't do that, ma'am. I mean, you ain't no—"

"Thief? Neither is Ellie. This is Wyoming and we pride ourselves on being fair, Mr. Wayne. This jury won't convict a woman of theft unless you can show us how it happened."

Josie swallowed hard, knowing that she was about to commit an illegal act. "I'm a little taller than Ellie, but tell me where she put her hands and where you put your hands."

Wayne looked at the judge pleadingly.

"Hug her," the judge said, a big grin now covering his face. "If that's what she wants, hug her."

What Josie wanted was to administer a little old-fashioned western justice to the judge. Instead, she waited for Wayne's response.

Awkwardly, Wayne put his arms around Josie.

"And where were Ellie's arms?" Josie said.

"I reckon they were around me." His voice cracked from sheer nervousness.

Josie slid her hands inside his jacket, fumbling a bit as if she were uncertain, embarrassed even. "Like this?"

"Yes, that's it."

"And where was your watch?"

Wayne patted his chest. "It was right in here, in this coat pocket."

Josie bit her lip to keep from smiling. "So you think she picked your pocket?"

"She did. That's why I had her arrested."

Wayne was beginning to sense trouble, but he couldn't figure out where it was coming from.

Josie removed her arms from Wayne's jacket and walked away from him.

"Let me ask you again, Mr. Wayne, are you sure you just didn't lose your watch or maybe—since you'd been drinking—forget where you put it?"

"Course not. I always put it right here, in this inside pocket." He poked two fingers inside and went silent. His eyes widened, and he seemed to have lost his voice.

"What's wrong, Mr. Wayne?" Josie stepped back toward the frustrated bridegroom and took his hand by the wrist, pulling his fingers from the pocket. Curled around the fingers was a gold pocket watch. His eyes grew even wider.

"Is that your watch?" Josie asked. "Better let me check the inscription."

She took it from his hand, flipped it open, and read aloud, *"To Poopsie from Sweetie."* Josie turned to the judge. "Looks like Mr. Wayne made a mistake, Judge. That's understandable. What do you say we dismiss the charges against Miss Allgood?"

Wayne began to stutter, "But . . . But . . . I know that girl had it. I gave it to her myself. I just meant to—"

"What's that?" the judge said. "Did I understand you to say that you gave it to her?"

"Well, yes. I mean, no." Wayne began to backtrack. "I guess I just lost it. But it appears to be found now. So I reckon I'd better get on up the road."

The judge shook his head. "Son, if you're going to marry Azzilee Gunther, I guess you deserve a break. Case dismissed."

"Not yet, Judge McSparren," Josie said. "In the interest of justice, I insist that my client be paid. She performed a service for which she is owed a fee of"—she leaned toward Ellie, then straightened up—"two dollars. But because of the trouble he's caused her, we're asking an additional fifty cents in attorney's fees to be donated to the Laramie City Fund for Women and Children."

Judge McSparren looked at Josie in disbelief, then burst out laughing. "You know, girl, I think you're right. Wayne, give *Miss* Allgood two dollars and fifty cents."

"But, Judge, I done said, I ain't got no money."

The judge pursed his lips. "What about this, Miss Josie, suppose I have a little talk with Miss Azzilee's pa. I'm guessing he'll be more than happy to discreetly take care of Wayne's bills."

"That would be fine, Judge," Josie agreed.

The judge leaned across the bar and gave Josie a stern look. "I don't know how you pulled that watch business off, but it was a pretty slick move, and I know you didn't learn it from a law book."

"I don't know what you mean, Judge, but I thank you," Josie said, and began to gather up her papers before he charged *her* with a crime. He had to realize that she'd committed a morally justified act.

"You do right good, for a woman," the judge said. "Course, it comes natural, I reckon, with a mama who's a doctor and a daddy who's a government official. Hear your little sister's smart, too. Guess it runs in the blood."

"Thank you, Judge." Josie could have told him that her sister, Laura, was the natural child in the family, while she herself was adopted. Josie's real pedigree would have put the judge back a step. And it wouldn't help her fledgling law career for the world to know she'd won her case because she was as good a pickpocket as she was a lawyer.

Ellie approached Josie with a grateful look. "I thank you, ma'am, fer getting me off," Ellie said. Her voice dropped to a whisper. "I know you put that watch back in his pocket. Why'd you do it, Miss Miller? You could have gotten into some terrible trouble."

"A person sometimes has to take a risk when she believes in her cause. You deserve to be paid."

Ellie nodded and gave Josie a sudden smile.

"Now promise me you won't earn any more money taking care of men."

A quick wince crossed Ellie's face, then disappeared. She nodded. "I promise."

Ellie was leaving through the side door just as Sheriff Will Spencer came in. "Josie?" Will said in a worried voice, "somebody just brought word there's a wounded man out at your house."

"Holy hell, Dr. Annie and Dan have gone to New

York. How'd he get out there instead of the office here in town?"

"That Indian friend of your mama's, Bear Claw, brought him."

Josie stuffed her law books and papers into her carrying case. "I'd better get going," she said as she pushed open the saloon doors and dashed across the street to the livery stable where old Solomon was still hitched up to the Miller buggy. Will followed close behind.

"I'll ride out there with you," Will said, "and we'll bring him back to town."

"Will, that's not necessary. I don't need protecting. I can look after myself."

Will reached out to help her up into the buggy, but Josie didn't wait. She lifted the mud-stained train of her walking dress, climbed up, plopped down on the seat, and gathered the reins. "Let's go boy, we've got an injured man at home."

Will jumped into the buggy at the last minute. "I'm sure you can take care of yourself, Josie, but I'm coming with you."

"All right," Josie said impatiently. "Let's go."

The sheriff smiled. From the time Josie came to Laramie fourteen years ago, she'd been the most talked-about, envied, and admired female in the territory— outside of Dr. Annie. Everyone knew that Josie Miller tried to be a stern lady lawyer. She even dressed like one, corseting her curvaceous frame into the hourglass dresses now in style. Her honey-blonde hair refused to be confined in the curls of the times, so she braided it and pinned it in a knot. But the knot tended to slip and the strands escaped regularly. With her wide blue eyes and disheveled dress, her attempt to look like a professional attorney was doomed to failure. But she was smart.

She knew the law and she knew almost as much about doctoring as her ma.

"What do we know about the patient?" Josie asked.

"Bear Claw said he found him west of the mountains. He kept talking about a black-and-white horse."

"Black-and-white horse?" Josie was afraid she knew what Bear Claw was talking about. Some of the Sioux believed Death rode a black-and-white horse. Others believed the horse was just a messenger from the spirit world. If Bear Claw was right, she'd better get home quick.

"Did anyone else see the horse?"

"Not that I know of. Could be it belonged to the man."

"Yeah. And it could be a maverick, running loose out there on the plains." Josie gave Solomon another sharp rap, urging him into a trot. The buggy bumped across the ruts. Her hairpins fell out and her face was streaked with perspiration.

Will didn't say anything else. And Josie concentrated on her driving. She had a peculiar feeling about this, a feeling of danger she hadn't had in a long time. Something was about to happen. And it might not be as easy to fix as picking a pocket.

2

The Miller ranch was an oddity in Wyoming. Dan Miller had designed it to look like a Spanish hacienda he'd seen in New Mexico, with a courtyard wrapped around the rambling adobe-brick house.

Josie drove the buggy up the long drive toward the house and smiled. Protected by the mountains to the east and the west, the trees were green and wild animals scurried away from the sound of the wheels. The afternoon sunlight gave the adobe a pink glow, and the smell of flowers caught by the summer wind brought a special kind of welcome. Dan had built the house the third year of his marriage to Dr. Annie, the year Laura was born.

Laura was ten now, the same age Josie had been when she'd picked Dr. Annie's pockets at the rail station and Dan had entered both their lives. That's where the similarities ended. Laura was calm and studious, with a voice as melodious as a bird's and beauty that caused people to stop and stare. Laura was the lady that Josie had tried to be—tried and failed.

There were two wings to the Miller house. One wing housed Dr. Annie's clinic, and the other contained the family's sleeping quarters. Connecting the two were a foyer, a large gathering room, and a dining area.

Josie urged Solomon to the clinic wing and climbed down, handing the reins to Wash, the old ranch hand who had emerged from the barn.

"Take care of Solomon," she said, moving toward the door to the clinic and nodding at Lubina, the Millers' housekeeper who hovered nervously inside.

Josie approached the unconscious man Bear Claw had brought to her mother's clinic. She took one look at him and felt a funny shiver run through her. He'd been laid out on the examination table. His clothes were caked with blood. His face was turned away and the side nearest her was obscured by a strand of thick dark hair that lay like a whip across his cheek. It was entangled in the dusty growth of his beard. He looked like a dark angel who'd been shot out of the sky. Josie thought that if she ever had to defend this man in court, he'd be convicted on his looks alone.

She pressed her fingers against the artery in his neck and felt the pulsing. Josie was once again struck with a sense of impending danger.

"Es too much blood, *señorita*," Lubina said, wringing her hands and wailing loudly.

"Stop that caterwauling, Lubina!" Josie snapped. "I don't want him scared to death." She tried to lift his shirt front, but the blood had stuck it tight to his shoulder. She didn't force it. "Looks like he was shot a couple of days ago. You know who he is, Will?"

"Never saw him before. And until we find out, I think

I'd better hold him in town, where I can keep an eye on him."

Even though he seemed unconscious, Josie had the uncanny sensation that the stranger could hear her. The danger she'd sensed skittered up her backbone and hovered somewhere behind her lungs, vibrating like the tail of a rattlesnake poised to strike. The feeling created a tension so strong she was surprised she wasn't visibly shaking.

"No, he can't be moved," she heard herself saying, "not until I treat his wounds."

Will looked at her with worry in his eyes. Josie tolerated him like an older brother, but there were times when she knew he wanted more.

Josie began to focus on the injured man's lower body. Most of the blood had dried on his trousers. "We'll have to get him out of those clothes," she said, glancing over her shoulder. "Lubina, help me."

"Lubina will not touch this devil," the housekeeper said, wringing her hands helplessly. "I ask the Holy Mother for strength, but she doesn't hear this poor feeble woman's plea."

"He's no devil, and I don't know about the Holy Mother," Josie said, "but when *my* mother returns—"

Will interrupted. "You hold his legs, Josie. I'll get the boots."

"All right. Lubina, please go get some hot water and clean cloths."

The housekeeper wasted no time getting out of the room.

Josie planted herself firmly against the man's right thigh and felt a shiver rush to the point of contact. She took a deep breath, nodded, and clasped the wounded man's knee while Will wrenched off his boots.

Josie might have spent a good portion of her youth assisting Dr. Annie in the sickroom, but she'd never been faced with treating a dangerous-looking man like this alone. Dealing with a simple wound was one thing, but for most of the last four years she'd been studying law in New York. The man on the table wasn't the only one in trouble.

Josie swallowed hard. She'd never totally undressed a man—certainly not in front of anyone. His skin was as rough as his appearance. Whoever he was, he'd been a man who worked for a living.

Will broke her train of thought. "Until we find out who this man is, I don't feel right about you having a stranger out here. I think we ought to send Dan and Dr. Annie a telegram in New York."

"We don't have time for that," Josie said, unbuttoning the wounded man's shirt. "Besides, this man is too near death to be a threat to me or anyone else."

"All right," Will said reluctantly. "I'll get back to town and make sure we haven't had any reports of a train holdup or a bank robbery. I'll be back to check on you in the morning."

Josie laid her hand on the hard plane of her patient's stomach. "He isn't an outlaw," she said softly, then wondered where that certainty came from. He might not be a criminal, but somebody was angry with him. Considering that one of his wounds appeared to be in the groin, a jealous husband could have shot him.

"You don't know what he is. You're just like your mama. You're the second stubbornest woman in the territory," Will grumbled as he left the clinic.

"That I am," Josie agreed, and pushed the door closed behind him. She unfastened the man's empty gun belt and his suspenders and then reached to unfasten his denim trousers.

The stranger's gloved hand shot across his body and caught her wrist.

Fear washed over her. What if she was wrong about him being an outlaw? She wished she hadn't let Will leave. "I'm only trying to help you," she said, "but if you'd rather bleed to death, it can be arranged."

He turned toward her with a cold, black-as-sin stare that held her motionless. Lines of pain—or menace—radiated from the corners of the stormiest eyes she'd ever seen. And despite his grimacing expression, Josie knew he was strikingly handsome and very dangerous.

The stranger let go of her wrist. He closed his eyes as if he had lapsed into unconsciousness again.

Josie relaxed her shoulders and let out a silent breath as she waited for her racing heart to slow. Swallowing hard, she took Dr. Annie's scissors and cut into his trousers, her fingers tucked beneath his waistband to guide the blades. As she inched downward, she brushed his thick body hair—and a mound of soft flesh.

She jerked back and lost her grip on the scissors. The blades slipped sideways.

The man let out a muffled oath, caught her shoulder, and pulled her forward. Josie suddenly found her cheek pressed against his thigh.

She froze.

Scream! Lubina will come, she thought. But when she felt him breathe, felt the warmth of his wounded body beneath her, she waited. "Let go of me," she said in a low voice.

He was only acting instinctively, she realized, and slowly she pulled from his grip. "You do that again and I'll let the sheriff have you," she snapped. Taking a shaky breath, she steadied her trembling fingers and finished clipping his trousers. Peeling the fabric open, she found a gaping wound. She worked her fingers beneath his body and located a smaller wound. What had happened? He didn't look like he could possibly be a victim—he was too big and mean-looking—though it was obvious from the wounds that he was being pursued.

Miraculously, the bullet hadn't hit anything vital. It looked as though it had simply gone through the back and out the front of his groin without nicking a major vessel. The man's wounds weren't fatal, but considering what he must have gone through, she didn't know how he had managed to stay alive.

Josie shifted her focus to his shoulder and quickly peeled off his rough chambray shirt, revealing a muscled chest covered with a mat of hair. She felt heat emanate from his body. He was feverish—or maybe she was the feverish one, she decided as she jerked back to study her patient.

Footsteps announced Lubina's approach. Quickly Josie drew a sheet over her patient's lower body.

"Thank you, Lubina," she said, taking the hot water and clean cloths from the housekeeper. Josie then waved her off, took a deep breath, and got to work.

Two pans of water and three cloths later, she'd washed away the dried blood. She then filled the groin and the shoulder wounds with sulfur and covered them with cloth pads to prevent infection.

The kind of sweat that came from physical exertion ran down Josie's neck and puddled between her breasts. She could hear the man's steady breathing in the silence. He was lucky. He'd be sore and weak for awhile, but nothing appeared to be broken and, if infection didn't set in, he'd probably be able to shoot a gun again.

Josie moved Dr. Annie's stool closer to the patient's bed and sat, letting out a long, exhausted sigh. She peeled back the clean sheet that she had draped across his body and took a quick peek at his groin. The bandage was tinged with blood. She closed her eyes for a moment, then covered him once more.

The urge to take another peek at the dark-eyed stranger was rapidly becoming a temptation.

3

For two long days and nights, Josie Miller stayed with her patient, watching him and studying her law books. The stranger was now her responsibility, medically and legally. Will would be after him soon, wanting to move him to the town jail. She'd better be ready to defend his rights if she wanted him to stay and recuperate.

Fact was, he still wasn't well. A fever had swept through his body and turned him into the devil. Josie fought him physically when periodic bouts of half-consciousness made his body convulse, and she soothed him with comforting words when his cries for someone named Ben turned into tears of rage. Ben seemed to give him the strength to survive, and she began to feel a growing admiration for her patient's unyielding determination to find him.

Who was this Ben, and how did he fit into this mysterious man's life?

Will Spencer was convinced that this was a dangerous man, but he'd had no report of any criminal activity on which to base his fears. He came by the Millers' house frequently, but he seemed to agitate the man, so Josie banned him from the sickroom.

Lubina was too frightened to enter the room at all and hovered outside the door renouncing Josie's patient as the devil.

"I saw the black-and-white horse the night he came," she said on the fourth day after the stranger's arrival. "The Indians believe the stallion es the death horse."

"That horse is just some maverick out looking for mares," Josie argued.

"Then tell me why he came in the middle of a storm, the very same night that devil in there came?"

"I can't." Josie walked to the open door and stared at the distant hills. A huge, dark cloud loomed on the horizon. "But maybe we'll see him again. There's another storm brewing."

As if fed by the energy of the storm, Sims Callahan began to wake. From behind closed eyes, he sensed the flash of lightning and heard thunder roll across the heavens like a herd of stampeding cattle. He thrashed wildly for a moment in a fit of confusion, but as the storm quieted he grew still.

A brisk wind blew across him, pushing away the darkness, bringing the fragrance of clean rain and, finally, awareness.

He opened his eyes and began to focus on the woman sitting in the chair beside his bed. She had slumped forward, apparently asleep. Her head rested against his shoulder and as her hair brushed against his chin, he could smell the sweet womanly scent of her.

He stroked her arm. "Am I dead?"

Josie jerked herself up and stared in amazement. "Not yet. But you've been a very sick man. I've done the best I can, but I'm no doctor. Your life is in God's hands."

Whoever the woman was, she had spunk. "Well, I hope His hands are gentler than yours, darlin'. You damn near killed me."

"Who are you?" she asked.

Wind gusted through the open window causing the lamp to flame. Callahan saw that her eyes were blue, the midnight kind of blue that cloaked the plains when a storm rode through the region. "Who are *you*?" he asked.

"I'm Josie Miller, but I asked you first. Are you an outlaw?"

No answer. The man had closed his eyes. He'd drifted off to sleep, or at least he'd pretended to.

"Coward!" Josie sighed in frustration.

The clouds emptied in torrents, rain hitting the mountains with a vengeance. She ran toward the window, reaching for the shutters to close them against the onslaught. Outside, a lightning bolt lit up the darkness, and she saw him, the ghost horse. The great black-and-white stallion stood on a ridge, looking down, his tail held high, and his mane whipping in the wind. He was just as Bear Claw had once described.

Her heart raced. She wasn't certain which had caused it: the violent storm, the ghost horse, or the dangerous stranger lying in her bed.

Then, just as quickly as he had appeared, the stallion vanished.

Will Spencer came by the next morning with an announcement. "I'm moving your patient into town, Josie, even if it kills him."

"Why?"

"I put out the word about a wounded man. There've been no holdups or bank robberies recently. All I've got is a herd of fancy, unclaimed imported cows at the rail yard. Apparently Sims Callahan and his younger brother, Ben, were delivering a saddlebag full of money to pay for them, but they never arrived in Laramie. I have a feeling your man may be one of the brothers or knows what happened to them. If he doesn't, I'll have to send the steers back."

"No, you don't. You can't send them back without a legal writ." Josie was already planning a defense, but something Will had said stuck in her mind. He'd mentioned Ben. She knew that name—all too well. The wounded man had called it out over and over in his feverish state. "Where are the Callahan brothers from?"

"Sharpsburg now," Will answered, "but I understand that they're originally from somewhere in the east—the Carolinas, I think. The two came up with the idea to invest in these cattle. They brought some other ranchers in on the deal, but the Callahans insisted on driving the cattle home. Now the money has disappeared, and your patient seems to match the description of one of the brothers."

"Well, then, how'd this one get shot?"

Will shook his head. "I don't know, and until I do I want him in jail. I'm sending a couple of the ranchers out here to identify your patient. They'll bring a wagon to move him."

"My *patient* cannot be moved, Will." Josie had battled to save his life and she wasn't about to lose it now. "The law plainly says that prosecution of larceny is based on proof of the defendant's intent to steal. My client would have had to make off with the money, and he certainly wasn't carrying a saddlebag filled with money. Bear Claw would have said so."

Josie knew she was protecting a man she knew nothing about. But she also knew that Dr. Annie had once done that for her. She now felt sure that this dark-eyed man was Sims Callahan. But until Will produced evidence, she refused to believe that he was a thief. If Dan and Dr. Annie hadn't rescued her from her life as a pickpocket when she was ten years old, she could well be the one the sheriff was after now.

This man was as alone and vulnerable as she had once been. Even if he was guilty, he deserved a fair trial. And Josie Miller would make sure that he got one. After all, she was the best lawyer in Wyoming, or at least she would be someday.

"You don't understand, Josie. Those ranchers are pretty darn mad. I'm taking him into protective custody—for his own good."

"No, Will. If I have to call Bear Claw and the Sioux Nation to protect him, that's what I'll do."

Will finally accepted, with one stipulation. "Promise me you'll send for Bear Claw and make him stay around until we know who your patient is. For now, be careful and keep that toothless old stable hand, Wash, close to the house."

"I will," she agreed. Anything to get him out of the house before her patient called Ben's name out loud. She led Will to the door, opened it, and stood impatiently while he walked to his horse.

"Oh," he said, turning back, "Ellie sent you this." He reached into his pocket and withdrew something wrapped in a piece of velvet.

"Ellie?" she repeated, knowing that his use of Ellie's

first name was out of character for Will, who was usually very proper. "What is it?" she asked, hurrying toward him.

"She called it a payment on what she owes you. Normally, I'd have refused to bring it, but considering the current situation in your home, maybe it's a good idea."

Inside the material was a lady's derringer, its finish polished to perfection. "I can't take this." She couldn't take a gift from Ellie, knowing how much of a sacrifice it had been for the girl. Josie had more money than she'd ever need. She'd made a lot of money playing the stock market with her grandfathers while she'd lived in New York. It was still sitting untouched in the Sinclair Bank, earning even more every day. She hadn't decided yet what she would do with the money, but a need would show itself eventually.

Will shook his head. "Don't think you have much of a choice. That saloon girl is a proud little thing. She's already quit her . . . job."

"Quit her job?" When Josie had told Ellie to change her life, she hadn't expected it to happen so quickly. "Will, you'll help her find something else, won't you?"

His expression spoke louder than his words. "Like what?"

"Like maybe at the general store."

He gave an uncomfortable laugh. "Josie, no self-respecting housewife is gonna buy from a woman like Ellie."

"I'm no housewife, but if somebody doesn't give her work soon. I'm going to open a store and hire her myself," Josie said. "If a woman wants to change her life, someone should help her do it."

Will shook his head. "You and Dr. Annie. Always looking for a challenge, mostly on behalf of someone else." He looked toward the clinic and his attention was drawn to the derringer. "You just be careful," he cautioned. "You can shoot it, can't you?"

"Every woman in the west knows how to shoot a gun, Will."

Long after Will's horse had left the courtyard, Josie was still dwelling on his words. *Be careful.* That's what her grandfathers had advised when she left New York to practice law in Wyoming. Of course, they'd added one more thing: *but don't let it stop you from taking a chance if it's a good one. Go with your hunch, Josie.* Josie thought about the times she'd beaten those two at poker and she laughed to herself at the memory. Nothing would stop her grandfathers from taking a chance—even a bad one. Roylston Sinclair was seen by many as a prissy intellect, and Teddy Miller never pretended to be anything more than the gambler he was. How the two lovable old rascals ever produced upstanding children like Annie and Dan Miller was a mystery. Josie should have been their daughter.

Her grandfathers would understand why she was taking a chance on her patient. Explaining her actions to her adoptive parents might be harder.

Still, she had a hunch about this man. In the absence of proof, lawyers set their defense on instinct all the time. She just wasn't sure if women should do the same thing.

The door opened and shut. Callahan heard her soft footsteps approach the bed. He didn't have to open his eyes to know it was her, the golden-haired woman who had flitted through his dreams. There was a spark deep inside him, in a place her fingers hadn't touched.

He'd been awake for awhile and when he was finally ready to open his eyes, she was the first thing he saw.

"I've come to wash and shave you."

"No!"

"No? Well I'm sorry, but I don't intend to touch you again until I get rid of the smell that's plaguing my mother's clinic."

"That's not all you're going to have to get rid of," he growled, "if you don't bring me a chamber pot."

Stunned by his announcement, Josie stared dumbly for a moment and then scurried to the washstand, returning with a china pot.

"Help me sit up!" he said.

She slipped her arm beneath his shoulders and lifted, avoiding his stormy gaze. It wouldn't be the first time she'd cleaned up after him, but he'd been unconscious then. Now he was—she looked at his heaving chest—one very conscious, virile man. She guiltily cast her eyes to the ceiling as she strained to lift his back.

"What the hell?" He swore and came to a sitting position. "I'm naked as a damn jaybird. Where're my clothes?"

"I burned them." She handed him the pot.

He took it, almost dropped it, and cursed again.

"Let me hold it," she said, trying to sound like Dr. Annie would have.

"Close your eyes," he demanded. He was hopping mad.

The sound she heard brought an unwelcome blush to her cheeks. She wouldn't have thought, after his fever, that he'd have stored so much bodily fluid. He must have swallowed more of the broth than she'd thought. Finally, there was silence.

"Are you done?" she asked.

"I am."

Josie covered the chamber pot and lowered it to the floor. She put her arm around him for support as he leaned back. His strength surprised her. Something almost physical sparked between them, hot and strong. He interrupted the moment by reaching for the sheet. "I assure you, Mr. Callahan, you have nothing I haven't seen."

"And I'll bet you took a good look, didn't you?"

Her face flamed. "I would never take advantage of you," Josie said haughtily. "After all, I am a well-respected member of the community. A lawyer, in fact."

He frowned. "None of the lawyers I know are women."

Josie fumed. "Well, if you are Sims Callahan, you'd better hope and pray that you've finally met one because the sheriff's got a posse out looking for a couple of outlaws—the Callahan brothers, Sims and *Ben*. Seems they've disappeared along with a saddlebag full of money that was supposed to have paid for a herd of cattle. When you were brought to the house, you were out of your head. You kept calling out for someone named Ben. I'm thinking that means you're Sims."

"They didn't find Ben?"

"You were the only one that Bear Claw found."

Callahan wrinkled his forehead. "Who's Bear Claw?"

"He's the chief of a Sioux tribe who lives on part of our land. He's a friend of ours—and yours too, now."

Callahan lay still, absorbing all of this new information. A sea of questions swept through his mind. What had happened to Ben? Did he get away? Or was he lying out there somewhere, full of bullet holes? He felt like a caged bear. Helpless. Unable to do anything. "Get me some clothes, Miss—what is your name, anyway?"

"It's Josie Miller," she replied. "Miss Miller to you."

"And my horse?" he asked, ignoring her response.

"You have no horse. At least, Bear Claw didn't bring it in. And it wouldn't matter if you did. You wouldn't get ten feet before you'd be food for the coyotes."

"You don't understand," he said, and tried to sit up once more. Dammit, he had to get out of here. Ben's life was at stake.

"No, Mr. Callahan, *you* don't understand. You've been more or less unconscious for four days, and you've lost a lot of blood. You're tough, but right now you're very weak. It's going to be a while before you can leave this house. Please be still, Sims."

"Call me Callahan," he said wearily. "And I'm not a thief, damn it."

He had admitted to being a Callahan. Fear washed over Josie. He *was* the man Will Spencer was looking for. But she still wasn't convinced that he had committed a crime. She knew how it felt to be branded a thief, even when you weren't.

Callahan knew she was right. He was too weak to go searching for Ben. He stopped fidgeting, then closed his eyes for a long, silent moment. "I really wasn't out of my head all the time. I kinda enjoyed waking up to my guardian angel lying next to me."

"I'm not an angel. Now lie still while I shave you." Josie lathered her hands with a cake of soap and plopped suds on Callahan's face. She'd never shaved a man, but she'd watched her adoptive father, Dan, shave often enough. Not much to it, she decided, working suds into Callahan's thick, black beard. His whiskers curled around her fingers and made her remember her initial reaction. Sims Callahan had hot hair.

She reached for the straight razor.

Callahan opened his eyes.

"I hope you know how to use that," he said.

"Nope," she admitted. "But I expect I will have learned by the time I'm done, won't I?"

After she got rid of the beard, she washed his face and neck and chest. Lord, he had a broad chest. He didn't complain when she changed his shoulder bandage, though she knew it hurt. But when she reached to pull down the sheet, her fingers hesitated. Viewing his manhood had been difficult enough when he was asleep. Now, he was awake and aware of every move she made.

"If it's your mother who is the doctor, why are you treating me?"

"She's away on a holiday. Since I've helped her over the years, Bear Claw brought you to me."

"How many men have you washed?" he asked.

"Plenty," she snapped, tugging at the sheet. "Now let go."

"First, let me have your hand, Josie," he said, ordering her, not asking.

He took her hand in his large calloused one and laid it on his stomach. She couldn't conceal the jolt of awareness that shot through her.

"Yeah, that's what I thought, Miss Josie Miller. It is Miss, isn't it?"

"Yes, it is. I've never married. And I never intend to."

"I take it that means you're a virgin?"

Josie gasped at the embarrassing assumption.

"Then you'd better close your eyes, or you're going to see a man's body announce its reaction to a woman."

Josie didn't have to ask what Callahan was talking about. The sheet that was resting on his lap began to rise and thrust forward as if it had a life of its own.

"It's called desire, darlin', and it's happening. Right now."

"No," she whispered, and fled from the room, bumping into Lubina, who was bringing clean towels.

"What's wrong, Josie?"

"He's alive," she said dryly.

"Of course he es alive," Lubina repeated. "You said he would live."

"Yes, but he seems to have a new problem," Josie announced loudly. "His male organ is becoming enlarged. He's a very sick man so it must be"—her voice got deliberately louder, enough for Callahan to hear it—"infection. Draining it is a medical procedure Dr. Annie never taught me. I'm going to have to study my medical books."

Lubina crossed herself. "Dear Holy Mother," she repeated, gazing heavenward. "Whatever you do, don't let Miss Josie figure it out."

4

Callahan took a deep breath and gritted his teeth as he pushed himself up. He'd been shot before. Hell, he'd been shot more than once, but this might be the all-time, flat-out most embarrassing hurt he'd ever been through. One bullet wound he could have managed, but two, in different parts of his body, should have erased any desire he'd felt. They hadn't.

He ought to be angry with his angel of mercy for running from the room. Instead, he couldn't stop himself from smiling. Miss Josie Miller might have been embarrassed by his erection, but he wasn't. *Everything* still worked.

Callahan's thoughts shifted to Ben, and for the rest of the day, he concentrated on trying to remember what had happened. The memories came back, one piece at a time. He and Ben had been riding north from Sharpsburg toward Laramie, when out of nowhere, three or four men on horseback attacked. The bastards had picked their spot well, hiding above them behind a formation of rocks until he and Ben were almost past. Then they started firing.

He'd been hit immediately, in the back, just below his belt, but he'd concealed it from Ben, throwing his brother the saddlebag filled with the money and yelling for him to ride like hell. Callahan had reined his horse behind the last boulder and returned fire, holding them at bay just long enough for Ben to get away. Then he headed in the opposite direction. That's when the second shot caught him in the shoulder. He still might have made it if his horse hadn't gone down.

After that, things got a little hazy. He remembered another horse, a big dun-colored animal with an odd scar on its haunch. The mark looked like a crescent moon with a circle at one tip. On the horse's back rode a shadowy figure, but he couldn't recall anything beyond that, except heat and pain. He didn't know how long he'd lain there before the Indian found him and brought him here.

If Ben was really missing and the money for the cattle was gone, they'd lose the ranch. Without the new cattle or the money they'd contributed to buy them, they wouldn't be able to survive. None of the ranchers would. This would be the second home the Callahan brothers had lost. The family plantation in South Carolina had been the first. Neither Ben nor Callahan could claim credit for that. But the loss of their ranch, as fledgling as it was, would be their fault. He could take losing the ranch, but he couldn't take losing his only brother.

Will Spencer and his men sighted the mountains in the distance and the grasslands to the south. He climbed off his horse and squatted, studying the ground. The rain hadn't washed the trail away, and with Bear Claw's help, he'd been able to trace the Callahan brothers' trek north. They reached a pocket of rocks where it looked as if there'd been some kind of confrontation. Faint tracks revealed that several horses must have converged with two horses splitting off, one riding west and the other going north, hell-bent for leather.

Farther up the trail they'd found evidence of another scuffle. Under a scattering of rock there were bloodstains. Either one of the riders had been shot or he'd fallen off his horse. This was where Bear Claw had found Josie's patient. The Indian told them that he shot a limping horse he'd found beyond the rocks nearby. An animal with a broken leg was always put out of its misery.

The posse doubled back, studying the first horse's tracks, and Will mulled over the evidence. There *was* the possibility that Bear Claw was involved. After the failed treaty of Fort Bridger in 1868, the Sioux, the Shoshone, and the Arapaho continued to wreck havoc on one another. Because of this, the settlers—including Will—had become distrustful of any Indian who was not living on the reservation. It was only because of Dan Miller that Bear Claw and the rest of his Sioux were tolerated by the authorities. Will knew that this tolerance would end if Bear Claw was in any way an accomplice of the Callahan brothers. But the Millers trusted him completely, and so Will would assume that Bear Claw was innocent—for now.

On the way back to Laramie, Will thought of a more likely conclusion. Suppose the whole thing had been a setup between the Callahan boys? From what he'd been able to find out, Sims Callahan's past was pretty spotty. For a short time, he'd ridden with Quantrill's Raiders, who were notorious for looting and killing in Kansas, all the while claiming to be fighting for the Confederacy. Some of the most infamous outlaws had ridden with the gang, including the James boys and the Younger brothers.

The older Callahan was a rough loner, always avoiding people. The younger one, Ben, was more civilized, always reading about new ways to improve their cattle. Considering that the other ranchers had gone along with his plan to buy the cattle, this Ben fellow appeared to be well-liked. Could Ben have shot his own brother? Perhaps there had been a falling out between the brothers, or maybe he had realized that not even new cattle would have been enough to bail them out of debt. It would have been a temptation for either brother to keep all the money and head farther west. But for Ben to leave his brother for dead? Will was stumped. He was inclined to believe that Ben was dead too. Nothing else made sense.

"Let's head back to Laramie, boys."

His posse turned their horses north and forced the tired animals into a gallop. Will was sure of only one thing: The wounded man was the key to unlocking the mystery.

Josie paced back and forth, trying to summon enough courage to enter the sickroom. She'd be the first to admit that she was a proud person, proud of winning her case before Judge McSparren, proud of the medical knowledge she'd learned from her adoptive mother—but since that man had come along, she'd become downright bashful.

She'd seen Callahan in *all* his glory and could still hear his laughter as she dashed out of the room like some kind of schoolgirl. But she wasn't a schoolgirl, and behind her embarrassed physical reaction lay suspicion. Most of her court cases forced her to interact with mean, dangerous men who had the same look in their eyes that Callahan did.

That look had turned Josie back into Joe again. Joe, the tough ragamuffin boy who'd tried to pick Dr. Annie's pocket at the Brooklyn train station. Though her real mother had tried early on to protect Josie from the truth about her own profession, in the end, Josie was no stranger to men and women—together. The walls of a house of prostitution were thin. There was little she hadn't seen or heard.

The physical mechanics of mating she understood, but the kind of desire Callahan talked about was something she'd never comprehend. Josie had vowed never to let a man make her lose control. None had.

Until now.

Her pacing took her to the kitchen. "Lubina," she asked hesitantly, "I know you've never married, but have you ever . . . been with a man?"

Lubina dropped the tin basin she was carrying and watched it roll down the corridor to a stop. "Been . . . with a man, *señorita*?"

"That's what I asked."

Lubina closed her eyes and shook her head. "Miss Josie, you should not even think about that. Dr. Annie wouldn't like it."

Josie thought about Dr. Annie and how she and Dan were forever touching and sharing secret smiles. "I may not ever have a husband, Lubina, but when Dr. Annie returns, I intend to ask her how it feels to want one."

A roaring voice reverberated down the corridor, followed by a crash from the hospital room.

"That devil is calling you, Miss Josie," Lubina said.

"You go see what he wants," Josie snapped.

"No, ma'am, es time for me to go to church." Lubina untied her apron and draped it over the hook beside the kitchen door. "I'll send Wash to look after him," she said, wringing her hands as she stood by the door.

"Lubina, you big coward. Come and help me."

A bang was followed by another roar.

"Hurry, *señorita*," Lubina said, "he es going to destroy your mama's sickroom. None of her other folks ever busted up the place."

Josie sucked in her cheeks. Lubina was right. The dark, angry man was *her* responsibility. She'd put a stop to his behavior—right this minute.

She marched down the hall and flung open the door. The bed had been dragged halfway across the room. Her patient was standing behind it, using it for a walker. Only sheer determination kept him upright.

"What on earth do you think you're doing?"

"I'm getting out of here," he said in a threatening voice. "Don't get in my way."

"And where are you going?"

"To find myself a horse."

She swallowed the obvious retort, saying instead, "But you don't have any clothes."

He looked at her smile and cursed. "You're right. And you know what? I don't need any."

He let go of the sheet and stumbled around the head of the bed toward her, as naked as the day he was born, except for his bandages. He made it about three steps before he exhausted his strength and fell back across the cot. His collapse occurred at about the same time the sound of hoofbeats in the courtyard announced the arrival of someone in a hurry.

"Josie?" Will Spencer's urgent voice came from the courtyard.

"Keep your mouth shut," Josie said, then moved to open the door and called out, "Sheriff. I'm glad you—and your men—are here. I need you to help me get my patient back into bed."

"I'll get back by myself," Callahan said, breathing hard.

Will burst into the room, gun drawn. He was accompanied by a posse of unidentified men. "Is it him?" Will asked.

One of the men nodded. "It's Callahan, all right. He's the thief who stole all our money."

"Keller," Callahan gasped. "You gone loco? Ben and I made an investment in those cattle, too. This was our last chance to make it as ranchers. Why would we steal our own money?"

"Because it was the only way you could get enough to pay for the cattle and the mortgage on your ranch."

"Don't move, Callahan. I'm putting you under arrest," Will said.

Josie felt her face go white. "Under arrest? You can't do that, Will. You have no witnesses and no proof."

Will ignored her protest, gave the rancher a nod, and they both moved forward, clasping Callahan by the arms. "We have a suspect, and that's enough for now. Turn your head, Josie."

"Why?"

"Because, in case you haven't noticed, he isn't wearing any clothes." Will picked up the sheet and flung it over Callahan, who could have spit gunpowder and fired away. "Give us a hand here, boys."

"What kind of sheriff are you? I'm not a thief," Callahan protested.

Josie moved in front of Callahan and faced the ranchers. "He's innocent until proven guilty."

Two of Will's men moved around Josie, lifted Callahan, sat him on the bed, and held him there. "Suppose you tell us where your brother is, Sims."

Josie took one look at the fury on Callahan's face and weighed her options. A legal argument wasn't going to defuse the situation. She reached inside her pocket and pulled out the derringer Ellie had given to her. "Stand back, Will. He may be a thief, but he's injured. You're not taking him anywhere."

With a shake of his head, Will signaled his men to draw back. "Put the gun away, Josie. I know you're trying to do what your mama would do, but this man is a suspected criminal. I have to take him to jail."

"*Suspected* criminal," she insisted. "Innocent until proven guilty. As his doctor, I say he can't be moved. You'll kill him."

Will looked at Josie's patient and frowned. "Kill him? I don't think so, Josie. He survived the trip here, slung over the neck of a horse. And he survived your treatment."

"As his attorney, I must warn you that if you remove him from the premises you're responsible for his life."

"His attorney?" Will's tone grew sharp.

"My attorney?" Callahan repeated.

"Your attorney," Josie insisted, hoping he'd shut up before he made things worse. "You see, Callahan, a woman can be a healer *and* a lawyer, too. *Fiat justitia*— let justice be done—*when* he's well enough to be moved. Now, get him back in bed, Will Spencer, and I'll put my gun away."

"You tell me how a *dying* man got out of bed and

moved it halfway across the room and I'll listen," Will said.

"You tell me where Ben is and I'll get back in bed myself," Callahan said.

"I came here to ask you that question," Will said. "If you don't know, we'll have to assume that he's either dead or he's run out on you with the money."

Josie was still searching desperately for an explanation, any explanation for Callahan's nudity and the bed being halfway out the door. But she didn't have to, because at that moment, Callahan fainted and started to fall forward. "Catch him, quickly," Josie snapped, tucking her derringer back into her pocket and rushing to Callahan's side. She wasn't at all certain that his faint was real, but she was willing to use it to her advantage.

"Say the word, sheriff," Keller said, "and we'll tie him over my horse and haul him to jail."

"And I'll have you prosecuted for murder," Josie warned. "Don't think I won't do it."

Reluctantly, the ranchers who'd accompanied Sheriff Spencer stepped back.

Will finally nodded his head and lay the unconscious man onto the bed.

"If you men will just roll his bed this way," Josie said, "we'll get him settled for the night. I was just moving him into the family wing of the house when he fell out of bed," she explained.

The men who made up the posse began talking in low, agitated voices. "I don't believe him," Keller said. "He knows where our money is."

Another voice argued. "Sheriff said that Callahan and his brother left the trail. Why'd they do that if they were heading for Laramie?"

"Maybe they had a good reason," another suggested.

"Ordering these cattle was Ben's idea, and you know he's smart."

"Ben, yes. It's Callahan I don't trust. Maybe he sent Ben on and staged getting shot so we'd let him go," Keller argued.

"And maybe the thief was one of you ranchers," Josie suggested. "All of you knew where the Callahan brothers were going. All of you need money."

The posse rolled the hospital cot down the hall to the family wing, all the while arguing over Josie's accusation.

Josie confronted the sheriff. "Will, you can't believe that he's a thief. Those gunshot wounds aren't self-inflicted, and they aren't flesh wounds."

"I know. But, Josie, I also know he's one of the Callahan brothers, and just like it's your job to defend suspects, it's my job to arrest them."

Josie changed the subject. "Will, where do you think his brother is?"

"I don't know. He may be dead or he may be halfway to California with the money. All I know is the Callahan brothers left Sharpsburg with over five thousand dollars in cash and jewels to pay for a herd of high-priced cattle imported from England. The cattle arrived, the Callahan brothers didn't. This one's wounded, and his brother and the money have disappeared."

"That doesn't prove they stole the money, and without stolen money, you have no case. The only thing you know for sure is that Callahan was almost killed."

Will looked uncomfortable. "When we find his brother, we'll find the money. Where's Wash? He's supposed to be protecting you."

"He's . . . around. Besides, I'm perfectly safe. Look at Callahan's wounds. He couldn't even get out the door."

Will stared at her sternly, conscious of the ranchers

standing in the doorway, watching. "When will he be well enough to move?"

"Dr. Annie would know," she said honestly, "but I don't. You'll just have to wait until she comes back for a diagnosis."

"I don't like it," Will protested. "I need to question him."

"That's going to be hard to do considering he's unconscious."

"All right, but I'll be back tomorrow. Until then, I'll leave a guard."

There was an almost imperceptible tightening of the muscles in Callahan's jaw. Josie had thought Callahan's collapse was too convenient. Now she was sure of it.

"You really going to leave that low-down thief here?" one of the older men asked.

"Looks like I don't have any choice. If we take him to town and he dies, we may never know what happened to that money."

"What if he runs off in the middle of the night?"

"He's not. I'm leaving Wash in charge to make sure he doesn't."

"If you think you're going to get him off like you did that bar girl, you got another think coming," someone in the group said to Josie.

Another joined in. "Yeah, and if we don't get our money back, you can forget a trial. We're going to hang the son of a . . . ."

"That's what I thought you had in mind," Will said. He turned to Josie. "Just so you know, I'm not going to let that happen. Arresting him may be as necessary to save his life as your doctoring."

Josie could only nod.

When Wash was firmly posted outside the door to Josie's room, Will finally left, taking his posse with him.

Josie walked back to her room, opened the door, and leaned against it. "All right, Mr. Callahan, I know you didn't pass out. You can open your eyes now."

He did. "Why'd you make up that cock-and-bull story about prosecuting them for murder if I died? I didn't ask for your help."

"I don't know. I guess it's the lawyer in me—anything to save a client."

"You really are an attorney?"

"I am. But saving you will cost you, and I could use a big fat fee."

"I'm broke, remember. And now we're going to lose the ranch and what few cows we have left. We're pretty well wiped out."

"What happened to your herd?"

"Our cows caught some kind of fever from a Mexican herd passing through last spring. Ben had read about some cows being bred in England to resist the fever. He thought if we brought in some new, stronger stock, we'd be better off."

"Go on," Josie said.

"A group of us pooled together all our money, jewels, and anything else we could come up with to pay for them."

"But you didn't coerce the others into making the deal, did you?"

"Ben and I didn't talk them into anything. I'll admit that I was worried about the risk, but the rest of the ranchers didn't think twice. Too bad. Now it's all gone. We've lost the chance to buy new cattle and we'll proba-bly lose our ranches. And Ben's missing."

"Callahan, who shot you?"

"Never saw a face. They ambushed us. I was too busy turning my back on trouble to get a good look."

She let out a deep breath. "And what did you intend to do when you reached Laramie?"

"Pay for the cattle and drive them back to Sharpsburg."

"And then what?"

"What do you mean? Each rancher got his share and we'd eventually breed cattle that resisted the fever."

"So everyone stood to lose if the money disappeared?"

"*Lose* is putting it mildly. Even with the cattle, we lose. Rebuilding our herds will take a year. We all have mortgages due in the fall."

One of the ranchers had mentioned it earlier. Now Callahan had just given Ben a motive for riding off with the money. "What do you think happened to your brother?"

Callahan let out a ragged sigh. "I don't know. I thought I held them off long enough for Ben to get away. But he should have made it back to Laramie by now. Damn it to hell, Ben doesn't know how to look after himself." Callahan was becoming irate. "I swear, if Ben's hurt, I'm going to find and kill the bastard who did it."

Josie shivered. This man was serious. He could kill a man—and would.

"Still want to be my lawyer, Miss Miller?"

The shadows around Callahan had deepened, casting a smear of darkness across his face. His jet-black eyes seemed to penetrate that darkness, pinning her to this moment of truth. Josie's heart raced. She could send Wash to catch Will. No, something told her not to. She was intrigued by this man. She needed to find out the truth herself.

In the silence, the kitchen door opened and slammed

closed. Lubina's voice called out, "Miss Josie! I just saw the sheriff go. Where are you, Miss Josie?"

"I'm in here, Lubina."

The housekeeper dashed into Josie's bedroom, took one look at the naked man in her bed and fell to her knees. "Mother Mary, when I asked you to help Miss Josie be a woman, this es not what I prayed for."

5

Later, as Josie was sitting with Callahan, he said, "You know, if the sheriff is right, you're taking a big chance bringing me into your bedroom."

"No, I'm not—you're forgetting Lubina."

"No, I haven't forgotten."

"Besides, I have a gun."

"Well, between a gun and 'the bulldog,' I'm scared to death." Callahan's eyes flared in mock fear.

Josie gave him a hesitant smile. "Your fainting episode was very believable."

"You're the only thing between me and jail. I thought I'd make it easier on you." There was a softness about his response that didn't match the piercing cut of his eyes.

"I sure hope you're a good attorney."

"I am. Unfortunately, the people of Laramie aren't as certain. The last woman attorney came into town to defend a horse thief. She walked up and down the street with a bullwhip, looking for her client, but he took one look at her and hid. Nobody in town wanted to point him out to her, so she finally packed up and left."

Callahan grimaced and cleared his throat. "Do you have a bullwhip?"

"No, but I know how to use one. You don't have to worry, Mr. Callahan. I know the law and I rely on it. I don't need a bullwhip to prove a point. The problem is, even after all this time, no one thinks that a woman can be a good lawyer."

He let a few minutes of silence pass, mulling over what she'd just said. "There's something I should tell you. I spent some time in a Kansas jail. During the war I rode with Quantrill's Raiders for a time. When I left, they blamed me for holding up a bank. The money wasn't found that time either, but I spent three years in prison for something I didn't do."

Josie's heart sank. What kind of defense could she offer to a man who had already been convicted of stealing money?

"I'm thinking that you believe you can save everyone, Miss Josie. The more blackhearted, the better."

"Blackhearted? No. Down and out with no place to turn, yes. Those are the ones I *want* to help," she said.

"If being down and out is a requirement, you've got your work cut out for you. But," he said softly, "don't fool yourself, Josie Miller. You'll just get hurt. I'm not worth it."

"All my clients deserve help, Callahan."

"Spoken like a true stubborn woman. Always right, even if she's wrong."

"Lubina was right," Josie said. "You're a devil, beyond saving. I don't know why I didn't let you die."

"Because you don't give up, Miss Josie. And neither

do I. But I am sorry if I offended you. I'm used to dealing with lower-class women."

Josie stood and started for the door.

"*Please* don't run out of here screaming," Callahan said. "I don't want that bulldog you call a housekeeper accusing me of having my way with you."

"Let's get this straight, Callahan." She turned back. "Lower-class women don't always choose to be lower class. I don't scream, and you can be sure I don't allow men to have their way with me."

He gave her what was almost a smile and held his hands palms out. "Okay. But maybe a good man might take some of the starch out of your petticoats."

"I don't have any starch in my petticoats, and I made up my mind a long time ago that I'd eat sagebrush and prairie dogs before I'd let a man take care of me."

"Can't say I've eaten sagebrush and prairie dogs," Callahan said, "but there've been times when either one would have been welcome."

A moment hung between them, a connection that asked for more than either could promise. Finally he looked down at the new bedsheets beneath him.

"I can smell you on the pillow."

She looked startled.

"You smell like flowers."

"It's soap and sunshine," she said, backing away, her words echoing from one wall to another.

Callahan knew she was thinking about his head on her pillow. Josie did smell like soap and sunshine, and every time he drew in a breath, he was reminded of her.

"For whatever it's worth, Josie, thank you. Not many people in my life have stood up for me. And I appreciate it."

"It's my job."

"No, it's your way."

Josie felt his eyes on her. In spite of the connection between them, she'd tried to keep their relationship on a professional basis, but her patient wasn't fooled.

She pursed her lips and walked back toward the window overlooking the mountains beyond their valley. It wouldn't be long before he could move himself. She closed that thought out. "You don't like my room?"

He took a long look around, studying the whitewashed adobe room with its round white fireplace in the corner and the Indian rugs on the floor. "Saw some adobe houses like this in New Mexico, built out of sand. Not many up here. Folks in Wyoming usually prefer wood."

"There's very little wood now. The trees were cut when they were building the Union Pacific Railroad. Then the farmers came in and now the sheep herders. Besides, Dr. Annie and Dan tend to use what's plentiful and we have plenty of dirt out here."

Callahan gave her a curious look. "Not many women would furnish a room this simply."

"I like things simple and free. No restrictions. That's why I like Wyoming," Josie said, softly this time.

"Have you always lived here?"

"No, until I was ten, I lived . . . back east."

"So did I," he said. "Why'd you leave?"

"It's complicated," she admitted, wondering what he'd say if she told him how much they had in common. They'd accused him of being a thief. She'd *been* one. "Out here in this open land, I can think clearly."

"I like Wyoming, too," he agreed. "And you're like this land, open and honest."

"And plain."

A silence ensued.

"I'll leave you now. I'm going to make a new poultice, something to take care of your soreness," Josie said, closing the door behind her.

There was nothing simple or plain about Josie Miller. Though she tried to hide her beauty behind her severe hairstyle and simple clothing, Josie Miller had a lot more to offer. He'd like to know just what that was.

It had been a long time since anyone had intrigued Sims Callahan. Too bad he wouldn't be able to stick around. If he wanted to find Ben, he'd better concentrate on getting his strength back. He smiled. On the other hand, teaching Miss Josie Miller to be a woman might be just what the doctor ordered.

The lost man stumbled forward.

"Have to keep moving," he mumbled over and over, his mouth so dry that the words felt like gravel. "Got to get back to—"

To what? To who? He didn't know.

The sun overhead was as hot as the night before had been cold. The heat clung to his injured body like grasping hands. He fell to one knee, then pulled himself up and glanced around in confusion. His vision was blurred, but by squinting he could see shapes and colors. Nothing looked familiar. Where was he? What had happened to him?

The only thing that stayed with him was the constant ache in his head, a rolling pain that stole his thoughts and filled those spaces with darkness.

He thought that three days had passed since he'd opened his eyes only to look straight into the face of a lean, beaked bird that squawked in protest at his waking.

At one point he'd followed the trail of a small animal to find water, but that was at least a day ago. He'd stopped being hungry, driven by some invisible force that he couldn't identify. He couldn't remember what had happened, only that he was running. There was someone he had to find.

Over and over he stumbled, until he finally reached the low flat plains of the prairie. In his confusion he imagined he heard something—a thudding sound and a woman's voice.

"Damn you! Damn you for dying on me!"

More sounds, then, "Well, this won't stop me. I'll get there by myself."

He moved toward the voice. One painful breath after another. One step after the other. Then his foot came down on uneven ground, a rut. He stumbled and fell.

The next time he opened his eyes a woman was leaning over him. "Jacob?" she said softly. "Welcome back."

In the clinic, Josie ground up seeds from the packet marked *wounds* and added it to the vinegar Lubina had supplied, turning the mixture into a dirty brown paste that smelled rotten. She didn't know what it was. She didn't even know for certain that it would help, but it was all she could find in her mother's notebook that might work on Callahan's injuries.

After she'd changed Callahan's bandages, she'd find him something to wear. She seemed to remember that Dan's mother sent him a fancy nightshirt last Christmas. It might be simpler to treat him nude, but she couldn't do that anymore. There was no point in pretending that he was just another patient.

Josie gathered her other supplies—bandages, sulfur

powder, and her wound medication—and headed for her bedroom. She met Lubina on the way out.

"Did he eat?" Josie asked.

"Not much," Lubina admitted. "He's asleep now. He's still not a well man. If it had been up to him, he would have eaten nothing. I told him that if he didn't open his mouth, I'd stuff them beans somewhere he wouldn't like."

"Lubina!"

The housekeeper grinned. "I wouldn't have, but he didn't know that. I think *you'd* better not trust him. He's a charmer, that devil."

Josie shook her head and moved past the older woman. Lubina might call Callahan a devil, but it was clear that he was getting to her. Josie had best get done with her doctoring before he won her over completely.

The problem would be keeping him from leaving. He was determined to find his brother. She couldn't fault him for that, but he wasn't ready to travel.

Callahan's eyes were closed when she entered the room. She hoped that he wouldn't wake up while she was changing the bandage on his groin. Letting go of a deep breath, Josie peeled back the sheet, folding it over to cover that part of him insistent on making itself known. She was glad that he couldn't see her inflamed face.

With trembling fingers, she lifted the bandage. The skin around the edges of the wound was dry.

"Be gentle, darlin'," he drawled.

Josie jumped, almost upsetting the basin Lubina had left on the table. "I wish you wouldn't do that," she said, pouring hot water from the kettle into the pan.

"Do what?"

"Pretend to be asleep."

"Why? If you want to fondle me unobserved, I'll close my eyes." In the wee hours of the morning he'd come to the conclusion that he wasn't physically ready to ride. If he was going after Ben, he'd have to make peace with his guardian angel. Besides, he liked talking to her and he liked teasing her. Callahan let out an exaggerated sigh. "I'm all yours."

Josie took her cloth and, without letting it cool, dropped it on his abdomen.

"Hell," he swore. "What are you trying to do, cook me?"

"Just reminding you that I'm the doctor and I can still hurt you if you don't stop playing games. Now, be still."

This time Callahan didn't argue and he didn't let her see his smile.

Using sweet-smelling soap from her own washstand and a plain bathing cloth, she washed the wound.

He made no comments during the process. Surprisingly, this disappointed Josie. She missed his flirting. She remembered just this kind of talk between her Aunt Ginny and Uncle Red—before they married. Uncle Red was a lot like Callahan, teasing Ginny constantly. And Ginny had given as good as she got. They'd married and kept on flirting—through five children.

Josie forced her attention back to Callahan's body and noticed a scar on the calf of his right leg. "What the . . . ?" she whispered aloud.

"Earlier bullet wound," Callahan said.

"That doesn't surprise me."

Callahan squirmed beneath her touch.

"How'd you get shot that time? A fight over a woman?"

"A fight over a woman? Not me. Never met a woman worth getting shot for."

"Not even your mother?"

He paused for a moment before saying, "My mother was killed during the war, trying to protect my sister from being raped by Yankees. Both of them were killed in the end."

Josie was touched that Callahan would share something so personal. "I'm sorry," she said softly. "My real mother died in childbirth. The baby died too." She didn't know why she'd told him that. She'd never told a living soul about the pitiful little boy that had taken her mother's life.

He changed the subject by asking, "How soon am I going to be able to ride? I can't lie here while Ben's out there, maybe wounded, maybe even dead."

"I'm sure your brother is all right. If he were dead, they'd have found him. Out here the scavengers direct your path, even when the searcher loses the trail."

He winced. "You mean the vultures, don't you?"

She nodded. "Look, if it'll make you feel any better, I'll ask Bear Claw to send out a full search party. The Sioux know this territory better than anyone. If Ben is out there, they'll find him."

"How can you be sure?" he asked.

"They found you, didn't they? Now, be still."

He let her dry his feet, pulling the soft cloth between his toes and working it along the limp muscles of his calves. "You have a special touch," he said.

"Actually, I'm pretty clumsy. Dr. Annie is the angel with feather fingers."

"This Dr. Annie, I guess she adopted you."

"Yes," she answered. "My real mother was a prostitute." Out of respect for Dr. Annie, she wouldn't normally have mentioned her real mother, but this conversation with Callahan seemed right.

He didn't appear shocked or try to ignore her confession, as most people would have. "She must have had a good reason for doing that kind of work. Can't imagine a woman willingly choosing that life."

As a young child, Josie had wondered the same thing. And later, when she'd collected enough courage to ask, her mother had just said that a woman does what she has to.

A silence fell between her and Callahan.

He caught her arm, running his fingers up and down the odd curve between her elbow and her wrist. "What happened here?"

"It . . . got broken. Didn't heal right."

He nodded, waiting.

"When my mama died, one of her 'friends' looked after me. He taught me how to pick pockets and open safes. I was better at opening safes."

"Is that how you got your arm broken?"

She was startled at his perception. "Yes. When I was clumsy, I was punished."

"And Dr. Annie treated your injury?"

"Oh, no. I met Dr. Annie later. We were working a scam on the platform outside the train depot. Dr. Annie was the target that day. Dan caught me in the middle of the con. But Annie wouldn't let them arrest me. Instead, she took me in and treated me like I was somebody special."

Josie rinsed out her cloth, emptied her basin, and refilled it with the remaining hot water.

"So what happened after she took you in?" Callahan asked.

"We came here to Laramie and Dr. Annie opened her medical practice. Later, she and Dan got married and adopted me. I had no place else to go, and this was the best home I'd ever had. I never had a last name so I took theirs. I'm not their blood, but they call me their daughter."

"I don't think it was as easy as you make it sound."

"It wasn't," she said, and began absently washing his arm.

After all she'd done to civilize herself, she was confiding details of her past life to a man she knew nothing about. *A possible criminal.* Was that what made her open up to Callahan? Did they share a link based on their common pasts?

Beneath her fingertips, Callahan's muscles bunched as she washed. Though he didn't speak, she had the feeling that this man was as caught up in the moment as she.

In a stern tone, she said, "I'm very lucky to have people who love me, who think I'm better than I am. They've given me a lot, and Dan and Dr. Annie have always expected a lot from me in return."

Callahan was listening intently. "Like what?" he asked.

She dropped the cloth in the pan and sat for a moment. "I was expected to learn, to do something with my life to help others. And"—she let out a sigh of exasperation—"to be a lady. I'm supposed to set a good example for my younger sister, Laura."

"But you're no more a lady than I'm a gentleman, are you?"

She cut him a quick glance. He wasn't insulting her; he was just stating a fact. "You're right. I'm not. I go around pretending all the time. But everyone can see straight through me, and I'm sure they're laughing behind their smug smiles."

"Look at me, Josie. Do I look like I'm laughing?" he asked softly.

Why was he doing this, forcing an intimacy between them that she neither welcomed nor understood? She didn't like the panicky feeling that swept over her. She felt as if he was the only person who'd ever truly seen her. "No. I don't think you are. You don't know how to laugh."

Josie reached for the dressing on his shoulder wound and jerked it off.

"Ouch!"

"Sorry," she muttered and washed the healing wound.

He deserved a little pain for forcing her to bare her soul like that. She softened her efforts. At least there was no putrefied flesh. She rinsed her cloth and wiped away the soap, vigorously scrubbing his skin.

Callahan groaned. "I think you were wrong about your past, Miss Josie Miller."

She looked up.

"You weren't a pickpocket. From the way you're going after my skin, I think you were a washerwoman. Stop pretending I'm a scrub board and you're doing laundry."

"I'm sorry, Callahan." She applied her bandage, then slid her arm around his neck and beneath his back. "You'll have to help me here," she said, urging him to lift himself.

He gritted his teeth and complied as she tied the bandage around the shoulder with a strip of cloth.

"I'm simply trying to do what my mother would do," she said, as she let him back down. The weight of his upper body pulled her forward. Her chin was only inches away from his lips. She could feel his breath against her neck and the wicked pulse of his heartbeat through her fingertips.

Slowly, she pulled her arm away and leaned back. They stared at each other, breathing deeply. She dropped her gaze to the bed, trying to break the connection that held them in an intimacy far too strong for her to understand.

But no sooner had her gaze landed on the sheet, *that* part of him began to rise.

She gasped and turned primly away. "And don't you start that again, Callahan. It won't work. I already know you're a randy devil who can't control himself when he's around a woman—even when she's only trying to help him." She jutted her chin forward and left the room.

"Wait," he called after her. "Please come back and move the basin so I won't turn it over."

She reappeared in the doorway. "It won't tip over if you remain still."

"I'm trying."

"Not all of you is succeeding."

He groaned. "It's just that you have a way of tempting my body."

"I do no such thing."

"Well, maybe not you, maybe it's your body. All I know is, mine seems to have a mind of its own."

"Self-control. All you have to do is exert a little self-control. That," she said sweetly, "will lower the pole. Without it, the flag can't wave."

"Flag?" he said in disbelief. "Darlin', it's been called a lot of things, but never a flagpole."

"Well, my apologies for insulting Old Glory." She gave a mock salute and left the room. This time, the door closed firmly behind her.

Callahan groaned again. How in hell was he supposed to react? She just kept coming back, touching him, her strands of blonde hair skimming his body when she bent over to dress his wounds. His response was intense and unexplainable. Everything about him hurt. Still, this woman reached out to him, her blunt words and honesty overriding his condition, invading his dreams, and teasing his body.

Josie slipped back into the room. "Put this nightshirt on."

Callahan took one look at the white garment she was holding and scowled. "You want me to wear a lady's nightgown?"

"This is not a nightgown," she said patiently. "This is one of Dan's . . . nightshirts."

"He wears this to sleep?" Callahan asked incredulously. "Tell me the truth, Josie. Have you ever seen your father in this garment?"

"Well, no," she admitted, feeling a flush of embarrassment color her face. "But I'm certain he would wear it if Dr. Annie asked him."

"The only kind of man who would wear something like this is a man who doesn't have a woman and isn't going to get one, angel."

Josie planted her hands on her hips and pursed her lips. "Well," she said, "I guess that fits your situation pretty well, doesn't it? Now, put it on or I'll do it for you. And don't call me angel."

"Give me that nightshirt," he said reluctantly, holding out his hand.

Josie placed the white nightshirt in it and smiled, then pulled her lips into a fine line. The nightshirt was a small victory.

Callahan found the bottom of the shirt and threaded it over his head. He might call her angel, but Josie Miller *was* a temptation. He joked about it, but it was a truth he ought to recognize and accept. He managed to get one arm inside the shirt, but the other one refused to lift itself.

"Here, let me help," she said, coming to his side. She threaded the shirtsleeve over his arm and the neck over his head, but smoothing the garment behind him wasn't going to be as easy. "Do you think you could lift yourself if you put your arms around my neck?"

"I'll try." He forced himself to a sitting position, hanging his arms around her neck and drawing his good side against her.

Reaching around him was a stretch for Josie because he was so big, but she finally tugged the gown down his back and braced herself with her hands on the bed. He was too tall, too intense. The clean scent of her soap on his body was almost intoxicating, that and his male smell. Helplessly she leaned against him.

He lifted himself against her and she jerked the nightshirt under his bottom, then reached away to brace herself. But his arms were still around her neck, and his hands were threaded through her hair.

Josie's breath caught in her throat, along with her voice. She gasped. "Don't."

"Don't what?" He fell back to the bed, pulling her with him.

"Don't . . ." But she didn't know what to say.

Callahan's mouth covered hers, and Josie instantly knew what it was she wanted. Just for one moment Josie forgot everything she'd ever told herself she didn't need or wouldn't allow. In that moment she allowed herself to enjoy his mouth on hers.

Callahan told himself he hadn't intended to kiss her. He must have gone light-headed or he would never have done it. God only knew how long it had been since he'd kissed a woman. Since a woman's mouth had opened shyly beneath his lips. But suddenly this one went stiff as a board and began to struggle. "What's wrong?"

"Don't you dare try to take advantage of me, Callahan. I don't kiss men."

He stopped trying to pull her back into his arms and softened his hold. "I've never taken advantage of a woman in my life, and I apologize if you thought I intended to now."

"Apology accepted," she said. "Now, if you'll just release me."

He rubbed her arms gently, moving up and down, touching loosely, reluctant to break the connection. "Why are you so frightened, Josie?"

"I'm not frightened."

"There's nothing wrong with kissing. You can leave anytime you're ready. But I'd like to say thank you for all that you've done."

His hands slid down to her waist, pulling her closer. He felt the fabric of her dress, simple, unencumbered by undergarments that foolish women wore for the sake of style. Not Josie Miller. She was what she was, with no pretense. "I bet you don't know how to kiss a man, do you?"

"Of course I know how," she snapped.

But she didn't. Deep down she was a shy, hesitant girl, not the in-charge doctor or the confident lawyer that she appeared to be.

"Callahan," she whispered, withdrawing in confusion. "You're sick. You don't know what you're doing."

"If you mean I'm out of my mind, you're probably right. You've been driving me crazy, touching me for the last few days. Now it's my turn. You owe me at least one kiss, Josie Miller."

"But—"

He kissed her again, and for a moment she stopped fighting.

Lubina's cheery voice came down the hall from the

kitchen. "Miss Josie, your supper's ready. I'll come and look after Mr. Callahan while you eat."

Josie's eyes flared and she jerked away.

When Lubina walked into the room, Josie knew she'd been caught making a deal with the devil.

6

Normally, Josie fell asleep quickly and rarely dreamed. Tonight, she couldn't be still.

It was the heat, she decided. Not Callahan. Not the kisses, or how they'd made her feel. She needed to breathe the night air.

Josie gathered the bottom of her gown, drawing it into a knot away from her legs, and padded through the house, across the enclosed courtyard. A full moon lit the valley, painting it with translucent silver. It was almost midnight, yet the heat was still ovenlike. The scent of roses hung sweet and heavy in the motionless air.

"Evening, Miss Josie." Wash's voice came out of the darkness.

Josie let the gown fall. She'd forgotten the old man was nearby. Though she was fully covered, her white nightdress made her stand out like a ghost in the moonlight. "Evening, Wash. Any word from Bear Claw?"

"Not yet, ma'am."

"You don't need to watch the house, Wash," Josie said. "I'm sure my patient is no danger to me." Her voice was a lot more confident than her convictions.

"The sheriff said Dr. Annie would have my hide if I didn't," Wash protested. "So I take a turn about every so often."

"Thank you," she murmured, grateful that the darkness hid the flush on her face, and kept walking.

Independence Day had come and gone. In another week Dr. Annie and Dan would be back, and she would have to face their censure if they didn't approve of her actions. But that was something she would worry about later. Right now she just wanted to find a cool spot. There was no dew on the grass, no moisture beneath her bare feet. The earth seemed parched.

No sign of the black-and-white stallion either.

At the riverbank, Josie paused, listening to the whispering of the current as it beckoned to the wild creatures who sought its coolness. She stepped into the water, and the hem of her nightdress tugged away from her, hanging on her ankles and pulling her forward.

She felt very strange tonight, out of touch somehow with this land that had adopted her and given her a new beginning. She didn't like the uncertainty of change unless she controlled the change herself. She had spent too many years turning herself into a woman who could make her own choices and carve her own way, as Dr. Annie had done. And, if the truth were told, she'd chosen a profession that gave her the right to be outspoken.

Sims Callahan signaled a change that was not of her own making. She looked up. A falling star streaked across the inky sky.

Perspiration rolled down her face and between her

breasts. The heat grew, not only from the stillness of the night, but from inside her own body. Desperately, she reached down, cupping the cool water in her hands and splashing it on her face and neck. Not enough.

She took a few steps out into the river and sank down to her knees, welcoming the sharp edges of the rocks on which she rested. Pain wasn't new to Josie. Pain had driven her life and reminded her that no matter how far she'd come, beneath the Miller name and the fine clothes she wore, she was still nobody. She'd tried her best to become a lady, to live an orderly life in appreciation to Dan and Annie. But the truth was, underneath, she was still Joe, the street urchin.

Her gown soaked up the river water and clung to her body. As it cooled down the heat, she felt her muscles begin to relax, her body breathe. Water tagged the rocks and seemed to laugh and move by. Life should be like that; a temporary meeting with an obstacle before sliding away and going on. She loosened her hair from its braid and leaned back, submerging her face in the water.

Josie shivered. This tingly feeling was with her constantly now and had been ever since Sims Callahan had come into her life. She wished she'd never met him. She wished he weren't an outlaw. She wished . . .

Callahan tossed, hot and sweaty. His skin stuck to the sheet. But the heat increased the smell of Josie. The room, even the linen beneath him, was filled with her sweet scent. He closed his eyes and imagined her in bed beside him, her bare skin against his, her breasts, full and pink, waiting to be sucked. The thought of Josie, just beyond the walls of his room, was torture.

If only he could get up and walk around, he'd put Josie out of his mind. He forced himself to his feet, and by taking slow, careful steps, he reached the covered courtyard. The scent of flowers that filled the night air was so overpowering that he could hardly breathe. A horse nickered softly, and from the mountains in the distance came the call of a coyote.

He waited until he'd marshaled enough strength to move again and made his way to the wall beneath the courtyard roof.

The moon was as bright as a million lamps, and Callahan felt exposed, even though he was hidden in the shadows.

What in hell had possessed him to kiss her again, and why was he worrying about it now? He ought to be worrying about Ben. But it was Josie who had him wearing a ruffled nightgown. Josie had officially turned his innards into clabber.

She might have been a wild street urchin who'd clawed her way to the top, but now Josie Miller was a member of the most prominent family in Laramie. Long ago he'd given up the right to care about a woman, especially one who'd achieved so much. There was nothing left inside him but the charred remains of a man who had lost too much, too fast. That life for Sims Callahan died when the plantation back in South Carolina had burned.

Callahan slid along the wall to the bench beneath Josie's window and sank down. He unbuttoned the front of his nightshirt. The hot night air dried the perspiration beading his chest. He'd been practicing moving about at night when everyone was quiet, but this was the first time he'd left the house on his own two feet. He wasn't positive, but he thought he'd been here for about a week. Now for a few moments out here tonight, he felt free.

But he couldn't fool himself. He wasn't free. He was tightly bound to this house and this woman by more than just wounds. Wanting her had made Callahan admit to a side of himself that he hadn't acknowledged in a long time. A deep longing, a need to belong, to have someone to touch, someone to connect with physically.

Frustration closed over Callahan, a frustration all the worse because he couldn't see a quick way out of the aftermath of wounds so incapacitating that he couldn't yet mount his horse and search for his brother without help. Suddenly, from the darkness, came a sound. Someone was walking in the courtyard. Bare feet moved across the hard earth like the kiss of a spider building its web. Sound turned into substance when a figure wrapped in sheer white fabric moved into the moonlight. Golden hair turned silver. Gown translucent, nearly nude. The woman looked like a marble statue he'd once seen in a museum. Except this woman was real.

She came closer, walking slowly, her arms crossed over her breasts. Then she stopped, not two feet from where he was sitting in the darkness. Her arms moved away from her body like unfolding wings. She began to sway. Her feet moved slowly, lifting her body as she danced on her toes.

Josie.

Callahan had never seen anything so beautiful. There was no music, except the magic of the inner song that moved her. More graceful than he'd ever thought possible, his clumsy Valkyrie became the angel he'd called her.

He must have made a sound, for she suddenly stopped.

"Wash?" she asked in a whisper. "Who's there?"

"The devil," he answered, more roughly than he'd intended.

"Callahan? How'd you get out here?" She ran toward him in quick mincing steps.

"I walked. I needed to move. Where have you been?"

"To the river. I couldn't sleep."

"Neither could I. Please, sit down."

She hesitated, then sat beside him and leaned back against the house.

"You're wet," he said. "God, how I'd like to lie down in the river, feel the fresh cold current roll over me."

"It's too far. Would you like me to prepare a basin of cool water for you to bathe yourself?"

I'd like you to lie with me, in that river, beneath the moon. "No." His voice was tight and low. "It wouldn't be the same."

"Here, let me help you get back inside."

"Yes" was all he said.

She leaned over and gently slipped one arm around his chest and the other on his hip. "Ready?" she asked a little breathlessly.

He could have told her that he could do it himself, but he didn't. "I'm ready."

Callahan knew he shouldn't lean against her, but he couldn't stop himself. At least that way he couldn't see her nipples peeking through her sleeping garment. Despite her wet clothing, she radiated an energy, an inner turmoil that fed the heat and the sweet scents of the night. She moved closer and her breasts pressed against his bare chest, nipples beaded like icy pebbles. Sweet torture.

"I have to let you go," Josie said, struggling to handle his weight. She let go of one arm and moved her hand to his chest where she felt the rapid beat of his heart beneath her fingertips. Unconsciously, she leaned against him, as if she were the injured one and he was her strength. It was as if they were the only two people on earth. But they weren't, and he wasn't strong enough to stand.

"Let me move around to your side," she said. "You can lean on me and the wall."

"Not yet," Callahan said, pulling her against him. And then he was kissing her again, just as he'd wanted from the start. A surge of passion swept over him, washing away every restraint, enveloping them both in its power like the current of that river he'd longed for. His hands slid down her back, cupping her intimately against him. Her womanly needs seemed to match his own.

His tongue sought the opening of her mouth, inviting, insisting, and she let him in, allowed him to taste her, to make love to her mouth as his body joined in the rhythm. His left hand moved downward, seeking and finding a full breast. She held her breath for one long moment.

Callahan found his way inside her nightdress and was soon rewarded by the touch of her bare breast. The tremors she set off as she caressed his chest almost undid him. He pressed his throbbing body against hers, refusing to let go, not without touching her—there, where he longed to be, inside her.

He slipped his hand lower and reached for the hem of her gown, lifting the wet garment. Then he pressed his hand against her womanhood, slipping his fingers into the V of her thighs. She shuddered at his touch.

"Callahan," she gasped, and tried to pull away. Callahan pressed his lips against hers once more, not gently this time, but with all the urgency he felt. After struggling for a moment, she met his motions thrust for thrust, tightening her muscles and arching her lower body. There was a deep moan and then a shudder. Her release came with a rippling intensity that surprised him and left Miss Josie Miller wide-eyed and stunned.

"What . . ." she whispered, "what did you do to me?"

"I just loved you, darlin'."

"But . . ."

Josie seemed frozen for a moment. As the last throb of her body dissipated, she shook her head and turned around, pulling his good arm over her shoulder and reaching behind her to clasp his back. "Lean on me," she said. "If you can't walk, I'll drag you."

They made their way along the wall. Once inside, she eased him onto the bed, then stumbled toward the open window.

Neither of them spoke for a long moment.

Finally, she said, "I don't want to talk about what just happened, Callahan."

"Good. Talking never does justice to loving."

"I'd appreciate it if you didn't call it that. In fact, I'd appreciate it if you never mentioned it again."

"I won't mention it, Josie. But it happened, and it won't ever go away. Every time we look at each other it will be between us."

"Then I won't look at you," she snapped, and turned around.

"Well, fine," Callahan said wearily. "But understand that tomorrow I have to get out of here. And you're going to help me. If you don't, this will happen again. Except the next time, it won't be my *hand* that loves you. Do you understand?"

She gasped and in a second was gone.

Callahan was more than willing to put what he'd done behind them, too—but his body would take more convincing.

Love was something out of a storybook for Josie. After all, she'd spent her childhood in a house of prostitution, seeing too much to believe that she'd ever want a man.

She'd never believed in the wild, overwhelming kind of lovemaking she'd just experienced until now.

And there was the issue of babies. Lovemaking made babies, and Josie never intended to have them. She felt awkward when she was around little ones. It had taken her a long time to hold her little sister.

Josie flung herself down on her parents' bed, but quickly rebounded when images of Dr. Annie and Dan making love flooded her mind. Of course they made love. They'd conceived a child, Laura.

Dr. Annie and Dan were so close that one could start a sentence and the other would finish it. What they shared was discreet, but Josie had seen the way they looked at each other, and she'd seen Dan give Annie an intimate pat on her bottom or a kiss when he thought they were alone. That had to be love.

Love was many things—from her aunt and uncle's lusty, I-don't-care-who-knows openness to Dan and Annie's quiet sharing. But it was not what she had seen from the men who visited her mother, seeking temporary satisfaction for only themselves.

Tonight, Callahan had given her pleasure without asking anything in return. And he'd called it loving her.

He'd been right about what had happened between them. Their need for each other was too strong to be ignored. It moved of its own volition and touched the other, spreading like a prairie fire burning out of control.

As the sun came up over the Laramie Mountains, Josie made a decision. She had to take drastic action. She would have to let Callahan go.

Josie found Bear Claw in the kitchen the next morning when she went in search of breakfast.

"Good morning," she said, having learned long ago that the Indian moved at his own speed. She'd find out why he was here when his stomach was full.

Josie poured herself a cup of coffee and sat down at the other side of the table. "Are you well?"

He nodded and took another bite of his biscuit.

"And your people?"

Bear Claw grunted.

Finally, when her patience was stretched to a fine thread, he put down his cup and let out a loud burp. "Good."

"Do you have news?"

"Missing white man ride in wagons with Men of White God."

"You found Ben Callahan?" Josie exclaimed. "How do you know this, Bear Claw?"

"Followed man's tracks. Wagon stopped. Tracks gone. Man in wagon."

"You're sure it's the right man?"

He grunted and stood. "Right man. Hurt, but he lives."

Josie watched her mother's old friend leave and ran to the bedroom to inform Callahan.

But that plan was taken out of her hands as Sheriff Spencer appeared in the courtyard with a man driving a wagon, cushioned and padded with blankets.

"I've come for my prisoner," he told Josie as he marched through the house toward Callahan's bedroom, the driver of the wagon behind him. His stride said he expected a fight over his announcement.

"He isn't ready to be moved yet."

"Doesn't matter," Will interrupted. "I can't leave Callahan out here. The ranchers are getting restless. I don't know what they might try, so until I get to the bottom of it, I'm taking him to jail. That's the only way he'll be safe."

Josie swallowed her retort. She knew he was right. "I won't try to stop you, Will," she said. "I'll send some medication with you if you'll treat his wounds and change his dressings."

Will looked at her in disbelief. "You will?"

"I'd appreciate it if you'd get him some regular clothes."

Will reached her bedroom, caught sight of Callahan in the nightshirt, and burst out laughing. "I think regular clothes might be a good idea. I'll send for some when I get him locked up."

"Now, just a minute," Callahan protested. "I'm not going to jail. You can't prove I've done anything except get shot. I've got to find my brother. Josie, you're my attorney, do something!"

"I'm afraid I can't do much until the trial. But without a witness or the money, they can't prove you're guilty."

He stared at her, his gaze filled with disappointment. "It isn't me I'm worried about. If I go to jail, Ben could die."

Josie saw the anguish in his eyes, and she knew she couldn't keep the truth from him. "Your brother has already been found," she said. "I was on my way to tell you."

"Found?" Will said sharply. "Where?"

"Bear Claw tracked him to the wagon trail north of here. He must have crossed paths with a missionary train that came by about a week ago."

"Then he's still alive," Callahan said, relief obvious in his voice.

Will frowned. "I'll send a telegram to the officials along the way and have them take him into custody. Then, as soon as I calm the ranchers, I'll go after him and the money."

"I'm going with you," Callahan said, poising himself for action. "I don't care what you say. There's something wrong or Ben would have come back."

Will pulled Callahan's arms behind him and tied his wrists together, then motioned for his deputy to help. Together, they carried him to the wagon, with Josie following.

"Maybe Ben just wanted it all," Josie speculated.

"You don't know my brother," Callahan said.

Josie didn't argue. She watched as they placed the agitated Callahan in the wagon. He'd seemed to calm down once he was tied up. But Josie had seen Callahan play possum before, and she thought he might be up to something. Then she saw perspiration bead up on his forehead and knew his body wasn't ready, even if his spirit was.

"Be careful with him, Will," she said.

"I intend to," Will answered, and laid his rifle across his saddle horn.

As the wagon rolled out of the courtyard and down the road, a feeling akin to sadness settled in Josie's chest, and she wondered if she'd done the right thing. And if she would ever see Sims Callahan again.

Josie leaned against the post at the front door and watched.

Behind her, Lubina's voice cut through the silence. "I heard the two of you in the courtyard. It es good that he es gone."

Josie felt the heat of embarrassment flood her face. She kept her gaze on the wagon, a speck on the horizon now.

"Dr. Annie and Mr. Dan will be back in a few days, and everything will be like it was," Lubina said firmly.

"No, it won't. Nothing will ever be the same again, Lubina."

The housekeeper came to stand beside Josie. "You saved his life. That makes a bond between two people stronger than we can know."

"I was thinking about what you said the other night, Lubina, something about a black-and-white horse that came to take Callahan to another place. But it wasn't the horse that took him away. It was Will."

Lubina sighed. "*Señorita*, I truly believe that it was the ghost horse who came. The Indians say that it always claims a soul. It's just that sometime the person doesn't die. Maybe the Indians are wrong. Maybe it returned a soul to a man without one."

Could Lubina be right? Everything in her life had been leading Josie to this moment—her past, her meeting Dr. Annie, and her schooling. But nothing had prepared her for the confusion. She didn't have to be with this man to know the need was there. Now the man was gone—but she was having trouble dealing with the aftermath.

"My grandfathers," Josie said quietly, "believe that sometimes a person has to accept what fate sends them. I guess I've always done that, but I'm just now understanding that there are some things I have no control over."

She thought about the two rascals she'd learned to love and knew that they'd been trying to teach her a life lesson. Both her grandfathers went straight for what they wanted and knew how to get it. If fate didn't provide, they gave fate a hand. She knew they'd want her to do the same thing.

Three days later Will Spencer propped his booted foot on the brass rail of the saloon called Two Rails and a Mirror. He looked past the bartender to the spidery reflection of himself.

"Hello, Sheriff Spencer." Ellie Allgood leaned on the counter next to him and smiled.

"I thought you had quit this job, Ellie."

Ellie tried not to flush. "I quit entertaining men. Now I just serve drinks. I wanted to thank you for asking Miss Miller to defend me, but you haven't been in. I hear you've been busy trying to find some missing money."

"I think it's with a missionary train heading for Oregon, but I haven't been able to find it. Apparently the wagons left the main trail, and the rain has washed away any tracks. I finally had to ask the army for help in the search. How are things around here?"

"Everything's uneasy since the townsfolk heard Miss Miller is defending your prisoner. You sure he's guilty, Sheriff Spencer?"

"I don't know. He and his brother were the last ones with the money. One brother is wounded and the other vanished with the saddlebags. It's up to the judge to decide."

"Josie doesn't think he's guilty. She'll get him off," Ellie said, with new confidence that made Will give her a second glance.

"Josie wants to prove to everyone that she's as good at practicing the law as her mama is at doctoring," Will said, frustrated. "She's going to be the death of Dr. Annie yet."

Ellie sighed. She didn't have to ask him why he was so cross. Everyone knew Will had been sweet on Josie Miller ever since he came to Laramie—everyone but Josie. But Will was just as blind, Ellie thought. Will never noticed *her* either.

She hadn't worried too much about her life, but since the trial she'd begun to look at herself differently. If what she'd heard about Josie Miller's past was true, then she, too, could change professions and become respectable.

She'd quit entertaining men in her room, and she'd started changing the way she dressed, but her reputation was marred in Laramie. She'd returned to serving drinks in the bar. But that was as far as she'd go. The only way to change her future was to separate herself from the past. So far she hadn't really found a way to do that.

"Funny thing about the younger Callahan," Will said. "Folks in Sharpsburg never thought Ben had it in him to run off with the money, but he got away with it—so far."

"So far," she agreed. "But you won't know the truth until you find him."

"And so far I haven't managed to do that. The people of Laramie are going to start asking what kind of sheriff I am."

She laid her hand on his arm. "You're an honest one. One the good people like and the bad ones fear. Everyone knows that, Will."

"Maybe I need to make you my deputy, just to remind me of the obvious."

"Maybe you do." She smiled. "I wouldn't ask for much pay."

"How much would you ask for?"

"A dinner now and again, away from here."

"I think Laramie can afford that."

"Deal." She held out her hand for a shake.

Will took it in his, and she felt his grip tighten.

"Thanks, Ellie," he said. "You really are a good person."

He started out the door, stopped and turned. "About that dinner, I was thinking that the hotel would be a nice place for a meal. Would you mind if Josie came along?"

7

"Do I know you?"

He was just waking up—though this could be a dream. Nothing seemed familiar, not even the woman leaning over him. She was young, small, with a heart-shaped face and sun-kissed skin. Her eyes, a deep brown, crinkled in concern at the corners, allowing, for just a moment, a hint of what might be called fear.

After a long silence that seemed to signal the waging of some kind of internal war, she answered softly, "I guess you don't remember."

"Remember?" All he could remember was pain. Every breath was sheer torture. His chest hurt. His ribs hurt. But mostly, his head hurt.

He glanced around. They were inside a small confined place with little light. At the end of their shelter he could see the night sky, glittering with stars, and below it the suggestion of a campfire. He was in a wagon.

She wiped his face, as though he were a child and she the parent. But he wasn't a child. He was a man. He reached up, catching her arm, pulling it down on his chest—not because it was his intention, but because he hadn't the strength to hold it up.

"Tell me," he whispered. His voice was graveled and strained. His tongue seemed to fill his mouth, making it difficult to talk. "Why? How did I get here?"

"You were hurt, Jacob. I found you in the mountains north of Laramie, in Wyoming. Then Brother Joshua Willis came along and said that it wouldn't be Christian to leave us stranded, so . . . well, we're . . . here."

"You called me Jacob?" he asked.

"You have to have a name. I couldn't go on caring for a man without one. I gave you a name I . . . I like."

The woman flinched. He glanced down and realized he was still holding her arm. He let go, but the colorless imprints of his fingertips remained. "Forgive me, I didn't mean to hurt you."

"You are forgiven. You've had a bad time, Jacob. You were half dead when I found you. You had a black eye and your face was badly bruised. I believe you were beaten."

He flexed his muscles, moving his legs cautiously. They were stiff, but seemed to work all right. Next came his arms. Functional. It was when he attempted to lift his head that he found the source of his greatest injury. His head felt like a huge egg, a heavy cracked egg. If he moved, it would break into a million pieces.

"How long ago?"

"Five days," she answered. "Would you like some water?"

He tried to nod but found it less painful if he remained still. "Yes."

She lifted a cup and a reed, studied him for a moment, then placed the reed into the cup and sucked water into it. Next she covered the top of the reed with her finger to trap the liquid before she inserted it into his mouth.

The water was tepid, but he thought it was the most welcome thing he'd ever experienced. Considering he had no memory of the past, that probably meant very little.

Twice more she drew up water and dribbled it into his mouth. "Enough?"

"Yes."

She pulled a muslin sheet over him and tucked it beneath his chin. "You should rest."

She started to move away.

"Wait!"

"Yes?"

"Your name?" he whispered.

"I'm Rachel," she answered.

"Where are the others?"

Tiny worry lines wrinkled her brow. "You mean the other travelers? They're in their wagons."

"And your husband?"

She averted her eyes. "I don't have one . . . any longer. He's passed on."

There was something wrong with her answer. He didn't know yet what it was. Then it came to him. "You found me? You took me into your wagon when you didn't even know me?"

She waited a long time before she answered. "I didn't have to. I always knew you would come."

She didn't know him, but she had been expecting him? Nothing made any sense. Suddenly he felt a cold rush of fear, as if he were stumbling through icy water, being sucked down by a current he could neither see nor touch. As he tried to line up his thoughts, a feeling of urgency swept over him. There was somewhere he had to be. "I thank you, ma'am, for taking me in and caring for me. But I have to get back home." He had to—

"Where is your home, Jacob?"

He started to answer, then realized that he didn't know. "I . . . I'm not sure. I can't seem to remember. I don't know. I don't know who I am."

"You're Jacob," she said softly. "Don't be afraid. I'll take care of you."

"Why? Why are you doing this? Why were you expecting me?"

"Because I prayed for a good man. And God sent you."

Josie walked into the Laramie City jail in the middle of the afternoon. She hadn't wanted to come, but after three days of assuming that Will was changing Callahan's bandages, she knew it was time for her to resume some responsibility for her patient. Now he was her client.

The town jail had started out as a store with two windows on the front. Dr. Annie had insisted that they be opened in the heat of the summer, so they'd covered the windows with bars. But the bars didn't keep people from looking in. From the sidewalk she could see Will Spencer. He sat in a rickety chair, his back to the street, his feet crossed at the ankles and resting on his desk.

She entered the open door, walked past him, and stood outside the only cell. Will snored lightly, his head leaned against the crude log wall behind him.

Callahan sat on his cot with his back against the far wall, watching her.

"How are you?" she asked.

"About as well as you could expect, considering I'm shot to hell and in a jail cell."

His reply made her feel like a schoolgirl. "I meant, how are your wounds?"

"You don't want to know."

"Yes, I do. I'm your doctor."

"You're my lawyer, too. Why haven't you gotten me out of here?"

Their conversation came in jerky sentences, as if they were strangers, instead of—what were they? He'd kissed her, that was all. No, that wasn't all. He'd called her darlin' and he'd touched her—'loved her,' he'd said.

In spite of her past, Josie had never heard anyone talk about a man loving a woman that way, not like Callahan had loved her. She shook off the rush of sensation those thoughts dredged up. He was out of her house now. All that was behind them. She understood he was just a man with manly needs that he expected to be satisfied. Yet, she was the one whose needs had been satisfied. What, she wondered, did that do to the man?

"You're right. I haven't done my job very well, have I?" Apparently Will had listened to her request and had found Callahan some clothes. He was wearing stiff new Levi's jeans, a chambray shirt, and scuffed boots. He looked different with clothes on—somehow more distant. And he needed a shave. She made a note to bring a razor and soap the next time she came, and a comb.

"Dr. Annie will be back soon," she said. "She'll be able to evaluate your condition and tell you when you can go."

"That's not the answer I'm looking for," he growled.

"Until Judge McSparren gets back, you aren't going anywhere," Will said, the heels of his boots thumping the floor. "Afternoon, Josie."

Josie wondered how long he'd been awake. "Good afternoon, Will. I've come to change Mr. Callahan's bandages."

"Yeah?" he said, eyeing Josie curiously. "Just a minute and I'll unlock the cell." He ambled to his feet and, from a nail beside the front door, lifted a ring with two heavy keys attached.

"Do you really have to lock him up?" she asked.

"Nah," Will answered, with a grin. "You wouldn't run off if I asked you to stay, would you, Callahan?"

"I think you know the answer to that," Callahan replied dryly. "Would you stay in a cell, Josie?" Callahan asked.

She felt foolish. She wouldn't stay in jail. In fact, she hadn't. On the several occasions when she'd been caught stealing, before she became a skillful thief, she'd played on the sympathy of the law by bawling her eyes out until they sent for her "mama." Never mind that Mama was dead. Once the policeman left to fetch her mother, Josie would pick the lock on her cell and escape. No, she wouldn't stay in jail either.

Will opened the iron door and held it back, his hand resting on his gun. "You can have fifteen minutes with your client," he said. "I'm going to have to lock this behind you. Just holler when you're done."

"Thank you." Josie nodded and slipped inside, then stood awkwardly by the door. There was no stool, and Callahan's large body took up the entire bunk.

"If you're still my doctor, get to it. I guess you're a better doctor than you are a lawyer. You've patched me up to go to my own hanging, or maybe my brother's funeral. Are you going to help me?"

She didn't have an answer, for she knew his question had nothing to do with her doctoring. "I . . . I need to check your wounds."

"Not necessary. They're fine. I don't need a doctor. I need someone to get me out of here—an outlaw."

"Too bad. What you've got is me and we have to talk. First, you seem to be using your arm better. Is the soreness dissipating?"

"I figure I can shoot now. By tomorrow I ought to be able to kill a man, if I need to," he said. "All I need is a gun."

"I said I could defend you against going to jail for stealing the money." She untied the cotton strips and peeled back the bandage on his shoulder. "Murder is another thing. Just who do you plan to shoot?"

"The son of a b—"

Will coughed.

"—whoever is responsible for getting me shot and Ben lost," Callahan finished.

"Will, I'd like to talk to my client alone," Josie said.

Josie could tell that Will wasn't at all happy about leaving them, but he finally nodded. "I'm right outside, if you need me, Josie."

"Talk about what?" Callahan asked, as soon as the door closed behind Will.

Josie jerked off the old bandage on his shoulder and cleaned the wound. "Your defense. I need to know exactly what you and Ben had set out to do. Tell me what happened that day," she prodded, applying medication to the area. "You told me that the ranchers around Sharpsburg were having a problem with sick herds."

"Sick is putting it mildly. Try dead."

Josie nodded as she began to button his shirt. "All right then, let's try something else. Did everyone know when you were leaving for Laramie?"

"Sure. And they knew the exact route, too."

She perched on the edge of the narrow cot. "You think any of them might have gotten greedy?"

Callahan frowned. It would be easier to keep his mind on his answers if she were still poking around on his injuries. "Maybe, they're all pretty desperate. Still, I don't think any of them would try something like this. It would be hard to keep a herd of cattle a secret."

"So you pooled all your money and jewels. And now you think you'll lose your ranches. Tell me more about that."

"Most of us have loans due in the fall. We won't be able to make the payments, and Banker Perryman isn't likely to let us slide. He's made that clear."

"Are you certain you didn't recognize the men who attacked you?"

"Of course I'm certain. They wore masks. It was difficult to hear their voices. Then my horse threw me and I crashed into a big piece of granite."

"But it could have been some of the ranchers."

"It could have been Will Spencer, for all I know. Just get me out of here, I'll find out."

"How?" she asked.

"I'll start by finding out if anyone from Sharpsburg's been spending a whole lot of money."

Callahan took Josie by the arm and forced her up and toward the head of the bunk.

"What are you doing?" she asked, trying to push him away.

"Getting up." He held on to her and pulled himself upright. "The thieves could be halfway to the Oregon Territory by now. You're a lawyer, Josie. All you know is books. Books won't find Ben, and they won't save me."

Callahan was right. Josie's lawyer mind kicked in,

overriding her frazzled emotions. "Callahan, are you sure you aren't fooling yourself? Ben had the money and now he's gone. Maybe he didn't want to raise cows anymore."

There was a long silence. "Ben would never steal, Josie. I'm the only one in the family who has ever been dishonorable."

Callahan caught Josie's arm, then let go and touched her cheek as he said softly, "You've got to help me, Josie. Get me out of here."

"I can't," she whispered, leaning against his hand. "I am an attorney and I've sworn to uphold the law. But I'll find a way to get you out of here. In the meantime I'll find out who's been spending money. Trust me, Callahan. I'm on your side."

Trust her? He did trust Josie Miller. It was the rest of Wyoming, making plans to hang him, that he feared.

Long after Josie left, Callahan paced his cell. His attorney was an exceptional woman. A beautiful woman who occupied much too much of his thinking. He could still feel the soft touch of her lips, and his face still burned when he remembered what he'd done to her on her veranda. She seemed to have put the incident behind her; why couldn't he? And why would this kind of thing be bothering him now? He must have had fifty women in the last fifteen years, and he couldn't remember a single face. Why this one? Why now when life was crashing down around him, his future gone and Ben was missing?

Callahan flinched, feeling the weakness in his body. She might not be a doctor, but he was still alive. And he trusted her. But finding the men who'd shot him and chased Ben to God knew where, was a job for a man. It was his job. He had to get out, to learn the truth. As much as he hated the thought of it, he had to use Josie to do that and he had to do it quick. Otherwise, some bounty hunter would believe that Ben had the money and go after him. Ben could be killed before Callahan could find him—unless Callahan found out the truth.

But where to start? Everybody in Sharpsburg had known what he and Ben were doing. Their mission had been the biggest topic of conversation in town. Even the drifters from the cattle drives knew everything, from the route they'd taken to the time they'd left. Any one of them could have been among the thieves who'd attacked them. But he hadn't recognized any of them. He had only a vague recollection of a horse with an odd marking.

Callahan forced himself to walk. He had to get out of jail. To do that, he had to move.

All that afternoon and the next morning he paced his cell, stopping only when the stranger showed up at the Laramie City jail.

8

———— ❧ ————

"I have a message for Sims Callahan," the stranger said to Will Spencer. "Understand you have him in your jail."

Will ambled to his feet and blocked the opening. "I do."

"What I have to say is private."

"Who are you?" Will asked.

"Name's Jerome. Work for Lester Perryman."

Will nodded. "Perryman? The banker over in Sharpsburg?"

"He owns the bank, yes. Among other things."

"And what business would Perryman have with Callahan?" Will asked.

"My message is for Callahan, sheriff. Now, will you open his cell and let me in?"

"Callahan?" Will called over his shoulder, "You have a visitor, works for Perryman. You know him?"

Perryman? Oh, yes, Callahan knew Perryman, knew

him well. He held the mortgage on his and Ben's ranch. He'd expected to hear from the man, but not so soon. The loan wasn't due until fall. "Yeah. Let him in."

"Guess you'd better let me search you," Will told Jerome. "Just in case you plan to break my prisoner out of jail."

"I certainly do not!" Jerome sounded offended. He held out his arms while Will checked for a gun.

Wearing a black suit and a small round hat, the man looked downright odd. As Callahan watched, it came to him that it wasn't the clothes so much as it was the man wearing them. He was lean and suntanned, not like a banker's associate, and his boots were those of a cowboy, not a clerk.

Will paused at the suggested bulge of a shoulder holster. "I'll take the gun," he said.

The visitor let out an oath, then handed over a small pistol concealed beneath his coat.

"And what do you have in your case?" Will asked.

"Just some legal papers." He opened it.

Will rifled through the case, then unlocked the cell door. "Go on in."

"I'd like to talk in private," Jerome said.

Will ignored Jerome and sat, assuming his resting position, feet on desk, head leaned against the wall. He closed his eyes. "You want to talk to my prisoner? Talk."

Jerome stood awkwardly inside the cell, facing Callahan, who was lounging by the window.

Callahan let him wait for a few seconds before asking, "Don't you think you're a little early, Jerome? I have until November to make my loan payment."

"No, you don't."

Callahan caught one of the bars in the window with his hand. "What do you mean?"

"That's why I'm here. Your mortgage has been paid. In full."

For a long time, Callahan simply stared at Perryman's lackey. "I don't understand. Who paid it?"

"Don't know. Just know they closed out the paper-work. I had business in Laramie, and Perryman asked me to tell you that you're out of debt. Too bad the other ranchers aren't as lucky." He smiled.

"Who paid it?" Callahan asked again softly, through gritted teeth. "I asked you, who paid off our mortgage?"

Jerome started backing up. "That's confidential infor-mation. I couldn't tell you even if I knew. And I don't. Too bad about your cattle. But it looks like you've still got your land. Let me out, sheriff."

Will opened the cell door, allowing Jerome to scurry out.

From his window, Callahan watched as Jerome tipped his hat to one of the bar girls walking down the wooden sidewalk. Then he climbed on a handsome dun-colored horse tied to the rail out front and rode off.

Callahan hit the wall with his fist and let out a roar. It made no sense. Ben was missing. Who the hell had paid off their mortgage? Why?

"Looks like that about sews it up, Callahan," Will said.

"What does that mean?"

"You answered your own question. Your ranch note got paid. What did you and your brother do with the rest of the money?"

"You think I'm that stupid, Spencer? Can't you see, someone is trying to frame me."

"Who?"

"I don't know, but I mean to find out."

"Since you're behind bars, you'd better hope Josie is as good a lawyer as she is a doctor," Will said wryly. "And while we're talking about Josie, there's something I want to say."

"Oh? What?"

"Lubina told me that you seemed . . . interested in Josie. I'm telling you to leave her alone. Dr. Annie and Dan are due back any day now. When they get here, they'll put a stop to what's going on. Josie doesn't know anything about men like you, and you don't know how to handle a woman like her."

Callahan felt an unwelcome twinge of jealousy. Josie was *his,* not the sheriff's. He wanted to claim her, strike out at the man who was scowling at him. But he couldn't. "You may be right, Spencer. In fact, I've told Josie that myself. But I have a problem. You see, she's the most stubborn woman I've ever known. She gets an idea in her head and you can't change it."

"Just so long as it isn't you giving her the idea," Will Spencer said. "I'm warning you. You just think you've got trouble now. Do anything to hurt Josie Miller and your neck might find its way to a rope."

Josie knew that Callahan was in trouble. He had a right to be worried. She could defend him from the charges of theft. She could pull out her law books and find cases and examples. But she was in Wyoming, where decisions were based on appearances. If a snake looked like a snake, it was a snake. The money was gone. Ben Callahan was gone. If she didn't find an explanation, that could be enough for a conviction. She'd already sent for Judge McSparren, but the truth was, she couldn't be certain the judge would be open to more legal maneuvering. This time she needed witnesses, facts. And the facts were somewhere between Laramie and Sharpsburg.

She needed to talk to her old law professors, but that was impossible. The only way out was to start asking questions. And the place to start was Sharpsburg. That decision made, she started packing. It was after midnight when she heard a pounding on the door. She wasn't expecting anyone, and the last thing she needed was another one of her mother's patients.

"*Señorita*," Lubina called out curtly, "there es someone to see you." It was clear from the housekeeper's voice that this someone did not meet Lubina's approval.

Josie let out a sigh and started for the door.

"Miss Miller." Ellie Allgood hurried down the corridor toward Josie. "I wouldn't have come so late, but I'm delivering a message." She stopped and glanced worriedly back at Lubina. "I was told we should talk privately."

"It's all right, Lubina. It's only Miss Allgood, one of my clients. Go to bed. I'll call you if I need you."

Reluctantly the housekeeper returned to her room behind the kitchen.

"Come in," Josie said.

"Thank you," Ellie said quickly. "I won't be long, I promise."

Once inside the parlor, Josie closed the door behind them. "What's wrong, Ellie?"

"I don't rightly know. Mr. Callahan asked me to fetch you. He's in a real tear."

"Callahan? Is he ill?"

"Ill-tempered, maybe, but I don't think that's what's got him stirred up. He says he's got to see you tonight."

"Did he say why?"

"He had a visitor this afternoon. Now he claims he may know who's behind the missing money. I'm supposed to bring you to the jail."

"Why didn't he send the sheriff?"

"The sheriff rode over to Sharpsburg."

"And you don't have any idea who his visitor was?"

"A man, a dandy in a suit. That's all I know."

Josie thought about her packed traveling case. "Let me change into my riding clothes and get my hat and my law books."

In ten minutes they were riding toward Laramie and Josie was deep in thought, mapping out her plans. She would ask for a jury trial. The evidence was all circumstantial. With any luck she could cast enough doubt about his guilt to get him off.

Josie realized that Ellie was prattling on about something. "I'm sorry, Ellie. What did you say?"

"I was asking you about Sheriff Spencer. Do you care for him?"

Josie shook her head, confused at the question. "Will? Care for Will? Is he sick?"

"Not his health, Miss Miller. Don't you know the man is crazy about you?"

That stopped her. Dan had suggested the same thing once, but Josie hadn't taken him seriously. "Why would Will be crazy about me?"

"I don't know, Miss Miller . . . Josie. Maybe because he's a man and you're a lady. Does he need a reason?"

"I'm not interested in Will, not that way. If a woman cared for a man, he'd know, wouldn't he?" She let her horse slow for just a moment, then said, "I mean, Will is just a friend. Actually, he's more Annie's friend than mine."

Ellie let a slow smile curl her lips. "It's Callahan, isn't it? You're sweet on him."

"Don't be silly, Ellie. I'm not sweet on Callahan."

"You can't fool me. I heard it in your voice. There's something between you two, I can tell."

Something between them? She tingled at the mention of his name. Her insides felt like Lubina's yeast dough, rising in the sun. It quite simply overwhelmed her when she allowed herself to remember his touch.

"Josie?"

She didn't answer Ellie; she couldn't. This kind of truth was private.

Ellie's whoop was her own response. "Good for you. You sure you know what you're doing? You could be getting yourself into a mess of trouble."

"Ellie, I'm not getting myself into anything. He's my client. Nothing else."

"Yeah, and Will Spencer's going to suddenly forget I work in a saloon and invite me out for a Sunday drive," Ellie said with a touch of bitterness in her voice. "I mean, he's too old for me, anyway, and I'm too . . . used for him. You'd do better to go after him and leave Callahan for me."

Josie finally grasped the reason behind Ellie's questioning. "You really care about Will?"

"Everybody seems to know that but Will." Ellie slowed her horse and glanced at Josie, frowning. "He doesn't even know I exist."

"If he doesn't know you exist, it's because you haven't made him aware of the real you, the woman who stood up to Virgil Wayne, the one who cares about other people. You've proved yourself. You even look different, Ellie. Just keep on standing up straight and looking Will in the eye, and he'll notice."

"As long as Will is interested in you, I'm thinking that he won't notice me. But maybe if you and Callahan—"

"There is no *me* and Callahan," Josie snapped. "I'm his attorney, nothing more. Tomorrow I'm going to Sharpsburg to talk to the banker who holds the mortgage on Callahan's ranch and anyone else I can find. I have to defend Callahan in court, and I need more than case law. I need facts."

"You're going to Sharpsburg alone? I can't let you do that. Look what happened to Callahan, and he's a man."

"But I'm not carrying five thousand dollars."

"That's not the only valuable thing a woman has to lose," Ellie argued. "I'll go with you. And don't worry, I know how to use a gun."

Josie patted her saddlebag. "You mean the gun you gave to me? So do I, if I have to."

The moon was high overhead when they rode into town—too bright for secrecy, Josie decided, riding straight up to the jail and dismounting. "Take your horse around back and wait for me, will you, Ellie? Leave mine out front. If anyone comes, you mustn't get caught."

"Yes, ma'am." Ellie climbed from her horse and started around the building, then stopped. "Are we breaking you in or Callahan out?"

Ever since the dandy representing Perryman had left, Callahan hadn't been able to stay still. Who had paid the loan, and why had Perryman thought it important enough to send someone to tell him? It couldn't have been because he was concerned. Perryman didn't know the meaning of the word. There had to be a deeper motive.

Reluctantly, Will had agreed to check out the loan payoff at the Sharpsburg bank, leaving Callahan in the care of the newly deputized hotel manager. He'd seen Ellie walking past the jail, and through the bars on the window, he'd convinced her to fetch Josie. But that was hours ago. Callahan caught the bars and shook them angrily. "Josie!"

Callahan's thoughts kept going back to Jerome. There

was something not quite right about the man. He'd been dressed like a banker, but he didn't seem comfortable with his mission. Callahan had been convinced something was wrong when Jerome left on a big dun-colored horse. The scene kept going around and around in his mind. Where had he seen a horse like that before?

Where? He started back across the cell, then stopped mid-stride. Damn! As clearly as if he'd been thrust back in time, he remembered. When he and Ben had been ambushed, he'd ridden away from the thieves, trying to divert them so that Ben could escape. Then pain. His horse had stumbled and he'd been thrown. Just before he passed out, he'd seen the horse, the dun-colored horse. He hadn't gotten a good look at the rider, only the brand on the horse's haunch—white, a shape like a crescent moon.

Now he'd seen that mark again. Perryman's lackey was riding the same horse as the man who'd shot him, or a horse with the same brand. Where was Josie? She had to get him out of this jail.

He heard the sound of a horse—no, horses. Someone was coming. The outside door opened.

He waited. He knew who it was without having to see her. He recognized Josie's scent—the same scent as on her pillow.

"Callahan?" she whispered. "Just hold on."

Callahan heard her fumbling with the lock. She swore again, talking to herself as she worked at the door. "You can do this, Josie. You still remember how. All you need is a hairpin," she muttered. A second later Callahan heard the rattle of the lock as it snapped.

The door swung open and Josie ran to the bunk. "Callahan, what's wrong?"

He grabbed her, jerking her forward so that she fell

across him. He intended to twist away and slip out the door. As much as he hated to do it, it was time to find his own answers. But there was one answer he needed first—from Josie.

He kissed her. She struggled briefly, but was no match for a determined man. It was a rough kiss, built of Callahan's frustration and the knowledge that he wanted this woman, wanted her badly, wanted her to the point of risking capture by delaying his jailbreak for a kiss. It was easy to tell himself that he was only interested because he needed her help—until he touched her. Then every lie went out of his head. He softened his kiss until he felt her tentative response.

That did it. He was lost. She hesitantly allowed his tongue inside her mouth. They kissed, over and over, twisting, canting their heads, hands pulling against collars, buttons, shoulders. Her mouth was hot, her breathing sporadic, her purring soft as she pushed herself against him.

He pulled back. "Damn! I didn't intend to do this. You drive me crazy, woman."

She stared up at him, her lips swollen with passion and her eyes filled with confusion.

Callahan drew in a deep breath, trying to focus on his escape plan. "Something happened today, Josie. I think I know one of the men involved in the holdup, but I have to get out of here to prove it, and you have to help me."

"You can't go," Josie whispered, dragging her shattered senses together. What was she doing? She reminded herself that she was here as an attorney, not some wanton woman whose body was nestled seductively against a man's. She jerked herself free and sat down on the bunk. "Until I reach Judge McSparren, there's no way you can be released."

"Josie, I can't wait. I have to get out of here."

"No. And if you sent Ellie to get me so that I could break you out of jail, forget it. Callahan, I'm sworn to uphold the law. You're a prisoner who happens to be my client. If you think kissing me senseless is going to persuade me to commit a crime, you're wrong."

"I understand your dilemma. But I won't lose Ben. Help me, Josie."

"You have to trust me, Callahan. I promise, I'll get you out another way."

Her respect for the law and her conviction that he would be exonerated was not only idealistic and misguided, it was downright foolish. He'd been on the wrong side of the law since before the end of the war. The law didn't protect men like him, even when its representative was Miss Josie Miller.

She was still breathing hard, and she knew as well as he did that she couldn't stop him if he really wanted to get past her.

Josie turned to look at Callahan. She couldn't see him clearly, for there was no light, but in her mind she could picture his face, hard and chiseled. His eyes were piercing in the darkness and his breathing harsh in the silence. She could still feel the touch of his hands on her face, his lips on her mouth, and she wanted nothing more than to turn around and recapture the moment they'd just shared.

"I'm leaving, Josie," he said, breaking the silence. "Before I go, I want you to know that I'm a man who wants you. But I know that this would be wrong—for me as your client and for you as my attorney. So you can scream for help or you can let me go and I'll never bother you again. Either way, I'm escaping."

Josie blinked, stared at him for a long minute, then stood up and backed away, still dazed by the tingling that made her lips feel as if they were connected to her kneecaps. Callahan had kissed her, yes. And she'd let him, welcomed it, and returned his kiss. He wanted her to betray her oath. She touched her mouth with the back of her hand.

"What did you say?"

"I said I'm leaving, Josie. I owe you my life, and I didn't want to go without setting the record straight. What I'm doing isn't fair to you. But I had to make a choice between you and Ben. You have a family, people who care, who will straighten this out and protect you. Ben doesn't. I'll lock you in this cell and you can tell them I overpowered you."

"Callahan," she sputtered, "if you break out of jail, you'll seriously compromise our case."

"I don't have a choice," he said moving toward her. "What happens to me isn't important anymore. I have to find out the truth, but I can't do it behind bars."

For Josie, searching for the truth was a powerful persuader. Callahan's life wasn't like Ellie's stolen watch. So far, she hadn't found any legal precedent on which she could argue for release. And sleight of hand wouldn't work here.

"Ben's life is at stake, Josie," he went on. "The Indian who brought me to you claims that a missionary train picked up Ben. If that's not true, I might be too late to save him. But I still need to prove he's innocent so that when Will catches up with that train, Ben won't be branded a thief. To do that, I've got to get to Sharpsburg. I had a visitor today, a messenger from Perryman, the banker. The note on our ranch has been paid in full."

That caught Josie's attention. "But . . . by who? Ben?"

"That's what I have to find out. I want to see those papers."

"And there's something else. I think Perryman's messenger's horse was wearing the same brand as the one that was being ridden by whoever shot me." He took a step toward her.

"You're not leaving," she warned, reaching behind her for the cell door. "As your attorney, I won't let you go."

All she had to do was slide out and lock it behind her. But in the time it took her to decide, Callahan reached out and caught her arm.

"I'm dismissing you as my attorney, Josie. You're fired."

"You wouldn't dare!"

He jerked her against him, gave her one last kiss, then, while he had her off-balance, turned around and slipped through the door, closing it behind him and snapping the lock fast.

"Don't do this, Callahan," she said.

"I'm truly sorry, darlin'. You saved my life and I'm grateful. Hell, I'm more than grateful. Under other circumstances . . ." His voice trailed off. There were no other circumstances, and there was nothing he could say. He glanced around, wishing the sheriff had left a gun, but there was nothing.

"My horse is in front, Callahan. Take him."

She heard the door open and close. Then there was nothing but silence. It was done. She'd picked the lock and let him break out without stopping him. Now she was an outlaw, just like him.

A few minutes passed and she went to work on the lock again. She heard footsteps and scurried to the cot to cover herself with Callahan's blanket.

"Josie, where are you?"

It was Ellie. "I'm here," Josie said, and flipped the blanket off.

"How'd Callahan get out of jail?"

"He broke out."

Ellie laughed. "Somehow I don't think your mama and daddy are going to believe that, Josie. I don't even believe it."

"Believe it," she said and went back to working on the lock. "Get me some light. I'm trying to get this lock open." She jabbed her hairpin into her thumb, dropped it, and swore.

Ellie fumbled along the wall until she found the lamp hanging by the front door. "Where's the key?"

"I didn't see it when I came in so I . . . uh . . . It's too complicated to explain, Ellie. Just give me one of your hairpins."

"You're picking the lock?"

"I'm trying."

By the time Josie got the door open, her hair was hanging loose over her shoulders and she was biting her lip and muttering in frustration. "I have to go after him. If he falls off that horse and rips open the stitches, he could bleed to death. I need a wagon."

"Callahan isn't a saloon girl you can save. You could get hurt."

"Callahan may be desperate, but he won't hurt me. You go on home, Ellie. I can take care of this."

"You stay put," Ellie said in a voice that realized argument would be fruitless. "I'll get the wagon."

Josie turned back into the jail, gathered up the blankets and a jacket that was hanging on a nail. Ellie's arrest had planted the bar girl on a new path, a path that she was following with confidence and gumption. Time passed and Josie began to fidget. She was about to light out on her own when Ellie slipped around the edge of the building.

"Let's go."

"What took you so long?" Josie grumbled as she put her blankets inside.

"I was arranging a little misdirection. Get in the wagon."

"You don't have to come," Josie said. "No point in you getting in trouble, too."

"Too late," Ellie said. "In a little while everyone is going to think that someone was hurt over toward Cheyenne and that you're heading up there. I'm going along to help."

Ellie's cool head was a pleasant surprise. "Well, if everyone believes there is an emergency, then I guess we'd better hurry."

Josie figured Callahan had at least a half hour's head start, and they would be moving at a slower pace in a wagon. She took the reins and gave them a flick. At the edge of town, Josie drove behind the buildings and doubled back, heading south.

"By the way, where are we really going?" Ellie asked.

"To Sharpsburg."

"But isn't that where Will is? Doesn't that seem a little chancy?"

"It's downright idiotic, but that's where Callahan is heading."

"Well, let's get moving." It would be morning when they got there, and riding into town would undoubtedly catch the sheriff's attention. That is, if they didn't meet him on the road along the way.

With the moonlight turning the plains into a silver carpet, they would never be able to conceal their presence. Luckily for Josie and Ellie, neither could Callahan. When they caught up with him, the horse was walking slowly down the road, with Callahan sitting so upright that he looked as if he were mounted on a pole. It was obvious that sheer willpower was keeping him that way. Thank heavens he'd been riding Solomon, who never traveled in a hurry. Josie pulled even, reached out, and took the horse's reins. "Whoa!"

Callahan started. "What are you doing here?"

Josie ignored his question. "Help me get him into the wagon, Ellie."

Together they pushed, shoving the protesting man into the back. "If we're arrested," Ellie said, "I'm going to swear I was kidnapped and didn't know what you were doing."

Josie made a pillow with the jacket and covered Callahan with the blankets. "I told you, you weren't strong enough to ride."

"The last time I knew, riding was exactly what I was doing. It's not my fault that nag is a hundred years old."

"Why do you think his name is Solomon? He's a lot wiser than you."

"I'm sorry, Josie. If you're determined to help me get there, stop wasting time and let's go. Here's what you'll—"

"No, this is what you'll do," Josie said, tying Solomon to the back of the wagon and climbing up to the wagon seat. "You'll shut up and rest. I'll get you to Sharpsburg. Then *we'll* decide what we're going to do."

Ellie, who'd been quiet up to then, turned to Josie. "And how do you plan to explain breaking a prisoner out of jail?"

"She didn't break me out." Callahan groaned as he stretched out in the back.

Josie ignored him. "I don't know. I'll figure that out when I need to."

Ellie sat for a moment. "Okay. Give me those reins

and you get back there and minister to your client—or patient—or whatever he is. I'll drive."

Maybe Ellie was right. Josie climbed in back and ran her fingers inside his shirt. "At least you haven't torn these stitches." She unbuttoned Callahan's Levi's.

He shifted his position. "Better watch where you put your fingers, darlin'."

"Stop that and be still," she retorted. "I have to make sure you're not bleeding."

"I'm not bleeding, Josie," Callahan said. "Besides you're my attorney now, not my doctor."

"No, I'm not. You fired me. Remember?"

"Well, until we find the money I'm supposed to have stolen, I'm rehiring you—provided you work on credit."

Josie remembered the nest egg she'd made investing her money on the advice of her grandfathers, money that was still drawing interest in the Sinclair Bank. "I'll take my chances on your credit," she said.

"Fine. You're rehired. At least you are until Will Spencer finds you with me. You think you can defend all of us from jail?"

"If I have to," Josie said, satisfied that Callahan hadn't damaged her medical work.

"I hope you mean that," Ellie called out. "I'm trying to make Will notice me, but I've had enough of jail."

Callahan let her fasten his trousers, then reached up and removed the man's felt hat she was wearing. He pulled her down beside him, resting her head on his good shoulder. "When we get to Sharpsburg I'm going to have to find a way to get into the bank and look at the loan papers."

"And how do you expect to do that, just walk into the bank and ask?"

"I haven't worked that out yet," he admitted. "I may

have to find a crooked locksmith, or maybe an out-of-work pickpocket."

Ellie groaned.

Josie looked up into the night sky that was full of stars. She wondered what Dr. Annie would say if she knew that her adopted daughter was lying in the back of a wagon in the arms of a criminal. She could guess what Dan would do.

"Your hair smells good," Callahan said, his voice slow and heavy. "I missed your pillow."

"Go to sleep, Callahan." Josie forced herself to remain focused. "I may have helped you escape, but from here on out, we're doing this by the book."

"By the book," he agreed, his breathing beginning to slow with sleep.

"And which book is that?" Ellie asked later, when it was obvious that Callahan was sleeping. "And what would it say about an attorney running off with a thief?"

"Not my law book, Ellie, the Bible. *Judge not that you be not judged.*"

"Somehow," Ellie said, "I don't think Judge McSparren is gonna accept that."

9

The wagon train had circled for the night, something they'd done every evening since leaving the main trail. Now the men were arguing about the shortcut their leader had taken. The scout had been certain he'd seen an Indian on a ridge in the distance, and so he decided they should leave the main trail. But this route would take weeks off their journey, and they'd been assured it was safe. In another two days they were supposed to reach a wilderness trading post, where they could replenish supplies—if they had money to do so.

Rachel went about her work as she did every night, without joining in the women's discussion. The others lighted cook fires to prepare the evening meal. Their movements were hushed. Even the oxen seemed quieter.

Inside Rachel's wagon the man lay half conscious, half asleep, trying to give form and substance to the vague shapes and sounds swirling through his mind. He still couldn't remember anything for certain. Hazy impressions of rocks and grass drifted through his dreams. And pain.

Through the opening in front of the wagon, he could see the western sky, tinged pink and orange, with wisps of purple clouds nestled across the mountain peaks like a thick patchwork quilt. It was a beautiful sunset, peaceful and reassuring. He could hear movement outside the wagon and smell something frying. The woman called Rachel worked hard. He could tell there were others around—cattle, horses, and children. But she'd been left alone.

Jacob forced himself to sit up, fighting light-headedness and pain. It was time for him to get out of the wagon and face whatever lay beyond, but weakness made him stop and wait. He watched the orange flames deepen into darkness and heard the call of a night bird as it signaled to its mate; he remembered Rachel telling him that God had sent him to her. What had she meant? Who was she?

A small, thin woman—wiry, rather than delicate—she might have been softer once, but the sun lines on her face and rough callouses on her hands told of her fierce determination to do whatever she had to do to make this journey. Deep, dark brown eyes darted about, seeing him but never directly facing him. Her dress was drab and wrinkled. On her head she wore a black-brimmed man's hat, the kind a banker or a preacher might wear. It was sweat-stained, but vanity didn't seem to be a characteristic she spent much time worrying about.

From the first time he'd opened his eyes and looked up at her, she'd been kind—caring for him, preparing food, and bathing the wounds on his face and head—yet she'd avoided his questions. No, she didn't know how he'd been hurt. No, she didn't know who'd hurt him.

"Just rest," she'd say. "You'll remember in God's good time." And she'd scurry away.

But as she'd driven the wagon across the plains, he'd heard her singing. Hymns and other songs she'd voice under her breath. Sweetly, but softly, as if she were singing for herself and didn't know anyone could hear. That voice had soothed him into and out of sleep, across the bumpy ruts and through the fretful dreams of violence that plagued his rest and vanished when he awakened.

Rachel. Just Rachel. No last name. And he was Jacob. A fine name, but not his real one, he was certain. Just as he was certain there was some terrible thing behind him. Still, for now, having a name gave him a reality. Until he knew who he was, he would be Jacob, because Rachel liked that name. Because she'd given it to him.

He pulled himself to his knees and crawled to the back of the wagon, pausing just a moment to look to the west, where a single star hung low in the night sky.

He clung to the sides of the wagon for a moment, testing his strength and his balance, then swung his feet to the ground. He was still weak, but he was standing on the prairie, holding himself erect for the first time in—he suddenly realized that he had no idea how long he'd been in Rachel's wagon.

There were wagons lined up side by side. In front of each was a small campfire—it reminded him of the welcome fires his mother used to have surrounding the plantation house every Christmas.

Plantation? At Christmas? Another vague memory came—and vanished just as quickly. This was not a land of plantations. It was a land of mountains and endless plains.

Rachel moved into his sight. She placed her hand

against the small of her back and stretched her shoulders. Too slight, she was, to drive a large wagon and four oxen across a rough terrain. But she did it, and she found enough joy to sing.

Here in the twilight, in a strange place he didn't recognize, the man who'd taken the name of Jacob felt unexpectedly happy.

"Miss . . . Rachel?"

She glanced up, surprised, alarmed. "You're up?"

"Almost. But I'm not certain I'll manage that for long." He felt himself sway and cursed the lightheadedness that turned him helpless.

"Here." She darted forward and slid her arm around his waist. "Let me help you."

She looked up at him, eyes wide with concern. And this time she didn't turn them away. He felt a shock run through him, like a fissure forming in the earth, the kind that shakes rivers and lakes. He'd felt those shocks before. But where? He didn't know. Now he was leaning against this woman, smelling her hair, her travel-worn woman scents seeming familiar, yet he had no recollection of holding a woman close. The only thing he remembered was a voice, a voice damning someone. Was it him?

"I'm sorry," he said, breaking the moment. "I guess I'm not as strong yet as I thought. I thank you for helping care for me," he said, fighting the confusion that muddled his choice of words.

She helped him over to a stool.

He sank down wearily and took a deep breath, warding off the blurry feeling that had swept over him.

"Being laid up for over a week takes a man's strength," she said, "even if he has no fever."

He hadn't realized how long he'd been ill and it surprised him. "I'm still a little unclear as to who you are and where we're going."

She turned back to the fire and took the big wooden spoon she'd been stirring with from the pot. "I'm Rachel Warren," she said. "And we're going to the Oregon Territory. We—I own a piece of land there I intend to farm."

"You're a kind and generous woman, Mrs. Warren, and I thank you for taking me in."

"You might not thank me when you find out the truth."

"Miss Rachel, I can't imagine any truth that would make me less grateful. I'm thinking I would have died if it hadn't been for you."

"You would have. That's what I told them. They don't approve, say it's not fittin'."

She looked around. He followed her gaze and saw the other travelers gathered in the middle of the circle. A large man wearing a black suit and hat like the one Rachel had been wearing came forward, holding something. Everything went silent, then a voice spoke out.

Jacob couldn't understand the words, but he suddenly understood what Rachel meant. The man speaking was a preacher, and the others were listening as he prayed. "A preacher?" Jacob said.

"You're on a missionary train," she explained softly. "They're going to Oregon, to preach to the heathens."

He let that sink in for a minute. "You aren't joining them in prayer?"

"No, I'm one of the heathens. My man got sick and the train we were with left us behind. He died. A few days later you came stumbling up to where I was burying him. We were somewhere north of Laramie. Somebody had beaten you bad. You didn't know who you were or what had happened. I couldn't just drive away and leave you, so I hid you in the wagon."

"Hid me?"

"That night, riders came. I think they were looking for you. But I'd camped behind some rocks, and they didn't find us. Then the missionary train came along."

"And I never said anything that would tell you my name?"

"The only name you mentioned was Sam, or maybe Sim. I couldn't tell for sure. You just seemed to be calling to him."

He tried that name on. "Sam. Sim." It meant nothing. "That's all I said?"

"No, you said over and over again that you had to get away."

He frowned in frustration. He couldn't connect that to anything. "Get away?"

"I didn't say anything to anyone, but I figured somebody was chasing you. Maybe you're a wanted man."

That hadn't occurred to him. "And weren't you afraid?"

She waited a long time before she answered. "I've been afraid for most of my life. When my man died, I figured that I'd die out here, too. I decided not to be afraid anymore. Then you came. So, Jacob Christopher, if you're a criminal, you just got yourself a second chance. Nothing you can do or say will frighten me."

"Rachel, why did you call me Jacob Christopher?"

"I named you Christopher for Saint Christopher. He's the patron saint of travelers and we're travelers in a strange land, and Jacob because in the Bible Rachel is the wife of Jacob."

"And the mother of Benjamin," he said, wondering how he knew Benjamin. He repeated the name and felt an odd flutter in the vast nothingness of his mind.

The call of a night bird came through the dusky air, sweet and clear. A sudden breeze rustled the tall grass, and the silky whisper brought Jacob an unexpected feeling of peace. This wasn't where he belonged, but this was where he was, and he'd do the best he could until he remembered.

If he remembered.

Suddenly, he did remember something that had puzzled him earlier; Rachel's comment about being "one of the heathens." He studied her.

She possessed a kind of resigned strength that came from living a hard life. He could still feel the callous on her fingers. As he listened, he touched his own hands. Calloused, yes, but it was obvious that his hands had been gloved. Hers had not. "Rachel, why do the missionaries consider you a heathen?"

She seemed to think about her answer, then said, "They thought you were my husband. I should have let them believe that, but before I knew who they were I'd told them we weren't married. The reverend said nobody living in sin could be a part of the train. That once you were in command of your faculties, he'd marry us. Else we'd have to go—both of us. I"—her voice strengthened—"I couldn't let that happen. I know now it was selfish of me, but I was kinda hoping you wouldn't come to your senses till we got to my farm. I could use the help there." She glanced at the gathering. "But I guess it's too late now."

Jacob looked up to see the preacher heading toward them, the others following like goslings behind the mama duck.

"I'm Brother Joshua," the preacher said when he reached them. "And I've come to perform the ceremony."

"I think we ought to talk about this," Jacob said quietly, coming to his feet. "I'm not sure that getting married would be wise."

"Suit yourself, Jacob. But we are God's people, and we don't condone living in sin. Either you marry this woman or she'll have to leave the train. Without help, she won't survive, and neither will you. This is Indian country."

"You don't have to do this, Jacob," Rachel said softly, coming to stand beside him. "I'll manage. I always have."

She was wrong. He did have to do it. She'd taken him in and saved his life. If he had a wife, he had no knowledge of it. Because he had no past, he had no future beyond repaying a debt to the woman who'd put herself at risk by taking him in. This was a question of honor. Looking from Rachel to the pious man with the threatening eyes, he saw no choice.

"Of course, Reverend," he said, stepping back to brace himself against the wagon. "I'll marry Rachel."

The others drew near. The women, heads down, nervously gathered their children while the men stared at Rachel's proud stance with accusing eyes, as if she'd planned her sin and dared them to criticize.

"What's your name?" the minister asked.

"I'm . . . I don't know." He looked at Rachel for assistance.

She frowned, then said, "He doesn't remember who he is. I gave him his name. He's Jacob . . . Jacob Christopher."

The minister opened his Bible. The ceremony was short and brusque. "Worship the Lord, else this union will be a punishment," the minister said. These words lingered in the groom's mind, for they were not a blessing. They were a warning.

It was almost morning when Josie felt Ellie stop the wagon. "Josie, we're coming up on Sharpsburg. Unless you want to be arrested, you'd better get out here. I'll drive on alone."

Josie slid out of Callahan's arms and sat up. "And how do you intend to explain having an escaped criminal in your wagon? Remember, Sharpsburg is Callahan's town. People are bound to recognize him."

"That won't matter. We aren't going into town. I've changed my mind. We're going to my ranch. That's where Ben would have gone."

Josie shook her head. "And that's the first place the other ranchers—not to mention Will—would have looked." Will was likely to check out the ranch again as soon as he heard that Callahan had broken out of jail.

"Maybe, but Ben's smart. He wouldn't let himself be found. He'll hide—and wait."

Josie didn't agree, but she hadn't the heart to point out the flaws in Callahan's logic.

"I have to know, Josie," Callahan said quietly. "I'll ride in east of the ranch and follow the river to the stand of cottonwood trees. They'll conceal my approach. When I'm sure it's safe, I'll ride in."

"If you don't fall off your horse and drown," Josie chastised. "You can't go alone, Callahan."

"I can and I will. If you run into the sheriff, you'll have a legitimate reason for being in Sharpsburg—you're getting information for my defense. Please, Josie. I won't cause anymore trouble for you than I already have."

The tenderness in his voice stopped Josie for a

moment. "And what happens if you do find Ben? You know he's been hurt. You may need me."

"He hasn't been hurt," Callahan said quietly.

"You don't know that." Josie argued, just as quietly. "Something has kept him from coming to you."

After a long minute, he nodded. "All right, we'll take two of the horses. One ought to be able to pull the wagon. Ellie can ride on into Sharpsburg and check out the situation."

"Me?" Ellie questioned. "And how do I let you know what I find out?"

"Just check into the hotel and wait. Josie will come to you."

Josie looked worried. "Somebody will telegraph Will as soon as they find out you're gone. What's Ellie's reason for being there if she runs into him?"

"She's to tell him that I escaped," Callahan said. "I've headed west in search of the missionary train."

Ellie shook her head. "He'll never believe that. And where is Josie supposed to be? Why isn't she with me?"

The horses moved restlessly in the silence that followed. Then came Callahan's terse answer. "You're right, Ellie. Just tell Spencer I kidnapped her."

10

—⚬—

Josie rode beside Callahan, who traveled at an easy pace. She had never been south of Laramie on horseback, so she was surprised to find the countryside so lush and green. Laramie existed because of the railroad. By the time Dr. Annie, Dan, and Josie had arrived, the town had saloons, a hotel, a store, a jail, a newly formed city government that had rid the town of its riffraff, a town marshal who was once accused of murder in Cheyenne, and soldiers at the nearby fort.

In the years since, Wyoming had given women the right to vote and serve on juries. They'd discovered gold in the Snowy Mountain Range, and the population was growing. But this section of the territory, near the Colorado border, was still sparsely settled cattle and farming country.

As the sun rose beyond the hills in the east, a peaceful glow was cast over the plains, and with it came a gentle breeze that ruffled the tall sage grass and spread its pungent odor. Had it not been for the danger, Josie might have enjoyed the ride. To be alone with a man like Callahan was something new to her, and the warmth she felt had more to do with the man riding beside her than the glow of the sun.

They followed the river, east to west, their horses scaring up wildlife nesting in the grass and insects hovering over the blossoms. For a while Josie kept an anxious eye on Callahan, and he seemed not only to be holding up well, but to be rejuvenated as they drew nearer his ranch. She didn't know whether it was the sun or the activity that was bringing faint color to his cheeks. The deep worry lines she was so accustomed to seeing on his forehead seemed to have relaxed, and he sat straighter in the saddle. How would he feel when he learned that Ben was not there? What would he do?

"We're on Callahan land now," he said with pride. "I never thought I'd own my own place. I know it doesn't look like much to you, but with the new cattle and a little luck it could have been."

"It still can, Callahan. Don't give up. A man who came back from the dead can do anything."

"Not without Ben," he said, and turned his horse into the stand of cottonwoods that bordered both sides of the small river. "All of this was his dream. I lost any hope for a future long ago."

He fell silent for a moment, then added, "I was surprised when Ben suggested raising cattle. I always thought he was more the schoolmaster type, or maybe a banker. In the beginning I thought he was doing this for me, but later he seemed almost happy. You know, we might have made it."

"You like raising cattle?"

"Cattle? Yeah, I do. It's the kind of thing a man can do himself. He doesn't have to rely on . . . workers. We hired an extra hand or two at branding time, but otherwise we managed." Callahan fell silent for a few minutes, then said, "We have to be careful now, Josie. The barn is just across the river, beyond the trees."

Josie didn't have to be told. On the flat plains she had already seen the outline of the ranch in the distance. "What do you intend to do?"

"First, I'm going to search the buildings. If . . ." He let his voice trail off. "If he isn't here, we'll stay here until dark, then we ride into town."

She noticed he didn't mention searching further for Ben. Perhaps he knew this was a futile trip. Still, with every word he spoke, he seemed more determined, more in charge, stronger.

He chose a wide, shallow spot in the river and signaled his horse forward with a nudge of his heels.

Josie followed.

Old Solomon balked at going into the water, until he saw Callahan's horse start across, then he trailed along at his normal, plodding pace.

They reached the clearing between the stand of cottonwood trees and the barn, and Callahan drew his horse to a stop, motioning that Josie should do the same. He slid from the saddle and leaned against the horse while he tested his legs.

Letting out a deep sigh, he said, "Wait here until I signal."

"And if you don't? Shall I come when you fall on your behind, or just wait around here until you get shot again?" she asked.

He didn't answer. Instead, he crouched down and ran in an uneven gait toward the back of the barn. His dexterity amazed her, though it shouldn't have. Callahan's speed announced his determination, his awkwardness betrayed the still tender injury in his groin. She could see his right hand as it reached for the spot where his gun should have been, but wasn't. The morning suddenly went silent. Since waiting had never been Josie's style, she certainly didn't intend to do it now.

As quietly as possible she slid off old Solomon, flipped his reins over a low branch, and followed Callahan's path. Something about the silence told her that they were alone.

The barn was empty, except for one lone chicken pecking seed from the grain in the corner. Josie heard the creak of steps in the hayloft overhead and was looking around for a place to hide when she saw Callahan's feet backing down the ladder. He tightened his lips when he turned and caught sight of her.

"Don't you ever do as you're told?" he asked.

"Of course. But I also do what I think is best in a given situation," she said patiently, "and I'm thinking, after what's happened, you ought to be glad that I do. Looks like the barn is empty."

"Yes." Callahan didn't seem surprised.

She hadn't expected to find Ben here. Bear Claw said Ben was with the wagon train, which was north of Laramie. She knew that Bear Claw was right. But she also knew that Callahan had to find out for himself.

"I'm going to tell you one more time, Josie, *stay put*. I didn't steal the ranchers' money, and with any luck I'll be able to prove it. But if anything happens to you, I'll be strung up to the nearest tree."

The stern look in his eyes slipped for a moment, and she caught a flash of something she could only interpret as worry.

"I don't want anything to happen to you," he whispered.

"Nothing will." She reached out, almost touching him, then stopped. As they stood, only inches apart, she watched him start to speak, then turn away.

"I mean it Josie, please."

She nodded and watched him walk toward his house.

Callahan moved slowly, refusing to stoop or run on his own land. Josie had been right. He'd virtually come back from the dead. He wouldn't have come this far if he wasn't supposed to make it. He'd been through a lot in the past, but had always survived. This time was different. He wasn't alone. Josie had saved him and she refused to give up, even risking her reputation by accompanying him here to the ranch. He could only guess how hard that had been. It was hard for him, too, in another way. He could feel the heat of her presence, and it had taken all his strength to turn and walk away from her just now.

He reached the house, put one foot on the bottom step of the sagging porch, and listened. He didn't have to be told the house was vacant; he sensed it before he pushed open the door and stepped inside. It looked exactly as it had the morning he and Ben left to transport the money to Laramie. He hadn't truly expected Ben to be here, but he'd hoped, and now that hope was gone.

Wearily, he sank down in the rocking chair Ben had insisted on bringing from South Carolina. It had been falling apart, but it had been the only thing left of his mother's, except for her cameo. Through the winter, Ben had spent hours replacing the cane in the chair. The chair was still here, but along with the missing money, the cameo was gone too.

Callahan leaned forward and covered his face with his hands. How in the world was he going to find Ben without getting caught himself? he wondered.

"Callahan, are you all right?" Josie's voice came from the porch.

Callahan cleared his throat and swallowed the lump that threatened to close it completely. But he hadn't moved quickly enough, because before he could erase the moisture at the corners of his eyes, Josie was before him, on her knees, her hands holding his. She looked like the angel he'd called her. A bit tattered and dusty, but an angel nonetheless. Now they were alone. The house seemed smaller.

He'd allowed himself to hold her last night in the wagon, telling himself that it would be the last time. Once they reached Sharpsburg, she'd be forbidden treasure— seen, touched, and relinquished. He couldn't be with her now, not when he was facing prison or worse, not after all they'd been through, not after he'd lost Ben.

"Don't worry, Callahan. We've come this far. We'll find him."

Her hands were soft against his rough ones, holding them gently. She gave him her strength and compassion with her touch. He pulled off her hat and studied her openly, allowing himself to see what he so badly needed now, the courage of those decisions she made regardless of the consequences.

Blue eyes looked back at him, clear and honest. This must be what a man could expect from a woman who cared about him. But he couldn't be sure because he'd never seen it before.

"You have to go back to Sharpsburg," he said in a voice so tight he wasn't certain she understood. "You've done enough."

"You know I can't."

He fought off the urge to put his arms around her. "If you go now, you can say I forced you to bring me here."

She cupped his face, rubbing her fingertips against the stubble of his beard, as if she were comforting a child. "I know now what Bear Claw's ghost horse meant."

Callahan was baffled. What did this have to do with Sharpsburg?

"The night you came to me, I saw it on the ridge in the storm. The Sioux—or at least some of them—believe that when you see the ghost horse it means a person is about to be claimed by the spirit world. But you didn't die. I don't know why, but I think it means that we are supposed to . . . care for each other."

Callahan didn't know what to say. He didn't know how to answer her, and he didn't know what to do about the closing distance between their faces as she leaned forward and kissed him. Her touch was light, gentle, almost shy. For a moment he allowed himself to feel her gentleness and the sweet illusion her touch inspired.

When he finally pulled back, she lifted her eyes in uncertainty. "What's wrong?" she asked. "I know I'm not very good at this." She lowered her gaze in embarrassment, and in that moment Callahan felt like the liar and thief he'd been branded. What she didn't understand was that her actions could hurt her even more than her embarrassment.

"Don't do this, Josie. What you're feeling now, it isn't real. You saved my life and now you feel responsible. But I'm tired, and I'm still weak, and it's been a long time since a lady kissed me. Go back to Sharpsburg, find Ellie and Will, and tell them I passed out and you got away."

She stood up and turned toward the window, her brow furrowed in uncertainty. He wondered how long it had been since Josie Miller hadn't known exactly who she was and what she was doing.

"You didn't find Ben, but you still need me to get into

the bank, to check those loan papers. That is what you came here for, isn't it?"

He gave a dry laugh. "And how are *you* going to get me into the bank, pick the lock?"

"If I have to. I don't know what's happened in your life," Josie said in low, tight voice, "to keep you from trusting people, but I can understand it. It took me a long time to learn that when somebody offers help, you should accept and appreciate it and try to become the person they believe you can be. I saved your life. That ought to be enough to have earned your trust."

"Trust?" he questioned, his body a mass of quivering muscles. "The last time I trusted you I ended up in jail."

"I couldn't stop that, Callahan."

And he couldn't stop his response. He'd punished his body and it was protesting. Even now, the air between them was turning as hot as a desert wind. "Josie. I trust you, but I still haven't earned your trust. And I won't be able to prove myself until this is over. That's the way it is."

"Callahan, I'm not judging you. Dan and Dr. Annie took me in when nobody else would. They didn't know how I'd turn out. They told me they cared. I still don't understand why. But they did. They taught me that caring comes from a kind of internal goodness. People either have it or they don't. Sometimes we can't see it or explain it, but when it's there, it's there. You just have to believe it in your heart. You don't have to prove anything to me."

With a stubbly growth of beard on his craggy face, Callahan looked every inch an outlaw. Josie knew that believing anyone cared about him was beyond Callahan's present state of mind. Her passionate speech came from the knowledge that she was beginning to believe in his goodness. The kind of goodness that comes from loyalty and love. Wherever he was, nothing was going to stop him from finding his brother and saving this ranch. Not her. Not bullets. Not the law.

Callahan might be an outlaw, but he didn't lie. She was the dishonest one, one minute pretending to be an outstanding member of the community, the next, reverting to her street-urchin, pickpocket ways.

"It's been a long time since I believed in anything, Josie," Callahan said finally. "Don't try to make me more than I am. I'm not a very nice person. I told you that before and now it's time for you to believe it. Years ago I went away to fight for the south, not out of any great sense of patriotism, but because I almost killed my old man. I didn't know until the war started that he wasn't my real father. He'd promised my mother that nobody would ever find out. She was the one with the plantation, you see. He was her pa's overseer. Once Ben came along, I was in the way. So when South Carolina seceded, I joined the army. I thought he'd be proud. But in the end he was killed by a band of Yankee soldiers who were raping and stealing from anyone who was still alive. The plantation was lost. I couldn't even save my mother and sister. And now I've lost Ben."

"You tried, Callahan. That's all that matters," she said quietly.

"The one thing I learned was that the victor reaps the spoils, even if they are criminals. The loser only loses. And pride? It's not worth the tin cup you use to spit it in. After the war, there were no graves for my family, and Ben had disappeared. I'd lost everything."

"Believe me, I understand about loss. But that's in the past. What we both need right now is food. Any chance there's something here to eat?"

"I don't think anybody's been here," he said, "but there ought to be cans in the storeroom. Maybe some beans and flour. Ben did most of the cooking." He brushed by her and opened a door off the kitchen. "Out here."

She followed him, her senses taking off at a wild gallop in the aftermath of his touch. "Is there coffee?"

"Over the stove. You get what you want out here while I start a fire. I'll go get fresh water from the pump at the back door."

Josie fidgeted. "I'll get the water," she insisted as she picked up the flour. "You've done enough walking."

"I told you, I'll go," he said. "The horses have to be put in the barn." He started toward the front door.

Josie stopped where she was and faced him with a look of chagrin. "Wait, Callahan, there's something you ought to know."

He stopped, but didn't turn around. "What?"

"I don't know how to cook."

When the reverend and his followers turned away, Jacob—he still found it hard to think of himself by that name—relaxed the protesting muscles in his body and sagged back against the keg where he'd been sitting.

"You didn't have to do that," Rachel said softly.

"Do what?"

"Marry me."

"I couldn't leave you alone, not after what you've done for me."

"Long before my husband died, I was alone." A sad look crossed her face. "Howell drank too much. He found a way to hide from his trouble."

"I don't mean to pry, Rachel, and if you'd rather not tell me, I'll understand, but what kind of trouble?"

"Howell had only one leg. In his eyes, that made him only half a man."

"A lot of fighting men came back from the war with missing limbs. I can imagine how hard that must have been."

"Yes," she said, without offering further explanation.

He smiled at her. "And you looked after him without complaint, didn't you?"

"It was my duty."

"You take duty very seriously, don't you, Rachel?" Jacob asked, looking off into the distance.

He wanted to know more about this woman. "Are you Catholic? Brother Joshua didn't seem to be a priest."

"No. He's starting his own church. And I don't suppose you'd call me anything. My father gave up on God a long time before I was born, but don't tell the reverend that. He'd probably turn around and go back to that salty lake we passed to baptize me. I may go to hell, but I'd rather not be pickled when I get there."

Jacob grinned. It seemed his *wife* had a sense of humor.

Just for a moment, when she smiled, he saw a different woman from the strong, silent little wren he'd thought her to be. Of course, his vision had been clouded before, but he'd thought her older. Her ample breasts couldn't be disguised by the plain, threadbare brown dress she was wearing. The worn spots looked almost honey-colored, matching the golden tints in her primly braided hair. He wondered how it would look loose on a pillow. A twitch in his loins reminded him that, in spite of his loss of memory, he was a man. And this woman was his wife. Wife? Had he ever had one before? This time, no flashes of memory came to him.

There was an awkward silence while he attempted

to remember the thread of their conversation. Parents. "And your mother?" he asked, moving reluctantly back to the present.

"I don't know. She left soon after I was born."

"I'm sorry, Rachel." The mention of her parents brought back images of his own. "I have a shadowy impression that my mother was quiet—or afraid. Maybe of my father. He was killed during the war, I believe. I don't think his death was a great loss."

Rachel wanted to be glad that he remembered, but she wasn't. She was afraid that he might remember too much, remember a life that would take him away from her.

"My Pa was a violent man," Jacob added. "He treated . . . people badly. I don't know how I know that, but I do."

The distant pounding in his head intensified, and he pressed his fingertips to the sore spot on his forehead, trying desperately to pull back something from the darkness. Nothing came.

"You just lean your head back against that wagon and rest," she said, "while I get our supper done. Whatever you need to know will come to you in time."

But when? Jacob cursed whatever fate had taken his past and left a shell of a man behind. This Howell that Rachel had been married to might have had only one leg, but at least he knew who he was. Jacob looked down at his clothing—typical ranchhand wear, but surprisingly clean. "My clothes?" he said, using the tone of his voice to turn it into a question. "You washed them, how'd you . . . I mean, did I . . . ?" He felt his face flush.

"Take 'em off? Nope. I did it. And I kept you cleaned up too. And yes, you were naked at the time. No way around that. You don't wear underwear. Makes sense to me. Why'd a man want to burn up if he doesn't have to?"

She'd taken off his clothes, washed them, and bathed his body? Jacob was speechless. He closed his eyes, drawing in the smells of the campfire, listening to the sound of the oxen and the laughter of children running through the camp in a game of chase.

Rachel began to sing. Conscious now of the woman behind the shadowy figure who'd hovered at the edge of his awareness for days, he listened to the words of her song. She sang a plaintive song of an Irish boy who went off to war, of the fair Colleen who'd loved him, and how she went to a rock on top of a hill outside their village to wait for his return. But he never came home, and she grew old alone. The boy's name was Fin, and as Rachel sang, that song permeated Jacob's awareness like the smell of a smokehouse in winter, tantalizing and somehow reassuring.

A stronger scent filled the air—coffee—and he realized that he was hungry. "Let me help you," he said, forcing himself to sit up again.

"No need. I'm making biscuits," she replied. "They'll be done in a minute."

"I can do that."

She looked over her shoulder, surprised. "You cook biscuits?"

"Did it every day." Her fingers were forcing the flour and lard together. He came closer. "Where's the milk?"

"In the cow," she answered.

He smiled, his face lighting up like a small boy who'd discovered a bee's nest filled with honey. He glanced around. "A cow? Where?"

"Rosie's tied out with the oxen, grazing. It might be harder than you think, Jacob. . . ." Her voice trailed off.

But Jacob, undeterred, picked up a bucket and headed for the animals.

Though his gait was unsteady, he felt a certain pride in moving, in being able to do something. Milking a cow was a simple thing—not manly, probably not even particularly helpful, but for the first time in days he was doing something.

Jacob pulled the cow around so he could sit on a stump and placed the bucket on a level spot. He realized he didn't have a clue about what he was supposed to do. The cow fidgeted, swishing her tail impatiently. Obviously, he'd done this before, otherwise he wouldn't have known to bring the bucket or where to put it. Gingerly, he clasped the teats in his hands and tugged.

Rosie snorted, lifted one leg, and brought her hoof down hard on Jacob's foot.

"All right, girl. So I'm doing it wrong. You could be a little more helpful to a man who's had a lick on the head."

She swung her head around and gave him a careless glance, as if to say it was up to him and he'd better be quick about it.

"Need some help, mister?"

An orange-haired boy with a dirty face peeped around one of the oxen. "I mean, if you'll let me have a cup of her milk, I'll show you how it's done."

"That's a deal," Jacob said to the boy and stood up. "Show me."

"Well, it's like this. You pretend there's a bucket full of ants down there and you got to drown them suckers. Then you just catch hold at the top of the tit and squeeze, like you're trying to empty it."

Jacob watched a stream of yellow-white liquid hit the bottom of the bucket and spatter the side, like the frothy surf kicked up by a storm. As he watched, he knew that he'd never milked a cow before. But he did have the uncanny sensation that he'd at some point lived near an ocean. It occurred to him that he didn't even remember where Wyoming was. But he was certain they were a long way from the coast. After a few minutes the boy leaned back. "You want to try it?"

As Jacob Christopher, he would have to learn a whole new way of thinking. He nodded and sat on the stump, clasping Rosie's warm teats and closing his eyes so that he didn't show his revulsion.

"Remember the ants," the boy directed. "One at a time, aim, squeeze, and let 'em have it."

The directions were good. Jacob followed them to the letter, and a short time later they had half a bucket of warm milk.

When Rachel caught sight of him returning, her eyes lit up unexpectedly and a smile curved her lips. The setting sun put a glow on her face, illuminating her warm brown eyes. Jacob held her gaze for a moment, then watched the smile disappear.

"I wasn't certain you'd be able to do it," she said in a voice that didn't match the tenderness he'd seen in her eyes only moments before.

"I didn't," he admitted. "I had help."

She glanced behind him. "Tell me you're not carrying a fairy in your pocket."

"No fairies. Sorry, only a little red-haired boy."

"No matter," she said, retying the string on her apron. "Never did believe in fairies anyhow."

Jacob couldn't help but notice that the buttons down the front of Rachel's shirtwaist gapped open. He tried not to stare, but he couldn't seem to stop himself. He took a step closer.

"What . . . what are you thinking, Jacob Christopher?"

He saw the sudden flash of fear in her eyes that came with realization. "Right now I don't think you want to know." He handed her the bucket and closed his eyes to block out temptation.

"Don't you go passing out on me," she snapped, suddenly beside him, her arm around his waist, those full breasts pressed against his chest. The ever-present throbbing in his head intensified.

He started to fade into blackness, all the while knowing that he'd never be able to control himself around this woman if he remained conscious.

11

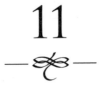

Josie looked down at the sodden mass of cornmeal and winced. "I should have stayed home and learned to cook," Josie sighed. But that wasn't what Dr. Annie had in mind for her daughter. Josie was to go to school, and it was there that learning became her passion.

Then Lubina was hired, and it was understood that no one was to trepass in her kitchen, which suited Josie fine. And when Josie went to New York to read law, there were housekeepers and cooks in both of her grandfathers' homes.

Josie had spent most of her life scavenging for books, and through her reading she'd discovered a world she'd never even dreamed of. But it was a world that didn't include cooking.

So be it. She found a skillet inside the oven, still greasy from its last use. With a small prayer for help from Lubina's patron saint of the kitchen, she poured the mixture into the skillet and plopped it on top of the stove where she could keep an eye on it.

Callahan snored in the room off the parlor–kitchen, exhausted from their ride and, Josie suspected, from the disappointment of not finding Ben. After they stabled the horses, she'd insisted he rest before they started back to Sharpsburg.

He hadn't argued. "All you have to do is start the fire," he said. "I'll just rest a few minutes, and then I'll help you make something to eat."

But as he slept, she became restless, pacing the small cabin, her thoughts focused on him. Not on his health, or even on what they'd done by breaking him out of jail, but on the man. Her heart hurt for the pain he felt because he thought he had let Ben down. Facing the possibility of losing your family must be devastating. She had better get used to that idea, she thought. After what she'd done, that could very well happen.

Josie continued to pace, torn between concern for her family's reaction to what she'd done and her feelings for this man for whom she'd risked everything. It wasn't just that Sims Callahan was an incredibly handsome man, it was the strong sense of connection she felt to him. The feeling of danger was gone. Whatever he'd done, it was to protect the people he cared about. He was simply trying to find a place where he could belong—just like her.

Josie didn't fool herself about how vulnerable she was right now. They were alone out here, and though he was still not back to his full strength, he could overpower her with nothing more than a kiss. Her heart moved like a wild mustang in a small corral.

She had to find something to do, else she'd wake Callahan, and that could be a mistake. How hard could making coffee be? She found a real coffeepot, filled it with water, and placed it on the hot stove. Next, she opened the can of coffee and measured out a loose handful, hoping it was enough to make a reasonable cup of coffee without having it walk out the door. Opening the top buttons of her shirtwaist, she fanned herself. How did women do this three times a day? The stove heated the July air, but it wasn't just the air that caused her forehead to bead with perspiration. It was the man sleeping in the other room.

Josie picked up her law books and tried to research cases that might be similar to Callahan's, cases where juries had reversed sentences, cases about breaking and entering and larceny, but if there was a case involving a man who was robbed while transporting money, she couldn't find it. Josie the attorney was out of her element; she'd become Josie the woman, and there were no books in her carryall to give her directions about that.

Josie's thoughts drifted to Ellie, and she wondered what had happened to her when she arrived in town. Did Will Spencer know that Callahan was out of jail? Was he still in Sharpsburg?

It would have made more sense for her to go into Sharpsburg and question Banker Perryman about Callahan's loan herself. But the truth was, she'd come to the ranch instead because she couldn't resist this man. In a matter of days she'd shed the fourteen years of training that had gone into making her a lady. She'd gone from upholding the law to breaking it. Now she was an outlaw, too. She'd chosen a different trail and she'd have to ride it to the end, wherever that might take her.

She let her gaze wander across the meager furnishings of the center room through the open doorway. Callahan lay sprawled across the bed like some loose-limbed child.

His new clothes, softened now by wear, were wrinkled. He'd removed the replacement boots Will had provided for him. Josie had had to cut the old ones off Callahan's wounded body.

This ranch wasn't much, but it was Ben's dream. By now, Josie had figured that it was as much Callahan's dream as Ben's. And suddenly it had become hers, too, because saving it would be the measure of her success as an attorney.

A burning smell brought Josie back to the present. She turned and reached out to pull the skillet away from the heat, letting out an oath of pain when the handle touched her bare fingers.

"Son of a—"

The skillet hit the floor in a clatter. Callahan jumped to his feet. "What's wrong?" he asked, reaching for the gun that wasn't there.

"Nothing," Josie said, dropping to the floor to conceal the evidence of her total incompetence. "I'm . . . I'm just a little woozy," she whispered foolishly.

"Careful!" Callahan started toward her. "If you're going to faint, don't fall against the stove." He covered the distance between them in long steps, and before she realized what he was doing, he'd knelt, pulled her up, and held her against him.

"I wasn't going to faint," she protested. Though now that she was being clasped to his big strong chest, she might be speaking a little too soon.

"No wonder you're feeling woozy. It's as hot as a Texas prairie fire in here. We're used to it, but that hacienda you live in is ten degrees cooler. Let's get you out of some of those clothes."

She looked at him in shock.

"I mean, we need to wash your face with some cool water. On second thought, the river will be quicker." Within seconds he was on his feet and pushing her out the door, down the steps, across the yard, and into the cottonwoods.

"Let me go, Callahan. I'm just fine," she said, but he wasn't listening, and she wasn't even sure she'd said the words.

He plowed directly into the river and sat, clothes and all, pulling her into the water next to him. The water level came only to his waist, but it came to her breasts. The current was strong enough to rock her, and she began to struggle.

"I thought the rivers dried up in summer," she sputtered.

"Not this one," Callahan answered, dragging her across his lap. "It comes straight out of the mountains underground."

She tried to keep herself upright, but the water kept pushing her against him. He realized what was happening and lifted her, letting the current settle her in his lap, then turned her so that her upper body was facing him and her legs were around him.

Her skirt rose like a bubble and floated loose about the tops of her thighs, exposing her stockings and her legs.

Josie had little choice except to slide her arms around his neck to balance herself. She was the weak one, not Callahan, and she found herself clinging to him shamelessly. Protests swirled through her mind and disappeared. She was pressed against him, against the strong wall of his chest. This was forbidden; she should stop him, pull herself out of his grasp, and run back to the house.

"Your wounds . . ."

"My wounds are finally cool," he said, sliding into shallow water and bringing her with him. "What about you?"

"Better," she lied. She'd been warm in the kitchen, but that heat didn't compare to the heat rushing through her body at this moment. She wouldn't be surprised if the water began to boil.

She could feel his heart beating against her breasts, the heat of his breath against her forehead and in her hair. "If bathing my face was your objective, then you've certainly succeeded. There's only one problem." She pulled her soaked blouse away from her skin, squeezed the water from it, then realized that the wet fabric against her skin was her only protection from the delicious touch of Callahan's chest.

"Only one?" he questioned, his brow furrowed.

She gulped in a breath of air, let it out, and said, "Our clothes are soaking wet and we have no more. We may draw just a little too much attention tonight when we ride into Sharpsburg, don't you think?"

"I can't say that I'm doing a lot of thinking at the moment, about riding into Sharpsburg, that is." His hands were moving against her back, his fingers pressing her closer to him. "But this is summer—in Wyoming—and wet clothes can be dried." He pushed her skirt up to her waist and a moment later pulled it over her head and slung it to the bank.

For a long minute they just looked at each other.

"Are you afraid of me, Josie?"

Her fingertips threaded through his hair, around his ear, and finally brushed the droplets from those long dark eyelashes. She became aware that his respiration had increased. Their eyes met in silent wonder. "Yes," she whispered, knowing he understood that her agreement had nothing to do with their clothes.

When Callahan kissed her, regrets and objections swirled through his mind. But this uncertainty soon turned into sweet response, blotting out any question. This woman filled a part of him he had walled off, a need to belong.

She opened her lips without hesitation, and Callahan plundered her mouth relentlessly. She returned his every move. Josie Miller was his equal, and she gave freely. She had already tainted her reputation; nothing would change that. She was here for him and he wanted to belong to her.

She pressed against him, then pulled back, looking up at him with stormy eyes that didn't back down. "Why are you doing this?" she asked.

He could have kissed her again and swept away her questions with passion, but she deserved better. She deserved the truth. "Because a man like me gets only one chance at loving a woman like you, Josie."

And I care about you, he could have said. He'd known it when she helped him escape, but he'd fought the truth.

Now he wanted to be inside her. They'd been heading for this moment from the beginning, and the sooner it was behind them, the sooner he'd be able to move on with his quest. And the sooner she'd go back to her safe, proper life.

There in the pulsating water of the river, he unbuttoned her blouse and dragged it from her shoulders, throwing it toward the bank to join her skirt. The ends of her hair hung against her shoulders like bronze swirls. He looked down at her chemise, the wet fabric clinging to her puckered nipples. His breath caught in his throat. She was so beautiful, and she hadn't pulled away. She trusted him. He cupped her breasts, taking one nipple between his lips. The feel of her—the taste of her inflamed him.

He paused and fixed his gaze on her beautiful face.

"You'd better stop me, Josie. Now, before this goes too far. You're too good for someone like me. I'm an outlaw and you're a lady."

"You think I'm a lady?" she asked in surprise. "I don't think my parents would agree."

"Too much of a lady for me."

He let go of her breast and slid one hand down her stomach between them, his knuckles rubbing the V between her legs. He lifted her with his knees and unfastened his belt and his jeans, freeing the part of him that strained to reach the place where it belonged.

"Let me know how you feel, or ride out of my life forever, Josie," he whispered.

She stared at him, bemused for a moment. Ride away? Out of his life forever? She couldn't go. She wouldn't leave him, no matter what he asked. How could she? Only now did she understand that she'd been waiting. Not for things or success or even the life she'd been given. Callahan was more than any of those things. He was the missing part of her. She was going to convince him of that.

Callahan untied the strings to her drawers and tugged them lower.

"Callahan," she cried, reaching for his shoulders to balance herself. And suddenly they were both back in time, to that night in the courtyard when he'd 'loved her.' She dug her fingers into his flesh, felt him flinch, and remembered his wound.

"Oh," she cried out, drawing back.

"Don't pull away," he rasped, twisting so that he could reach her nipples with his lips. "I want to show you what it means to have a man love you, Josie Miller," he said, nuzzling the underside of her breasts through her chemise, then moving upward until he found a spot behind her ear. "And you want me too," he growled. "Admit it."

"Please, Callahan," she whispered.

"Please what, Josie?"

"Please love me, Callahan."

And there, in the middle of the afternoon, a river that should have flowed sedately, churned with the desire of two people. Josie knew that this man was what she wanted. All she'd done—learning medicine from her mother and studying the law—all she'd become was meant for this man. She'd saved his life that very first night. The ghost horse could have taken Callahan, but it hadn't. He belonged to her and she would have to save his freedom.

Josie leaned forward, kissed her outlaw, and lifted herself. She felt him tense. He thought she was leaving, something she never intended. Instead, she stripped off her chemise, then pitched it toward the bank and lowered herself, taking the tip of him inside her.

Callahan tried to pull back, to give her more time to accept him. He slipped his hands around her waist and held her very still, whispering words of concern, but as her breathing grew more rapid, he knew she didn't hear him. Callahan watched her beautiful face as, tentatively, she began to move. He tried to slow her but realized that she was as caught up in the feeling as he.

With a will of their own, his hands and his body guided her, up and down. Her fingertips caught his face, curling and letting go. Then she arched her back away from him and let out a wild cry of release. He felt everything inside her explode.

His own release followed, the sensation rocking him with intensity. And when he was spent, he pulled her close and held her for a long time.

In the silence, he heard the song of the river, the wet

slap of its current against Josie's bare back. He felt the expanse of her chest as she breathed and the puckering of her nipples against him. Then reality hit. What in hell had he done? He'd known she was innocent, vulnerable, caught up in some kind of false sentiment that came from saving his life. Yet he hadn't stopped.

He felt a rush of unwelcome cold as she pulled away. Apparently she, too, was beginning to understand the enormity of what they'd done. Good. It was time she admitted what he was.

The last thing he expected was for her to lean down and cup his face with her hands. She smiled, and then she kissed him with such tenderness that he felt his heart take a painful lurch. As he looked into blue eyes as bright and open as a Wyoming sky, he knew something had changed. A feeling of wonder formed, growing in intensity, knocking around in his head and his heart until he felt his bones turn hot. And then he understood. He'd damn-it-to-hell fallen in love with Josie Miller.

At last she pulled away.

"You know that was a mistake," Callahan finally said as she leaned back and smiled once more.

"Are you sorry?" she asked.

"No. But that's not the point."

"What is the point?" she asked, wiggling her bottom against him.

"The point is," he growled and caught her waist, attempting to hold her still, "the point is that this isn't smart, Josie."

With her hair wet and hanging behind her, she looked like some siren on Poseidon's ocean rocks, and he was sitting here on the river bed, his jeans pulled down mid-thigh, with a rock digging a hole in his bare bottom, and he was beginning to get excited again.

"Breaking you out of jail wasn't smart either," she said. "But that didn't stop me. Sometimes it's instinct that is most important. A person doesn't always do what's smart, does he?"

"I'm smart enough to know that there's a big difference between wanting a thing and being fool enough to justify having it."

The sun cut through the trees and covered Callahan's craggy face with sunshine. Josie didn't know if it was what they'd just experienced or something deep in his eyes, but she knew she'd reached a place that he hadn't intended to let her go. "And you never think you deserve good things, do you?" she asked. "Well, neither do I. I've tried to be smart, but just this once I've got to let go and be myself. I think you're like that, too, Callahan. We're more alike than you think." She stood and held out her hand.

For a long moment Callahan stared at her in amazement, then took her hand and came to his feet. "This is about as clumsy as a man ever gets," he roared, pulling up his pants and limping to the bank, where he stepped out of them. "Any other woman would take one look at me and run."

She glanced down at his erection and grinned. "I'm not any other woman, Callahan."

Prompted by her sultry glance, he dropped to his knees, pulled her down, and laid her back on the bank. "God help me, you most certainly are not."

His grin was suddenly replaced with a grimace that spoke louder than words. "I may never clear my name."

"You will. You have a good attorney, remember?"

"I have to find Ben."

"I'll help."

His voice was tense with desire. "Josie, suppose none of this works? We have to think about that."

"Later," she said, sliding her arms around his neck. "Why don't we take care of now?"

And they did. Not once, but twice, proving that the physical is sometimes more powerful than the logical and that given enough time, wet clothes dry, even when they're not in the sun.

Later, back in the house, Callahan took one look at the kitchen and came to the realization that Josie Miller was not cut out for day duty as a wife. But hell, any man married to her could hire a cook and housekeeper to take care of the days, so long as Josie was in his bed at night.

Marriage? Wife? That was the last thing he needed to think about. But it was the only thing on his mind. By the time he went out to saddle the horses, he knew he had to decide between what he should do and what he wanted—there were no in-betweens. It was dusk when they were ready to head out. He figured it would take an hour to get to Sharpsburg, and by then it would be dark enough to hide their approach.

Josie gathered up their things and turned for one last look at the house—this might be the last time she'd ever see it. Fantasy time was over. She tried to substitute logic for the self-doubt that plagued her. Josie the woman had to change back into Josie the lawyer. She straightened her back and headed for the barn. Callahan stood, silhouetted by the light coming from the open door at the other end of the building. She stopped for a minute to memorize a picture of the man.

"Callahan, I don't know what will happen when we get to Sharpsburg, but there are two things I want from you before we leave."

"What?" He tightened the strap on the saddle and turned as she walked up behind him. They were so close that they were almost touching.

"I know you have a mission that takes precedence over anything you might want. I can understand because I had—*have* one, too. I never planned on you, so I didn't allow for the possibility that my life goals could be altered. I don't expect you to change anything, but you need to know that I love you."

He hadn't expected this, but her approach was pure Josie. Honest, straight to the point, no playing around. For her own good, he'd have to make her understand. "Listen to me, Josie. We just made love and it was spectacular. That doesn't happen often for a woman or a man. But," he lied, "it doesn't mean we're in love. It just means our bodies are good together."

She'd known when he went out the ranch house door that he hadn't intended to touch her again. Everything about the way he held himself said he was rebuilding walls, getting ready to close out their time together. The tightness had returned to his face.

Josie thought of her childhood and all the men she'd seen going in and out of her real mother's bed. Back then she didn't understand the difference, but now she knew. She thought of Dr. Annie's fierce determination when she'd decided to come out west and be a doctor. She hadn't let anything stop her, and neither would Josie. She reached out to touch him, but he was as rigid as a statue. Hesitantly, she slid her arms around his neck. "Kiss me, Callahan. Please?"

"You're treading on dangerous ground, Josie."

She knew she was, but she couldn't stop herself. The ground she'd walked on for most of her life had been unsteady, and this afternoon she'd discovered that the only thing that made her feel safe was Callahan's arms. She whispered, "Please love me again, Callahan."

Slowly, Callahan kissed her.

This time it wasn't a savage kiss of desire; it was sweet and gentle and sad. And she knew that he was saying good-bye with every touch. Finally, he pulled back, let her go, and drew in a ragged breath.

"There will be no more kisses, Josie. We'll go back to Sharpsburg, and you'll forget this ever happened. And so will I. It has to be that way."

He waited as she mounted her horse, then dragged himself into the saddle, refusing to look at her for fear she'd know that he'd lied.

"You can stop kissing me, Sims Callahan, but you can't stop me from wanting you to," she said softly. "And I'll never forget it happened."

12

In his dream, he was riding hard across a rocky ledge, his heart pounding in time with the horse's hooves. "Go! Ride fast!" a voice yelled. "I'll decoy them."

And he'd ridden, the horse flying through the piles of rocks. He heard a shot, and that's when he woke, his breath hard and frantic. Where was he? Then, as he forced himself to take even breaths and still his flinching muscles, he remembered.

Rachel. He was married.

As he lay, dawn came out of the east, casting a softness across the range grass and a pink glow on the mountains in the distance. The cattle and the oxen moved noisily inside the corral formed by the circled wagons, grazing lazily on the lush summer grass. Jacob had spent the night on the ground beneath Rachel's wagon. This morning everything seemed peaceful.

For the last few days, Jacob had grown physically

stronger, and with the help of the orange-haired boy, whose name was Eli, he'd learned to milk the cow. His next chore would be learning to yoke and drive the oxen. Big stubborn beasts they were, but at least they were sturdier than the cattle he'd seen die in his dreams.

He shook off the memory of watching them bellow in pain and fall, just one of many pieces that teased him and vanished into the vast nothingness of his mind. It would be easier, he decided, as he crawled out from under the wagon, if yoking the oxen didn't start at six o'clock in the morning. And it would be easier on his stomach if Rachel hitched the team and he did the cooking. That was one thing he was comfortable doing.

He heard Rachel moving about the wagon, singing to herself as she did every morning. He tried to imagine how she'd start her day, pulling on her work dress and balling up her hair under the black hat she wore. Climbing down from the back of the wagon, quietly, as if she were tiptoeing. She'd start her fire. Then she'd fry salt pork and mix flour to make the lumpy biscuits that were the staple of their meals.

This morning, if he worked quickly, he'd have everything ready for her by the time she left the wagon. From the pile of dried grass and twigs, he built up the fire. From the supply box he retrieved the coffee, added it to the pot, and slid it onto the flames. Next came the flour and the lard.

"What are you doing, Jacob?"

"I'm making your breakfast," he answered, turning to face her.

Her mouth dropped open. "You're making breakfast? When you said you could make biscuits I didn't think you were serious."

"Making biscuits is a serious business."

"Who—who did you make them for?" Rachel asked.

"For Callahan," he answered, automatically, then stopped.

"Who's Callahan?"

"I don't know."

A three-quarter moon hung low in the sky as if it had no energy and was holding on only because of the clouds it was riding. Its brightness made the trail look like a faded ribbon strung across the prairie. Callahan set a steady pace, too fast for the rider who didn't know the area. Solomon protested, but, like the moon, allowed himself to be pulled along through the darkness.

Callahan seemed deep in thought. "Don't you think we ought to talk about what we're going to do?" Josie finally asked.

"You're not going to do anything."

She didn't argue. He was a man, and getting his strength back translated into looking after himself. She'd have to teach him that working together was better, but that would come a few kisses later. After all, she'd had two good examples of how a man and woman worked together—her adoptive mother and father. "All right, but I believe I have a right to ask what your plans are."

"I've been thinking about that," he said. "The first thing I want is to have a look at the loan papers Perryman's holding."

"You can't just walk into the bank, Callahan. If Will is still in town, he'll be waiting for you."

"I suppose you have a better idea."

"Let's wait until morning and I'll go to see the banker. After all, I'm your attorney. For me to ask to see the papers is appropriate."

"And I suppose Will isn't going to wonder where you've been?"

That aspect of the situation was worrying her, too. "I'm hoping Ellie will have taken care of that, which is why we have to see her before we make any move."

"Well, this should be very interesting," he said with sarcasm in his voice. "Just think about it, Josie. First Ellie turns up in Sharpsburg with a very flimsy excuse. Then Will finds out I've broken out of jail and I've kidnapped you. I just don't think he's going to believe it."

Josie nodded her head. "You're right. I think we ought to take our chances and tell him the truth."

"Taking our chances will send me straight to jail, Josie."

"You may just have to go back to jail for awhile, Callahan, at least until Will and I get to the bottom of this."

Callahan was beginning to feel jealous and irrational at the mention of Will and Josie working together. "You and Will? What are you going to do when he asks you if you're defending me because I'm innocent or because you've let me make love to you?"

Josie winced. "Because you're innocent, of course. I wouldn't have made love with you if I didn't believe that. But that's between us, Callahan. I don't intend to tell him that we—it has nothing to do with the situation."

"And you don't think he'll know? We've been alone to-gether for a night and a day. You want them to believe you're a loose woman, Josie Miller? Under any other cir-cumstances I probably would have to marry you."

"I don't much care what people think," she said in a low, tight voice. "And I'm not ashamed of anything I've done. If you feel differently—well, so be it."

Josie had thought Callahan was softening, that she'd made a dent in the wall he'd built around himself. She'd been wrong. He said he'd *have* to marry her, not *want* to marry her. Something in his life had left a hard cold core, a darkness she still hadn't penetrated. "I . . . I don't know what to say. But I don't believe you. Dr. Annie and Dan have never cared what the world thought about them, and they've brought me up to believe that I can be anything I want to be. If I want to—care about you, they won't turn their backs on me."

"You aren't in love with me, Josie. And I'm not in love with you."

There, he said it, what they'd both been avoiding. "You're a sensual woman who's never met a man who made you feel like one. Those feelings just made you get caught up in what happened. I was wounded and you were there for me to lean on. But I'm strong now and I don't need you anymore. I'll do what I have to do to clear my name and find Ben."

"If you're trying to protect me, I don't believe a word you're saying. You didn't steal the money. You're not a criminal. And nothing you can say will convince me otherwise."

"Don't lie to yourself, Josie. I'm not what you think."

Josie desperately wanted Callahan to stop what he was saying. "We need to talk about our plan," she said in an attempt to change the subject. "Right now, we should forget about Ben. We know he crossed paths with a wagon train, that they picked him up. By now, Bear Claw may even know where the train is. The army will catch up to them and bring Ben back. So, now we need to find out who stole the money before both Callahan brothers end up in jail."

Callahan looked at her for a long minute, his eyes narrowed. She was right.

"Perryman," he said. "He has to be behind this. There's no other answer. He holds the mortgage on all the ranches in this area. Without cattle to sell, none of us would be able to pay off our loans. He could foreclose on our ranches, which would make him the owner of all the land up to the territory line. With the railroad carrying cattle to market and bringing new settlers, he could easily sell the land all over again. Since we weren't the first owners, he may have done this before."

"And if he paid off your loan, it would look like you had a lot of newfound money to spend," Josie deducted. "That makes you and Ben the most obvious suspects for the holdup. That way he gets it all—the money and the land. Perryman may be a rich banker, but if the ranchers don't have money to put in his bank, then eventually he won't either."

Callahan chimed in, "He needs cash. And if we don't get a look at those papers fast, he's going to spend that five thousand dollars—and get away with it."

At least this time, he said *we*. They'd figured out Perryman's plot together, and now they had to stop him.

The horses settled down into a slow lope. The shadows of the Laramie Mountains loomed to the east and north, casting dark shadows of purple and inky black with each cloud that swept across the moonlit sky.

In spite of his air of disinterest, Callahan loved Wyoming, with its ever-constant landscape at war with nature's determination to change it. It wasn't soft and slow like the south, but wild and strong. A man's country. At least that's what Ben had called it that first fall when they'd ridden in, before winter left two homeless men discouraged and hungering for roots.

Callahan and Josie reached the outskirts of town, almost too soon. Unless there were cowboys in town, taking a few hours off from a cattle drive, they'd likely be the only strangers. Sharpsburg was little more than a crossroads between the stagecoach from Cheyenne and the cattle ranches to the south. With only a hotel, a livery stable, a general store, and the bank, Callahan had to wonder why Perryman had ever come here in the first place. If Will Spencer was waiting, he'd have to use the hotel as the jail because there wasn't one.

At the edge of town, Callahan drew his horse to a stop, then cut off on the path behind the first building.

"What are you doing?" Josie asked.

"I'm hiding. You ride on in, stable Solomon, and see if Ellie has checked into the hotel. Find her room and wait."

"Why? What are you going to do?"

"I'm going to get into that bank."

"And how do you plan to do that?"

"I told you I was an outlaw."

"Oh? Without tools?"

"I'll find a way."

"Listen, Callahan. Do you hear any noise?"

"No."

"Nobody else does either. You break a window or batter down a door and it will sound like a gunshot. You'll be caught before you even get in."

"I suppose you have a better idea."

"I'm working on it. Where is the bank?"

"Next building down."

"Fine. You stay here and let me check out the front. I'll be back in a minute."

Before he could argue, Josie slid from her horse, grabbed her carrying case, and ducked around the edge of the building.

The roof over the sidewalk cast a shadow of darkness across the front of the building. Josie would have preferred to pick the lock at the back, but burglars and lock-pickers couldn't be choosy. She'd learned early on that child thieves were expendable. Survival depended on how good you were. She'd just never expected to use those skills as an adult.

She hugged the darkness, wondering about Ellie. Was she all right? Was Will still here, and if so, had he believed that Callahan had forced her to accompany him? She'd been right when she'd called attention to the quiet. There was no sound. Only lamplight down the way signaled the presence of people—the hotel, probably. Callahan had been right. Sharpsburg was not much of a town. But the fact that it had survived meant that it had a future.

Picking the lock on the front door of the bank wasn't easy. It took longer than she'd expected. Longer than Callahan expected too, for suddenly he was standing behind her. "What's the matter, Josie, lost your touch?"

She gasped. "Callahan. You scared me to death."

"Sorry. Can you open it, or do I break the door in?"

"Shush! Perryman must have a lot of money in his bank. This is a pretty sturdy lock." One more click and it opened. "Quiet now, the bank might not be empty."

Once inside, Josie allowed her eyes time to become accustomed to the darkness, then made her way to a caged area across the back. The lock there wasn't any easier. Callahan said nothing to distract her this time. Still, he was there. She dropped her pick twice, thanking whatever muse had inspired her to bring a few tools in her reticule. She had to hurry, they'd already been inside too long.

"How'd you learn to do that?" he asked in an admiring tone.

"It wasn't easy. I had incentive. Let's just get into Perryman's office."

They located the door and opened it.

"There aren't any windows back here, so we can light a lamp. I have matches in my pocket," Josie said, fumbling until she found one of the wooden sulfur sticks and handed it to Callahan.

"This is too easy," Callahan said. "I don't like it." A moment later he lit the lamp on the desk, casting an eerie light around a luxurious room.

"Would you look at this," Josie said. "A rosewood desk. Our Mr. Perryman has great expectations."

"This desk is new. Seems pretty rich for a Sharpsburg man." Callahan moved behind the desk, pulling out drawers and holding papers up to the light.

Josie walked over to the safe. Though she'd opened wall safes in rich people's homes, she'd never encountered anything like this. It took her more time than she expected, but finally it clicked open. Even in the poor light, she could see that there was no saddlebag inside, only a stack of bills. If the money had found its way back to Perryman, they'd never identify it. And there was no sign of any jewelry. Letting out a sigh of disappointment, she closed the safe. "Nothing here, Callahan."

"Well, well," Callahan said. "Here's the file on the Callahan brothers in this drawer. And here's my signature on the loan attached to a letter that says it's paid in full. It's signed by Ben."

"Let me read it," Josie said, reaching for the paper.

"No need. This isn't Ben's signature."

"Are you sure? I mean, if he was wounded, it might look a little different."

"His normal handwriting already looks different. Ben is left-handed. Look at his original letter of inquiry about the land. The letters lean to the left. Whoever signed this payoff note didn't slant them in that direction. Besides, whoever signed this has an ornate handwriting. Ben would never have put a tail on the C in Callahan. Somebody forged his name."

Josie studied the paper. "You're right."

Callahan leaned back in the banker's chair. He'd always known Ben didn't steal the money, but now that he had the actual proof in his hand, he didn't know what to do. Could he convince Will Spencer that the banker was somehow mixed up in this?

Josie obviously thought so. "Let's find Will," she announced.

"Not necessary, Josie. I'm right here." With gun drawn, Will stood in the doorway.

"Will," Josie began, completely surprised, "we've found proof that Ben didn't pay off the note on their ranch. Show him, Callahan."

"Thanks for getting him here, Josie. Ellie said you would," Will interjected.

Callahan looked back at Josie in disbelief. "Getting me here? You had this planned all along? Why?"

Josie was just as stunned. It had to be jealousy making Callahan blind. "You can't believe that. Not after . . ." But she could tell from the look on his face that he believed what Will had suggested. Either that, or he was protecting her.

"After all that big talk about being on my side, you arranged for me to walk right into a trap. Well, it won't work. I'm leaving."

"There's only one way out, Callahan, and I'm blocking it," Will said. "And I have a few of your former partners outside, just in case you decide to try."

Josie moved as close to Callahan as she could. "You know I didn't arrange this, I swear. Will's doing the same thing you are—protecting me. Tell him, Will."

"Yeah, tell me, Will. How'd you just happen to be waiting for us? How, Sheriff Spencer?"

"That was easy. When Ellie told me that you'd kidnapped Josie, I knew she was lying. I know how Josie's mind works. Coming to Sharpsburg to see the payoff note was the logical thing to do. I had no doubt that you'd come with her."

"But, Will," Josie began, trying to bring both men to their senses, "in the interest of justice, you have to listen. No matter what you think, we really do have proof that—"

Will frowned and cut her off abruptly. "Breaking into a bank?" He was clearly uncomfortable. She could almost see the wheels turning in his mind. Then, he said, "Josie, if I hadn't known what you were up to, I'd have to arrest you, too. Thanks for your help."

"She didn't have any choice," Callahan said. "I forced her to come along."

"Stop this, both of you!" Josie protested. "Nobody forces me to do anything."

"Josie, shut up. You, too, Callahan," Will said knowingly. "I'm locking Callahan up. Josie, you get on over to the hotel. Ellie is waiting. I'll get back to you later." He stood aside and waited for her to go, his gun pointed at his prisoner.

"I'm going with you," Josie argued. "After all, I'm his attorney."

"Get out of here, Josie," Callahan barked. "I already told you, you're fired."

"We'll just see about that."

13

Ellie was waiting in their hotel room. She hugged Josie. "I was so worried. Are you all right?"

"I'm fine. What did you tell Will when you came into town?"

"Just what Callahan said—that he'd kidnapped you and headed for the missionary wagon train." Ellie looked worried. "I told Will I'd followed him to Sharpsburg to tell him because I figured he'd want to go after you. Did I do something wrong?"

"Of course not. But Will just told the men in his posse that I'd arranged to have Callahan caught breaking into the bank."

"I guess I'm not a very convincing liar," Ellie said biting her lower lip.

"No, it's not that. Will lied in front of the ranchers so that I wouldn't have to be arrested. But now Callahan believes him."

"Oh, Josie. I'm so sorry."

Josie patted her friend on the arm and moved toward the window. "It's just as well. I need to do some investigating, and I couldn't do it in jail." Through the hotel window, she saw Callahan, his arms trussed up like a Christmas goose, walking up the street ahead of Will Spencer. Several other men closed in behind them.

"I wanted to ride out to warn you, but Will was camped out at the livery stable all day, just like he was waiting. I couldn't get the horse. I'd planned to try again, but now you're here. What's going to happen to Callahan?"

"Will's put him under arrest. Looks like he's locking him up in the livery stable."

Ellie came to look out the window. "Josie, what are we going to do?"

"What we set out to do," she answered wearily. "We're going to find out who is responsible for this mess. And I think we have our suspect."

"Who?" Ellie asked.

"The banker, Mr. Perryman. He gave himself away by pretending to pay off Callahan's loan. I just don't know how I'm going to prove it."

"Mr. Perryman?" Ellie asked in disbelief. "But he's a very important man. He owns everything in Sharpsburg, even the hotel. The proprietor said he's planning to get himself appointed territorial governor of Wyoming. He's built himself a fine new house. He's even throwing a ball for all the important folks in the territory on Saturday night. They've been arriving for days."

"So that's why he needs money—to buy the governorship. Callahan's jail sentence is his ticket to the appointment."

Will and the other men came out of the stable and headed for the hotel. Josie's first inclination was to lock the door. The last thing she wanted to do was face Will Spencer, but she had no choice.

A few minutes later there was a knock on the door. "Josie?"

Josie looked down at her still damp, wrinkled clothes, gave a deep sigh, and opened the door. "Come in, Will."

He stood there for a moment, then stepped inside. His lips were narrowed; he was steaming. "Can you excuse us for a moment, Ellie?"

Ellie protested, "But, Will, don't you think—"

"I think you spent most of today telling me how smart Josie is and how I should forget about the law and let her take charge. I know Josie Miller. You don't have to tell me she has a mind of her own and knows how to get what she wants, including an outlaw."

"What do you want, Will? I guess you know your little story turned Callahan against me."

"Somehow I don't feel real bad about that." He gave Josie a long look. "Stop playing games with me, Josie. I intend to get some answers to some questions that I sure as hell don't want to ask." He glanced again at Ellie.

"I'll be all right, Ellie," Josie said. "Go on."

Reluctantly, Ellie left the room.

"What have you done, Josie?" Will stared at her wrinkled clothing and the broken pieces of dried grass clinging to her skirt. "Besides breaking a criminal out of jail?"

"I don't understand what you mean," she said, brushing her hands against her skirts.

"I think you do. Why him? Any one of a dozen men in Laramie—and probably more in New York—would have gone through fire for you. Why this man?"

"I don't know," she said softly. "I love Dan and Dr. Annie. They took me in and gave me the kind of life any woman would want. But I'm different. I've always known that. I pretend to be a lady when I'm really just an out-law. The irony is, Callahan's a gentleman hiding under-neath that dangerous exterior. Maybe I care about him because we're both alike—we're frauds."

"Alike? You and Callahan?" Will's voice bounced across the room.

Someone next door pounded on the wall. "Keep it down in there."

Will walked over to Josie and stood before her. "I knew I was too old for you, that you weren't interested in me, and I accepted that. You were a Miller. I expected you to settle down with a younger, more educated man, someone with a future. But Sims Callahan? You're no outlaw; Sims Callahan is. He even served time for bank robbery." Will groaned. "I can't believe he sweet-talked you into breaking into Perryman's bank."

"He didn't."

"Don't excuse him, Josie. I don't want you falling for a man who isn't good enough for you."

"You're too late, Will," she said softly. "I think I'm al-ready in love with him. But that isn't why I've done what I've done. I believe in the law and enforcing it. And I'm going to prove he's innocent."

"By breaking the law?"

"If I have to. In the end, I intend to see that justice is served, Will. What I've done is morally right."

Will slammed his hand against the wall beside the window.

"If you don't keep it down in there, I'll call the sher-iff," the voice roared from the next room.

"I am the sheriff!" Will bellowed. He took a deep breath. "You do realize what you've done?"

"What do you mean?"

"Ah, come on, Josie. Dan told me a long time ago

about your career as a pickpocket. Nobody else could have picked the lock at the jail. Now there's the bank. Tell me what you expected to accomplish."

"To prove he is innocent. To find the real thief."

"If he's innocent, it's up to you to prove it in court."

"I would have, if you'd done anything to help me. I still will, once I find the money."

"I've done everything I can. I've sent telegrams to every office west and north asking for information about that missionary train. Nobody has seen it. I can't even prove that it exists. Then I came down here and talked—separately—to the ranchers whose money was stolen. They're angry. Not only have they lost their money, now they're about to lose their ranches—all thanks to your *client*."

"Not Callahan, Will."

"Not Callahan? Okay, so it was the kid brother, Ben."

She walked back over to the window and glanced down into the street. Even at this late hour, the ranchers were still milling around, their voices growing louder. Josie didn't like the picture she was seeing or the possibilities that existed. In the last year, Judge McSparren and the law officers had done a lot to civilize the west, but this was still an untamed territory. She knew what a group of ordinary men could do if they were desperate enough to believe that Callahan was responsible for their losses. She needed to get Callahan out of Sharpsburg and back to Laramie where she had people she could call on to protect him.

"It wasn't Ben either, and I can prove that."

"How?"

"I've seen his signature on the paperwork settling the loan on their ranch. It's a forgery. Neither of the Callahan brothers paid Perryman."

"Probably not," Will agreed. "I wouldn't take a chance on coming into the bank and paying the debt either. I mean, folks in Sharpsburg just might notice that the man they'd given their life savings to was spending it. You want to hear something funny? I even interviewed Perryman."

"I'd expected you to, Will."

"I asked him if you were the one who'd paid off Callahan's mortgage. After all, as Callahan's attorney, you'd legally be able to do things on his behalf, wouldn't you?" He didn't wait for her to answer. "Perryman said it was Ben who paid the mortgage, the same day as the holdup, before anyone knew what had happened."

"You can't believe Perryman," Josie said. "This is a clear case of forgery."

"I didn't say that I did, Josie. But Callahan's jailbreak certainly makes him look guilty. At the moment it's Callahan's word against Perryman's. Who do you think the ranchers are going to believe?"

"I was hoping they'd feel more sympathy for Callahan."

"Not when they owe Perryman money. What's your plan now?"

Her answer was simple and devastating. "I don't have one. All I know is that I have to stop Perryman from winning."

Any further discussion came to a dramatic stop when Ellie pounded on the door, then opened it. "Josie! Will! Come quick. The hotel manager says those men are about to string up Callahan."

Will swore. "Now look what you've done. There's no way in hell I can stop a lynch mob."

"I'm the one responsible," Josie said. "Let me talk to them."

"What makes you think they'll listen to you?" Will

asked, turning to the door and making his way down the stairs.

"Because . . ." The solution came to her in a blinding flash as she trailed after him. It had been there all along. "I'll pay for the cattle myself," Josie announced.

"Think about that," Will said. "Even if you wanted to, it wouldn't be smart. How would you explain where you got the money?"

Josie took in a deep breath. She realized that by coming up with the money, she had just given Will more evidence to make Callahan look guilty. Either she was in it with Callahan or she'd been duped. Either way, the woman who loved him would be buying him out of his mess.

From the hotel counter she took a piece of paper and began to write. "Will, go wake up the telegraph operator and have him send this message to the Sinclair Banking Company in New York. Just so you know, Will, this is my own money. I made it investing in the stock market while I was studying law."

Will took her scribbled message. "You know that won't be what people think."

"I don't care what people think."

"And it won't get Callahan out of jail."

"No, but it'll buy some time, maybe keep Callahan from a hangman's noose until I find enough evidence to dismiss the charges of theft and escape from jail."

"I'd just like to remind you that as the sheriff, that's my job," Will said.

"Will, we've run out of time. And right now, I have to get to the livery stable in a minute, or I won't have a client to defend."

———

"We're running low on supplies," Rachel said. "Brother Joshua says that there's a trading post about two miles west of here. I'll borrow Eli's horse and ride in with him, if you'll keep the wagon moving."

"No, I'll go," Jacob said, then frowned. "Of course, I can't pay. I don't even know if I have any money. You've just married a man who might not be able to support you."

"We'll figure it out," she said. "I have some money. Enough, I think."

"I'd like to think that I might able to contribute something, Rachel, but I'm not sure how. Maybe someone at the trading post knows who I am."

Rachel blanched. He shouldn't go. Somehow she knew this. Or maybe she didn't want to take a chance. She'd watched him regain his strength, turning into a handsome young man. Even as the thought came to her, she tugged at her skirt. She wasn't so old—she just felt old. Looking at Jacob's dark eyes and thick curly hair, she wondered again how he'd come to be so badly beaten. There was something southern about him, his slow way of talking, his polite manners. Jacob Christopher, or whoever he was, was a gentleman. Wherever he'd come from, he was her gift from God, and she intended to protect and keep him, no matter who he was. By going to the trading post, she might be able to avoid Fort Bridger, the next place they could buy supplies. Fort Bridger was the federal law in this part of the territory. Fort Bridger had a stockade.

She felt a tinge of remorse at her need to protect Jacob from the truth. But as she thought about how diligently he'd tried to fill the role she'd assigned him, all the while struggling with his memory, she strengthened her resolve. Jacob might not be a farmer, but he belonged to her now, and she intended to keep him. It wasn't that he was unaccustomed to physical labor—he was no well-heeled easterner who'd never gotten his hands dirty. He was a gentle man, taking a real interest in Eli and making certain the boy always got a portion of the milk.

Jacob's memory was returning in snatches, and that worried Rachel. She knew it was selfish of her, but if he never knew who he really was, she'd find a way to make him happy. Still, she heard him in the night, talking in his sleep, calling out in fear as he thrashed restlessly. The man who'd been sent to her was fighting his own demons, and she was afraid for him.

Rachel had to persuade him to let her go to the trading post instead. "Jacob," she began, "I appreciate your offer, but I think I should go. And we'd be better off getting supplies here than waiting until we get to Fort Bridger."

"Fort Bridger? There's an army fort ahead?"

"About two days away. But Jacob, you have to be careful. We don't know who beat you. They might still be out there. You could be in danger."

He shot her a quick look, a frown marring his face. "What are you saying, Rachel? Do you know something you're not telling me?"

"Know something? No. I just think it would be safer if I went, just to check it out. Then if you're . . . wanted or something, I . . . we'll know."

"Wanted? You think I'm a criminal?" Jacob saw something in Rachel's eyes he'd never seen before. Fear? Uncertainty?

"Of course not. It's just that sometimes, in your sleep, you cry out, as if someone were chasing you. I keep remembering how badly you were beaten, and we can't be sure whoever was responsible isn't looking for you." She moved closer and put her hand on his arm. "Until we know, I'd feel better if you stayed with the wagon. Please?"

"I know you're right. I don't know who beat me, or why." He felt her fingers tremble and frowned. "But I hate hiding behind a woman."

"I know."

"I promised you I'd help get you to your farm," he said, trying to convince her of his usefulness. "Even if my memory comes back I'll keep my promise. Will you ask the storekeeper if anyone's been reported missing?"

"But suppose . . ."

Her grip tightened and he saw her eyes go dark. The laugh lines at the corner of her eyes deepened in concern, and before he realized what he was doing, he put his arm around her. "I'm not a criminal, Rachel," he whispered.

She stiffened and glanced around, obviously self-conscious. It couldn't have escaped the attention of their fellow travelers that even though they were husband and wife in God's eyes, he still slept under the wagon. Everyone knew the marriage wasn't real.

Jacob understood her fear that he might leave. Reverend Joshua had already made it plain that without a husband and supplies, Rachel would be left behind. And now that he was well enough to ride, there was nothing to keep him from going.

Except honor. Their marriage vows were a lie and yet he felt bound by them. Rachel had taken him on as her responsibility, and she'd become his.

"Don't worry, Rachel," he said, pulling her close. "You're right, maybe you'd better go into town with the reverend. I'll drive the wagon."

14

Callahan swore and kicked the door. The room in which he'd been placed was too big for storage, too small for a stall, and too dark to find a way out. Spencer had locked him in the sleeping quarters that had been built into the stable. The livery owner had made it as snug as possible for the Wyoming winters and sturdy enough to keep out any liquored-up, cattle-driver cowboys. The sheriff had taken no chances with locks that could be picked; he'd laid a heavy timber on brackets across the door to prevent his prisoner from escaping. The only light in the room came from a glimmer of moonlight that shone through a crack in the wall opposite the door.

Moving forward, Callahan stumbled over what he discovered was a bucket and a . . . chair? An object caught him mid-knee, plunging him forward—an iron bed. He groaned. At least he'd found it with his uninjured side.

Callahan wasn't sure he was ready to accept the word of an Indian on his brother's whereabouts, no matter who the Indian was, but Josie had been certain. He clung to that hope. It was all he could do. Now, thanks to that same Josie, he was back in jail. And if the ruckus he could hear coming from the other side of the wall was any indication, he was about to be strung up—with or without the benefit of her expert legal help. He climbed up on the rickety bed, balancing a foot on either side of the frame.

A sliver of light came from a crack in the wall where the window might have been, if there'd been one. If he could just get his fingers behind the plank . . .

His hands were too big. He needed something to rip it off, an ax or a good knife. Too bad he didn't have either. Too bad he didn't have Josie Miller in here. He'd use her stiff backbone to pry it open or just let her argue the boards off the wall. The more he thought about what had happened, the more frustrated he became. It made no sense. The logical portion of his mind told him she hadn't set him up, but his heart wasn't so certain.

Callahan swore. Whatever the reason, he'd let a woman distract him, and now he was locked up again when he ought to be on the trail of the wagon train. Then again, what good had he ever done? They'd lost the plantation back in South Carolina. He hadn't saved his sister and Ben from the horrors of the war. Now their cattle ranch was on its way to ruin. He hadn't even been able to protect the money entrusted to him by the ranchers. Even worse, Ben was missing.

And then, there was Josie.

Will had caught both of them red-handed. He'd chosen to overlook Josie's part in the break-in, protecting her by insinuating that she'd been part of a plan that would result in Callahan's arrest. But Will knew she'd implicated herself legally in the crime for which Callahan had been charged.

Involving herself, Callahan now knew, was something of a given from the start. Josie looked after every stray in Laramie, but up to now they'd mostly been women and drifters down on their luck. This time she'd taken on an outlaw. And he didn't think that her normal rescue services included making love in a river. Once she'd kept Will Spencer from removing him from Dr. Annie's clinic, the die had been cast. He hadn't wanted her help; he hadn't wanted to be obligated to any woman. But it seemed as if fate had taken a hand and determined that they belonged together.

Miss Josie Miller, his guardian angel, was the adopted daughter of the most prominent couple in Wyoming, in a time when women were coming into their own. They could vote, they could hold public office. Josie was an attorney, and she was a better doctor than ninety percent of those hanging up a shingle. But more than that, she was a woman who knew what she wanted and went after it. The last thing he'd ever expected was that someone like her would want a man like him.

Or that he'd drop his guard to trust her. Loyalty was a rare quality in anyone. He respected that. He respected Josie. Hell, he was probably in love with her. That made it impossible for him to let her suffer for her big heart. Or allow her to take charge and protect him by making sure he stayed in jail. He'd look after himself—if he could just get out of here.

Callahan pressed his eye to the crack. He caught hold of a splinter of wood and stripped it out, widening the opening so that he got a clear view of the men milling around outside. He'd known most of them for three years, and he'd trusted them. They were desperate now or they wouldn't believe that he and Ben had stolen their money. Desperation made men crazy. He should know. For a time after the war, when he understood how much his family had lost, he'd been crazy too. Nobody knew about that, except Josie. Not even Ben.

A shout drew his attention, and he saw a man carrying a torch walk into the middle of the street. "I say we string the son of a bitch up!" the stranger yelled.

Another man appeared with a rope in his hand. "I'm for it!"

He wasn't one of the ranchers whose money had been stolen. But there was something familiar about him. Then Callahan knew. Perryman's messenger. Jerome. Stirring up the town seemed to be Perryman's purpose. If he managed to get Callahan hung, he would pull off his thieving scheme. He'd keep the money and foreclose on the ranches he'd financed. And not even Josie could stop him.

The crowd noise grew. Things were about to get ugly. And Callahan had had more than one run-in with ugly crowds. Some people went to jail. Some people died.

Callahan hit his hand against the wall. "Spencer, get me out of here!"

At that moment Will Spencer appeared in the doorway of the hotel across the street, with Josie right behind him. "Now, wait a minute, men," Spencer said. "Let's not do anything foolish."

"Foolish? Is it foolish to protect what's yours?" a man carrying a torch demanded. "Winter's coming. We have no supplies, no cattle, and no way to pay our mortgages." His voice rang out and other men joined him. They were disgruntled and angry, waving their torches in the air.

"How do you figure killing Callahan is going to solve that?" Spencer asked, chewing on a piece of straw as he leaned against the post supporting the roof over the hotel sidewalk.

"It'd make his lying brother come back here," Jerome said, egging them on.

"How's that?" Will asked quietly. "If Callahan is already dead, why would Ben come back?"

" 'Cause he ain't brave, that's why."

The voices grew angrier, frustration feeding the illogical arguments of Perryman's man.

Josie disappeared into the hotel and returned moments later, holding something in her hand. "Gentlemen!" she called out several times before she lifted a small pistol and shot over their heads.

One bullet lodged in the livery wall about six inches from Callahan's shoulder.

"Hellfire, woman." Callahan jumped back from the crack. "You may be a fine lawyer, but you're no marksman. You damn near shot me."

The crowd quieted.

"Well, well, lookee, lookee," someone in the mob called out. "What do we have here—Callahan's woman. She's standing behind her man."

"Callahan's attorney," Josie corrected. "Some of you may not know me. I'm Josie Miller. Dan and Dr. Annie's daughter. I think I have a way to straighten this out."

Disagreement rumbled through the crowd, but they were willing to listen.

"You need five thousand dollars to pay for your cattle. If you had the cattle, would you have enough income to settle your debts?"

A swell of agreement seemed to rise. Then one rancher

said, "Maybe. But now that I think 'bout it, if Perryman's figuring on foreclosing, the cattle might not be enough, at least not soon enough."

"If you had the cattle and enough money to make your next mortgage payment, would you have a chance?"

Callahan couldn't see where she was going, but she had their attention now.

"All right, I have a proposition for you. I'm organizing the Sharpsburg Cattleman's Association. Each of you will own shares in it according to the amount of money you contributed to the cattle fund. I will buy those shares *and* advance you enough money to make your next mortgage payment."

There was a stunned silence. "So what's in it for you, Miss Miller?" one of the ranchers asked.

"Sims Callahan is my client. He did not steal your money, but since we have been unable to find out who did, I'll make restitution. When the missing funds are found, I will be reimbursed. When your herds prosper, you can repay the remainder of your loan. If they don't, I've just gambled and lost. Fair enough?"

"She's up to something," one of the men called out.

"I'm trying to save you!" she shouted. "I'm sending a telegram to my banker in New York for the money for the cattle and a little extra to pay the notes. The funds will be transferred to Laramie within a few days. The bank in Laramie will send the money to Sharpsburg."

"Why would you do this?" one of the ranchers asked.

"Don't trust her," Perryman's lackey called out. "It's some kind of a trick."

"No trick. I'm doing this because . . ." She took one look at the stance of the men—hands on their weapons, eyes narrowed—and knew they wouldn't believe her, no matter who she was. "Because . . ." She faltered and began again. "Because Sims Callahan and I plan to be married. I would prefer that my husband not be in jail."

A loud guffaw exploded in the crowd like a gunshot.

"Well, you sure have a peculiar way of treating the man you're gonna marry. A woman wouldn't ordinarily turn her husband in to the law—unless she was scared he was about to run out on her."

"Yeah!" someone agreed. "Looks like Callahan will get the Miller fortune and our money, too. If she wants him, maybe we'd better listen."

The men milled around for awhile, talking among themselves, then dropped their torches. "When do we get the cash?"

"You can come for it in a couple of days. I'll see Mr. Perryman before I leave town and make arrangements to take care of the mortgage payments."

Callahan heard her, but he didn't believe it. Their acceptance came too easily. He never really believed that she'd turned him in to keep him around. Was her reputation as a lawyer important enough to her for her to bail him out with marriage? No way he'd have any part of that. This was one Miller woman who had to learn she didn't run the outfit. She could talk her way around most men; she'd just done that. But he'd be damned before he let her talk him into marriage. When he got ready to marry—if he ever did—he'd be the one to decide.

The door to his cell opened and Josie stepped inside.

"Josie!" he roared as someone closed the door and dropped the timber in place behind her. "What the hell do you think you're doing?" he demanded, blinking in the sudden brightness of her lantern.

She set it on the floor by the door. "Buying us time until we find Ben and the missing money."

"From what I heard it sounded more like you're buying *me*!"

"Relax, Callahan. I know you don't care about me—as a wife, that is. You don't have to marry me."

"You don't know what I have to do—what I want. Hell, I don't know what I want. You've got me so turned inside out that I feel like a snake with a half-shed skin."

She took another step closer. "Well, I'm ready to talk about this when you are. But unless you want Perryman to hear our plans, I think you'd better lower your voice."

"I will not lower my voice. If I want to yell, I damn well will!"

She was as calm as a cucumber, but he was so full of pure frustration that he couldn't deal with Josie, not when all he could think about was where and how they'd spent the afternoon.

"Let's talk, Callahan," she said in a controlled voice.

He looked at the ground, pressed his lips together, and looked back at Josie before he finally spoke. "After all that conversation you just had out there in the street, I'd think you ought to be ready to be quiet."

"Well, I could stand a few minutes of . . . silence." She let out a little sigh.

He could feel her breath.

"Unless there's something else you'd rather do," she added tentatively.

What he wanted to do was throttle her. What he did was reach out and pull her into his arms. "You're the most aggravating woman I've ever known."

His mouth covered hers, kissing her ruthlessly for seconds. Then he let her go, groaned, and said, "Is that what you wanted? Every time we disagree, I end up kissing you and you get your way."

"And so do you," she said softly.

"Damn it, woman. You get inside a man's mind and you don't even know you've done it, plying your soft woman's ways to get what you want. You rush out and do things without asking or even stopping to think what the consequences may be."

"Do I?"

"You know damn well you do."

His mouth was only inches away from her lips but he'd stopped kissing her. She shivered. *I don't know any soft woman ways.* Callahan was wrong. She was very different from women like her mother. She always considered the consequences and made her choice. And her choice was to reach up and pull Callahan's face down so that she could kiss him again. But this time he held himself stiff, refusing to return her kiss until she slid her tongue into his mouth.

Then he growled and met her thrust for thrust.

She moaned, smiled, and stepped back. "What consequences don't I consider?" she asked.

His breath was as tight as hers. "Don't you understand? You could be arrested, Josie."

"For what? You kidnapped me, forced me to accompany you to your ranch, to get you into the bank. As far as the ranchers are concerned, I'm the innocent bystander here."

"Only until they find out you can't come up with the money you promised."

She wondered if Will listened from behind the stable wall. "But I *can* pay for the cattle, and I think I can meet all the mortgage payments, too. I'll have to find out for sure, but what I don't have, I'll get."

"And how do you plan to do that? Dan and Dr. Annie may be wealthy, but they aren't likely to finance your little peccadillo with an outlaw, and I don't think fifty-cent legal fees add up to much."

"Callahan, I have money—my own money."

"Considering what I know about your life of crime as a child, dare I ask where you got it?"

"I earned it myself, in New York."

There was a long silence. "And it didn't come from being a lawyer, did it?"

"No. From investments. I started with a hundred dollar birthday gift from my grandfathers. They taught me how to invest it. They're gamblers, both of them, and I did a lot of gambling on the market, too. Found out I was as good at picking the stocks that would double in value as I was at picking locks. I made a lot of money, Callahan. Money I intended to use to help people, to help women like Ellie go to school and learn how to take care of themselves."

"And now you're going to use it to pay back the money I'm supposed to have stolen? I won't let you do that."

"*Estoppel*," she snapped.

"*Estoppel?* What's that?"

"That's Latin legal talk for saying you can't stop me, or close enough."

Callahan glared at her, emotion feeding his anger once more. "Josie Miller, this is a good example of what I was talking about. You're like an avalanche just rolling over everything in your path. I don't understand about the law, and I don't trust it. Don't you understand, I have to do this? I have to get out of here and find that money and the missing jewelry. Or did you intend to replace that too?"

Josie turned away, crossing her arms over her chest as if to stave off a chill. Callahan was a force to be reckoned with. She'd seen enough of his anger to fear him if he really let go. He was like the storm that came the night she saw the ghost horse, all power and danger. Then his anger changed into something else that filled the space between them with sheer desire.

She had to be careful, lest she push them both too far. Taking a deep breath, she tried to regain control of her emotions so that her words would calm him. "You just gave me an idea. Tell me what the jewelry looks like."

"Why?"

"I don't want to tell you just yet, not until I get it all worked out in my mind. Please, Callahan"—she reached out and touched his hand—"we have to work on your defense. Let's not argue. We're liable to be interrupted any minute. Just tell me."

He looked away, his brows furrowed in the lamplight, his eyes wide. Josie waited. Lubina had called him a devil; maybe she'd been right. The shadows beneath his eyes reminded her of how near he'd come to death. Now he was locked up again for a crime he didn't commit and in danger of being hung. She could understand his frustration.

"Trust me, Callahan. I need to know what the jewelry looks like."

"I don't really know what the other ranchers had, I never looked. Ben handled that. But one of the pieces was my mother's cameo. It belonged to her mother, and it was the only thing she managed to hold onto during the war. My father sold everything else. I don't know what it looked like. It was just a cameo, with little pearls around the outer edge, I think."

"That's enough. When I see it, I'll know." She could have heard a pin drop in the silence that followed.

"When you see it? You aren't going to break into Perryman's safe, are you?"

"If I have to, but that's not what I have in mind."

Josie had a mischievous glimmer in her eyes. "Ellie says that Mr. Perryman is giving a party, and I've decided to attend."

The Oregon Territory Trading Post was just that, a rustic building dating back to the time of the French trappers and traders. The proprietor carried supplies and provided a corral holding a few horses, a tent that doubled as a washhouse, and sleeping quarters for the stagecoach that still ran twice a week.

Rachel rode past the post, beyond the stagecoach office. She climbed down from her horse, led him to the water trough, and looped his reins over a fence post at the corner of the corral. Hanging back, she waited until Brother Joshua, his scout, and the committeemen representing the rest of the wagon train entered the post, then she walked toward the door. There was no way she could inquire about missing men without being overheard. But she'd promised Jacob, and she didn't take her promises lightly.

Then she saw the thing she'd dreaded. Posted on the stagecoach wall was a flyer.

WANTED FOR ROBBERY
SIMS AND BEN CALLAHAN
BROTHERS FROM SHARPSBURG
REWARD
Telegraph Sheriff Will Spencer
Laramie, Wyoming
ARMED AND DANGEROUS

Rachel's heart sank.

Sims and Ben Callahan. Wanted for robbery. Rachel glanced around, making certain that no one was watching, then reached out and grabbed the paper. As if she were holding the handle of a hot pot, Rachel jabbed the paper inside her carryall. With heart pounding, she turned and moved into the store. If Brother Joshua had any idea that her Jacob might be one of the wanted men, he'd turn him over to the law. The flyer had to be a mistake. Her Jacob was too kind and gentle to be a robber.

Her Jacob. Even his name was a lie. Everything about their relationship was a lie—except the man himself. He'd married her out of a sense of obligation, telling her that he might even be married already. He'd been honest and she'd accepted that—because she needed him. He'd treated her with respect. She owed him something in return. But in spite of this, she realized that the pieces were beginning to fit. The name he'd called out was Sims. Her Jacob *was* one of the robbers.

What should she do?

Nothing, she decided. Not yet. Jacob wasn't well enough to be subjected to jail and a trial. He needed to be protected. He didn't know who he was, so as far as she was concerned, until he did, he wasn't the man on the poster. Inside the post she gave her eyes time to adjust to the darkness and she listened.

"I'm Brother Joshua, God's messenger," the minister said.

"Hoke Pierce. This here's my place. What you folks need?"

"You call this the Oregon Territory Trading Post," Brother Joshua said. "But I thought the Oregon Territory was still more than a hundred miles away."

"Yeah, well, it is now, but when folks first come out here, all the land from the Wyoming Territory to the Pacific Ocean was called Oregon."

The proprietor looked up and caught sight of Rachel. "Afternoon, ma'am," he said. "What can I get for you?"

"I need just a few things: flour, coffee, cornmeal, salt." She stepped farther into the room and caught sight of some canned peaches. "I'd like two cans of those peaches, please," she said, and fished her change purse from her reticule. "And maybe five cents worth of that hard candy."

The men continued to talk among themselves while Rachel's order was being filled. "Lot of excitement," the man behind the counter said. "Did you run into any of those renegade Indians?"

A worried look crossed Brother Joshua's face. "Indians? No. What happened?"

"Who knows what's got 'em stirred up," Hoke said. "But you'd best be careful. The last stagecoach driver through here said he saw several raiding parties."

"Did they hold up the stage?" Brother Joshua's scout asked.

Hoke shook his head. "Funny thing about that. Just looked in the coach like they were searching for some-body, then rode off. Driver said he didn't have no passengers. Guess they weren't interested in the mail."

"Here you are, ma'am," Hoke said, and gave Rachel a total.

She winced while counting out the money. Perhaps her concern over the Indians was unnecessary, unless they were looking for Jacob. But that didn't make sense. Why would Indians be looking for him? Their unrest was probably just more Indian unhappiness over the loss of their land. Still, she was anxious to get back to the train.

Thanking the storekeeper, she carried her supplies back to the horse she'd borrowed from Eli's father and led him over to the shade of a tree.

If it were up to her, she'd ride back alone. But the

threat of nervous Indians made that impossible. Brother Joshua wouldn't allow it. She was neatly boxed in, Jacob and whoever was looking for him behind them, Fort Bridger and the Army ahead. An army fort would certainly be on the lookout for a robber. At least the wagon train would head north, avoiding the fort. And by coming here, Rachel had been forewarned. She'd keep Jacob in the wagon to avoid calling attention to him.

She reached inside her carryall and made sure the flyer was still safely hidden. It was just a matter of time until someone else saw one. When they crossed the Green River, she and Jacob would leave the train. Once they made it to her land, he would be safe. After that, they'd just have to take things one day at a time. Deep in thought, she barely heard the crying. She tilted her head to listen. The sound came from an animal, not crying so much as whimpering.

She followed the noise to a sorry little fenced area lined with sagebrush. Inside, tangled in the brush, was a small hound-like puppy. At the sight of Rachel, his brown eyes lit up and he wagged his long tail limply.

"Oh, you poor little thing," she whispered, picking him up and holding him close. "You're half starved, aren't you?" The word *half* was an understatement. No animal should be treated like this.

She started toward the trading post in strides that meant harm to Hoke Pierce or whoever had penned up the dog. Then she stopped. No telling how long the little thing had been out there with no shelter, no food or water. It was obvious that whoever was responsible didn't deserve him.

Voices announced the return of the men. Rachel whirled, turned back to her horse, transferred her supplies to her saddlebag, and slipped the dog in her carrying case. "Be quiet, little one," she cautioned.

As if he understood, the dog allowed Rachel to mount her horse and hang the handle of her case over the saddlehorn.

"Ready, Mrs.—what is your name now?" Brother Joshua asked.

"Christopher," Rachel answered. And somehow she had become Rachel Christopher, who, with her husband Jacob, was heading out west to their farm and to start a new life. The pup let out one soft little sound of contentment, and as if he knew, he complied with her silent request for the rest of the ride. Now Rachel was guilty of theft, too. She hadn't stolen money as Jacob was accused of, but taking a small brown pup was just as much a sin.

Rachel Christopher, she repeated to herself. She liked the sound of that name. As they rode back toward the train, Rachel Christopher began to sing a familiar old hymn about going home. To her surprise, Brother Joshua joined in.

"Maybe he ought to sing his sermons," the scout said under his breath, and gave Rachel a wink.

Brother Joshua was returning to his flock.

Rachel was returning to Jacob.

15

Tired of tossing and turning, Ellie eased out of bed and went to the window.

Through the gauzy curtains, she could see Will across the street. After the crowd had dispersed earlier, he'd dragged a bench outside of the livery stable, lit up a cigar, and settled in to keep watch over his prisoner.

Did he know she was watching him now? Ellie wondered, then decided it didn't matter. The only watcher he was interested in was Josie. And Josie was interested only in Callahan. Ellie knew that hoping for a life with Will was a dream she'd never realize. Ellie had decided to take Josie's offer to finance a small restaurant back in Laramie—that was, if Josie still had enough money after this ordeal.

A restaurant wouldn't be the same as having a husband and a family, but she'd have respectable work. Cooking might not be her best talent, but she could learn. And maybe she'd be able to employ other women who needed to support themselves, an idea she would have never thought about had it not been for Josie.

Opening the buttons of her gown, Ellie fanned herself. Wyoming summers were intense and hot. A slight breeze broke the stillness, and she could smell Will's cigar, rich and pungent. She liked it. She didn't smoke, but many of the girls she worked with did. The men seemed to enjoy it, and it was one pleasure they were willing to share without expecting anything in return.

Hoping to catch more of the breeze, Ellie stepped through the window and out onto the roof over the sidewalk. Though the moon was near setting, the stars were so bright that they sucked up the darkness. She sat, covered her feet with her gown, and rested her elbows on her knees, listening, feeling a sadness sweep over her.

Across the street, Will watched. He'd sensed movement for some time before the shadowy figure stepped through the window. For a moment he thought it was Josie. Then he caught sight of the darker hair against the pristine white of a nightgown and knew he was looking at Ellie. The pale starlight showered over her, recreating the kind of painting he'd once seen. She was beautiful, and he wondered why he had never noticed that before, and why she looked so dejected. She bent forward and rested her chin on her drawn-up knees.

Lonely, Will thought, settling back to study her while he smoked his cigar. Her pain reached out and touched him in a way he didn't understand. He'd never thought much about Ellie, never paid for her services or even noticed her. Not until she'd been accused of a crime. Who was she, this Ellie Allgood who had been a saloon girl defended by Josie Miller?

Remembering that defense, Will smiled. Virgil had

given Ellie the watch; he was certain of that. But Will hadn't been able to find it when he searched her room, and he knew damn well it hadn't been in Virgil's pocket all that time. Josie found a way to get Virgil to hug her and somehow managed to put the watch in his pocket.

He thought back to when he had searched Ellie's room. It had been neat and clean and dignified, despite its pitiful furnishings. She was a proud woman. He wished he knew what was making her so sad now.

She stood, and for a moment Will feared she would go back inside. Instead, she moved to the edge of the roof and looked across at him, almost as if she were waiting.

Will eased to his feet and walked out into the middle of the street. "Is something wrong, Ellie?"

"No," she replied quickly. "I just can't sleep. I feel like I'm the one in jail."

"Maybe you've been cooped up in the heat too long. Come on down and keep me company for a spell."

"I don't know," Ellie said hesitantly. For years she'd dreamed of Will being one of the men who led her up the back stairs at Two Rails and a Mirror. But she didn't want that now. She would never let any man, not even Will, touch her that way again. She wanted to be loved.

"Please." He held out his hand.

Unable to resist, Ellie walked barefoot along the roof to the steps at the end and down to the street.

When Will touched her fingers to lead her to the bench, she hesitated for a moment, then let out a deep breath. "What if someone sees you?" she asked.

"Sees me?"

"With me. I mean, you're the sheriff. Your reputation is important."

"Well," he teased, "I guess I could get into trouble

meeting a beautiful woman wearing a nightgown in the middle of the street."

Ellie gasped and made a move to leave.

"Don't go. It's *your* reputation we need to protect. I know—if we have to explain, we'll just say you were sleepwalking," he said, chuckling.

"There was a girl once, back in Cheyenne, who walked in her sleep."

"Where did she go?" Will asked curiously.

Ellie realized that Will was still holding her hand. "To church. She never set foot inside a church in the daytime, so far as I know. Bar girls weren't allowed to attend services. But when she was upset, she'd get up and walk there in her sleep. I used to follow her inside. She'd run up to the altar, just stand there listening, as if she were hiding or maybe waiting for someone. Then she'd start to cry and wake herself up. 'He promised he'd come,' she'd say."

" 'Who?' I'd ask. But she'd never answer. Finally, I'd take her back to bed."

"Do you think whoever she was waiting for ever came?" Will asked.

"I'm not sure if he was who she had in mind, but there was a man who came for her—a big, mean man. He beat her, then put her on a horse, and they rode out of town. I never saw her again, but I never forgot the sound of her crying. . . ." Ellie finished, her voice trailing into silence.

Will squeezed her hand. "At least she had you to care for her, for awhile. Some people never have that."

Ellie's throat was tight from holding back her tears. Everyone needed someone to lean on, she thought. And now, just for awhile, she had Will. He made her feel safe.

They didn't talk about Josie or Callahan or what might happen. They didn't talk about Ellie and what she had been and done. Every once in a while one of the horses in the livery moved or there was a creak from the settling building. But for the most part, Will and Ellie simply sat, quietly, peacefully.

They knew the hour was late when a cold breeze swept by and Ellie shivered. Will let go of her hand and put his arm around her. She snuggled against his side and they sat, two people alone in the quiet night, strangers who now shared the simple story of a woman who walked in her sleep and the warmth of each other's company.

Josie was headed down the stairs to begin her search for a ball gown when the door to the hotel opened and her father, mother, and younger sister, Laura, stepped into the lobby.

"Father! Mother! What are you doing here?"

"A better question," Dan said sternly, "would be what are you doing here?"

"Yes, Josie, when we got off the train yesterday, we were told that the outlaw you were caring for broke out of jail and kidnapped you. Though I'm positive there's more to this story," Dr. Annie added skeptically.

"Of course there is," Teddy Miller said, pushing past his son and sweeping Josie into his arms. "She escaped. Told you our Josie could take care of herself."

"Hello, granddaughter," Roylston Sinclair said, patting her on the back. "We decided to return with your parents for a little visit. You're looking very well—in spite of your ordeal."

Josie groaned. Not only were her parents here, but they'd brought along both grandparents and her younger sister. She felt like this was a town hall meeting and she was the problem they were about to discuss.

"You do look surprisingly well," Dr. Annie observed shrewdly. "You're practically glowing. No doubt due to your success in court. We ran into Judge McSparren in Cheyenne. He told us about your defense of Miss Allgood. Apparently you did well."

"Thank you."

"I also heard that you saved Mr. Callahan's life. I'd like to have a look at him if you don't mind, Josie."

"I told him you would," Josie said, hoping to divert her mother's attention from her illegal escapades to his medical condition. But one look at Dr. Annie's face told her that wasn't going to happen.

"And I'm told that you are taking on this thief as a client," Dr. Annie persisted. "Lubina is convinced you saved the devil's life, then he bewitched you into running off with him."

"Ah, we don't believe that," her chubby Papa Miller said and turned to the other grandfather. "Do we, Sinclair?"

"Absolutely not," her thin, proper Grandfather Sinclair answered. "The people in Laramie said an outlaw kidnapped her. Personally, I think that makes more sense. Josie's smart. If she'd run off with the devil, we wouldn't have found her."

Feeling as though the walls were closing in on her, Josie began to back up in an attempt to escape, stopping abruptly when she hit an object behind her. It turned out to be Will Spencer.

"And where are you going, Josie?" he asked.

"Nowhere. I mean anywhere. I was coming to find you. I think I'm going to need protection. Is there enough room in Callahan's cell for two?"

He looked past her to see everyone standing around a large table, waiting. "A bit like the Christians being thrown to the lions, huh? Well, you knew it would happen. You shouldn't have broken him out of jail. I'm Will Spencer, sheriff in Laramie," he introduced himself to the grandfathers. "Mr. Miller—Mr. Sinclair. I believe we met when you came to Laramie in your new Pullman car." He held out his hand and smiled as he shook first Teddy's, then Sinclair's hand.

"Hello, Will," Dan said.

Dr. Annie nodded. "We are about to have something to eat, Will, would you join us?"

"Yes, do," Dan said, with a twinkle in his eye. He turned to the proprietor. "Is there somewhere we can sit to talk and get some food?"

"We have a dining room, sir," the man said proudly. "Built just for the upcoming events in Sharpsburg. My cook is already preparing for the extra guests Mr. Perryman is expecting for his party. I'll have it opened for you immediately."

Led by Dr. Annie, the group walked toward the dining room.

"Bring us whatever you have in the kitchen," Dan told the proprietor.

The man nodded and scurried away.

"Now, Josie, sit down and tell us first about the 'medical emergency' you and Miss Allgood left town to take care of," Dan said. "Then you can explain how you happened to meet up with your client, Sims Callahan. Seems to be a difference of opinion on how he escaped jail."

"There was no medical emergency. And I wasn't kidnapped," Josie said quietly as she found a place at the table. "He locked me in his jail cell and . . . I escaped."

Dan looked at Josie, a quirked smile on his face. "Still have the touch, do you?"

"I . . . I don't understand what you mean," Josie began.

"When we arrived in Laramie yesterday, we learned of Mr. Callahan's escape and found Will's wire saying you'd been kidnapped and that he suspected you'd be heading for Sharpsburg. We arranged to take the next stage," Dan said.

"But," Dr Annie added, "we were intercepted by our banker who said he'd received a wire from the Sinclair Banking Company saying they were transferring funds to Josie's Laramie account. That she urgently needed six thousand dollars. Since a transfer takes time, he suggested— due to the unusualness of the situation—that your father might want to use his own funds and deliver the money personally. Why do you need seven thousand dollars, Josie?"

Josie had been wrong. This wasn't a town hall meeting, it was an inquisition. She knew now how Ellie Allgood had felt. "Did you bring the money?" she asked.

"Of course," Dr. Annie answered. "But we need answers, Josie."

Josie stood and walked to the window, trying to find a way to justify her actions.

"I don't suppose it has anything to do with the ranchers' missing money, does it?" Dan asked. "You can understand why we're a bit concerned about your involvement with an outlaw."

"Quit worrying, Dan," Sinclair said. "I'm sure Josie can explain."

Now it was Dr. Annie's turn to smile as she said, very pleasantly, "Father, I don't think you're in a position to criticize. I can see your hands all over this money Josie seems to have mysteriously acquired without our knowledge *and* kept in your bank."

"Mother, it's *my* money, at least most of it. I made it playing the stock market while I was reading law and I needed it because . . . because I intend to start a cattleman's association."

"You see, Annalise?" Teddy Miller said brightly. "I told you she could explain. Got a good mind for the market, our Josie has."

"Cattleman's association? A good head for business, too," Sinclair added.

Annie shook her head. She wasn't buying Josie's story, but for now she was obviously willing to let her explanation go. "All right, that explains the money, now tell us about your . . . client."

"Why don't you tell me about your trip, first," Josie suggested, delaying the inevitable confrontation with her mother.

Laura, who'd been uncharacteristically quiet, beamed. "Oh, Josie, it was wonderful. We went to dinner parties and had tea at a fine hotel, and, Josie, we saw a real stage play. I've never seen anything so wonderful. That's what I want to do, sing on the stage."

"Laura," Annie interrupted, "we'll talk about New York later. Right now, I'm more interested in hearing what Josie has been doing. Josie, please, this is very serious."

The doors to the kitchen opened, and a man wearing a soiled white apron came through, carrying platters of food. He put them on the table, then went back for more.

Dan opened his napkin and spread it over his knees. "Will, maybe you can help us understand. It seems Mr. Callahan was well enough to be moved from the clinic to the jail. Is that right?"

"Not in the beginning, but eventually," Will agreed.

"And you left Laramie with your prisoner locked in a cell?" Dan continued.

Will nodded. "But . . . somehow he broke out."

Annie lifted her napkin and gave it a flounce before placing it in her lap. "But you've recaptured Mr. Callahan. You have him locked up here in Sharpsburg?"

"Yes, ma'am."

Josie let out a deep breath and prepared for the worst. She had no defense for what was coming.

Dan looked straight at her. He wasn't going to make this easy. "Just for the record, you picked that lock, didn't you, Josie?"

Josie nodded. "Yes, I did."

It was Teddy who spoke with authority, "And if you did, I'm sure you had a good reason. Just tell us."

Josie looked at Will, then back toward her parents. "Because he's innocent. The man behind the trouble is Lester Perryman. I'm sure of it. The only way I can prove it is with Callahan's help. And we can't do it while he's locked up."

"Now, just a minute, Josie," Will protested. "I'm doing everything I can. You're just determined to do it yourself."

Teddy beamed. "If our Josie's sure the man's innocent, I believe her. I'll always back a sure thing. What about you, Sinclair?"

Josie watched Grandfather Sinclair look at her mother. He was the more conservative of the two, and she knew her willful actions were reminiscent of Dr. Annie's decision to leave New York to practice medicine out west. He'd never quite forgiven his daughter for that. Though Annie had married Dan Miller as he'd hoped, Josie wasn't certain what Grandfather Sinclair would say.

"I agree with you, Miller. If Josie says he's innocent, he's innocent."

Dan looked at Annie and nodded. "If this is true, Annie and I will support your convictions. Maybe not your methods, but your instincts."

Teddy patted Josie's hand. "Then that's settled. I say, let's eat. Josie can tell us her plans for the money later."

Thirty minutes later they'd filled their stomachs and enough time had passed for Dan to make a show of support for his adopted daughter. "Will," Dan said, "why don't we take a little walk. The rest of you can get settled."

"Fine. Josie, you come with me," Annie said. "Laura can take a nap and we'll talk."

"A nap! Oh, Mother, I'm almost eleven years old. I don't need a nap, for heaven's sake. I'd much rather take a walk with Daddy."

Annie's voice was weary. "We've just had a long train ride, and we didn't even have time to get unpacked before we had to get on the stage. And . . . we have a party to attend tomorrow evening. You are going to take a nap, or you will stay in your room until we are ready to return to Laramie."

Laura choked back a sniffle and nodded.

"Party?" Josie said in surprise. Her mother cared little about social affairs. "You're going to Perryman's ball?"

"We received an invitation, for which I'm grateful. As a matter of fact, that's what brought us back to Laramie early. A number of people have asked your father to check Mr. Perryman out, including Judge McSparren, who will be here tomorrow."

Josie felt as if the floor had caved in beneath her feet. She was dangling out in space, her downward plunge inevitable. Judge McSparren was coming to Sharpsburg.

Dr. Annie stood and nodded at the hotel proprietor.

"Thank you for opening the dining room and for preparing food for us," she said. "We would also like a room."

"Three rooms," Roylston corrected. "One for Dan and Annie. One for Mr. Miller and me, and one for Josie and Laura."

"But, Mother—" Josie began, trying to tell her about Ellie.

"Of course," the proprietor agreed, cutting Josie off. "It will take me a few minutes to rearrange some of our other guests' accommodations. I'll have your things taken up."

Josie didn't have to guess what that meant. From what she'd already seen there were only five rooms. Rearranging meant evicting anyone who might not be on the same social level as the Miller party.

"Mother, I think you ought to know, I already have a roommate."

Dr. Annie stopped in mid-stride, dismayed. "Who?"

"Ellie. Ellie Allgood is sharing my room."

"Your client?"

"My friend, Mother. She is my friend. She came with me to Sharpsburg to get evidence for Callahan's defense. But that's not a problem. We'll make a pallet on the floor. I'll get Laura settled, but we'll have to talk later. I have to do some shopping."

Annie blinked. "You? Shopping? Now?"

"For a party dress, Mother. I'm going to the ball."

It was mid-afternoon, and Sharpsburg's businesses were surprisingly busy. Dan was worried. As they crossed the street, he eyed the horses tied up outside the general store and the saloon. "You think these people are here for Perryman's party?"

"No," Will answered. "Some of these horses belong to ranchers who will probably be attending, but most of them are here because they heard that Callahan's here. They want their money or a piece of his hide. I don't know if he's guilty or not, but I haven't been able to find the money or Callahan's brother. Last night things got a little rowdy. Some cowboys and ranchers still believe in taking the law into their own hands. After a few drinks they were ready to save the trouble of a trial and take care of Callahan personally."

"Lynching party, huh?"

"Yes. And there is no way I could have stopped it. If Josie hadn't come up with the idea of a cattleman's association, Callahan would be swinging from the nearest rafter. Josie had me wire the Sinclair Bank and ask them to arrange for the bank in Laramie to send the money. Obviously, she didn't know the transfer would come through so quickly"—he raised a skeptical eyebrow—"or that you'd be the one to deliver it."

"It didn't. Let's just say that we worked it out. But, tell me, Will, what's going to happen when they have time to think about how convenient it is that Josie Miller just happened to have the same amount of money they lost?"

"I thought about that, but now that you're here and they'll get their money, they won't cause any trouble."

"Maybe . . ." Dan mused. "Why don't you start at the beginning and tell me what happened."

"It started when the ranchers lost most of their cattle to some kind of sickness they caught from a Mexican cattle drive last year. Ben Callahan—he's the younger of the two Callahan brothers—read about some cattle bred in England that are resistant to this sickness. He talked the other ranchers into pooling their money and investing five thousand dollars in new stock."

Dan nodded. "I've heard about some new imported steers. Sounds like a good plan."

"Might have been. Ben and Sims took the money and jewels collected by the ranchers and headed for the rail yards in Laramie. The problem is, the cattle arrived. Ben and Sims didn't."

"I see," Dan said. "Go on."

"Then that old Indian, Bear Claw, found Sims Callahan wounded and brought him to your house for Dr. Annie to treat."

"We were gone, so Josie stepped in. Where's the brother?"

"That's the trouble," Will said. "Nobody's seen Ben since."

"So the younger brother stole the money and left the older one to take the blame?"

Will shook his head. "Honestly? I don't think so. Bear Claw says that Ben was hurt, too. He tracked him to where he crossed paths with a missionary wagon train and his trail disappeared."

"You think they took him in?"

"I do. And I don't think Ben shot his own brother. According to what I've been able to find out, they kept to themselves, ran the ranch alone. Weren't the most successful ranchers here'bouts, but they were brothers and they were close."

"So you find the wagon train and you find the truth."

"That's what I figured and what I'm trying to do. I've sent word to all the telegraph stations from here to Oregon and all the forts and law officers from here to California. Nobody's seen them. Then Josie broke Callahan out of jail and brought him here. I caught them inside Perryman's bank."

Dan swore. "Josie must have been desperate. Is there more to this than compassion for a client?"

"I think Josie has fallen for the outlaw, Dan, and she's determined to get him off. I've locked Callahan in the livery owner's quarters. We had to construct a lock that Josie couldn't pick. Unless she takes it apart board by board, I think he'll be safe until the judge gets here."

"What about the man Callahan? How do you read him?"

"He's a tough case, prickly as a cactus. Ellie says he's in love with Josie—he just doesn't know it yet."

"This Ellie, she's the saloon girl?"

Will bristled. "She was. Folks can't call her that anymore."

Dan smiled at his old friend. It was good that Will was finally getting over his quiet crush on Josie. Josie had always looked at Will as a friend. And because of the difference in their ages, Will had never pursued her. "Do I detect a touch of defensiveness in your voice, Will?"

Will studied the ground for a moment, then nodded. "Yeah, I guess you do. Ellie's too young for me, but she doesn't seem to care."

"And you, Will? Do you care about what she was?"

"Hell, no. Out here I figure every person can be whatever he can be. Guess that means women, too. Otherwise, you and me would have been in a peck of trouble with Dr. Annie and Josie."

"You're right about that," Dan said. "At least Laura is still a little girl, though this infatuation with HMS Pinafore and the stage when we were in New York makes me a little uneasy. Still, we have plenty of time to direct her otherwise." He let out a dry laugh and started toward the bank. "But then, I thought the same thing about Josie. By the way, apparently Josie ordered an extra thousand dollars. What's that for?"

"Josie's not only going into the cattle business, she's going into competition with Perryman. She's lending the ranchers the money to pay their overdue notes. I'm thinking that the candidate for territorial governor is going to be one angry banker."

"What do you think, Teddy? Is Josie in over her head?"

"Sinclair, I'm worried. I know we've taught her how to handle herself, but I'm thinking she might need a little help here."

The two grandfathers watched Annie, Josie, and Laura climb the stairs. They pulled out cigars and matches and, under the guise of "having a smoke," started out the door.

Teddy Miller stopped and turned back to the hotel manager. "By the way, where does the sheriff have Mr. Callahan locked up?"

"Directly across the street."

There were several horses tied along the rail in front of the buildings. Rough-dressed cowboys gathered in clusters, eyeing Teddy Miller and Roylston Sinclair on one side of the street and Dan Miller and Will Spencer on the other.

Sinclair took in the calm and recognized the unrest beneath it. "Maybe we'd better have a little talk with the prisoner, just to see for ourselves."

"Agreed," Teddy said, and sauntered casually into the street. "We're going to need transportation to the ball. I suppose we'd better see what we can rustle up in that livery stable."

"Bad choice of words," Sinclair muttered. "It's just as

well these men don't know you're still a master criminal when it comes to finding cash when you need it."

"At least that runs in the family," Teddy said, and lit his cigar. "Look at Josie. Who else do you know who could turn a hundred dollars into ten thousand and never spend a penny of it?"

"Not Annie," Sinclair said with a smile. "If she had it, she'd give it away, just like Josie is about to do."

The men stopped on the other side of the street and nodded at each other.

"Josie isn't a blood relative to either one of them. I think we did real good in teaching her to be the best of both," Sinclair said. "But this Callahan fella may be a problem."

They both made a beeline for the livery stable.

16

Eli sat on the hard board seat next to Jacob, holding on to the edge as the wagon lurched down the rutted trail. The oxen plodded, swishing their tails to discourage the ever-present swarm of insects that flew along like escorts, vying for a choice spot on the oxen's rump.

"How come we haven't seen any other wagons?" Jacob asked his young companion. "You'd think there would be a lot of people going west."

Eli grinned, showing a wide space where his two top teeth should have been. "There are. Lots of them ride the rails now, but we couldn't bring Mama's things on the train. And she wouldn't come out here without them. You ever ride a train?"

"I don't know. There are so many things I don't remember about my life before. I guess trains are just another one of them. But I'd think a train would be a lot better way to travel than this."

"Me, too, but Brother Joshua talked to the Lord, and the Lord gave him a vision of the way to do things. The scout he hired back in St. Louis said we could save a whole month if we go this way."

Jacob didn't have to have his memory back to understand that the wagon train was also cheaper. He suspected that money, along with control, directed Brother Joshua's actions. "Your pa agree with him?"

"Pa, he ain't much for knowing things like that. He just believes in Brother Joshua."

"And your ma? What does she think?"

Eli's eyes dropped. "My ma, well, she ain't strong like Miss Rachel. Whatever Brother Joshua and Pa says, she don't argue 'bout."

Strong like Miss Rachel. Jacob smiled. The boy was right. Rachel was a strong woman. She knew what she wanted and she went after it. They needed supplies, she had said, though from what he could tell they still had plenty. In a few more days they'd reach the fort, where they could replenish their stores, but she had insisted on riding to the trading post with the others. She never made an issue of it, but he understood what she was doing. She was protecting him. A trading post was less of a threat to a man who didn't know who he was. A fort was bound by laws.

But the post was isolated and there were Indians about. "Isn't Brother Joshua worried about Indians? I heard one of the other men say that some of them are still pretty unhappy with our invasion of their land."

"Brother Joshua says the Lord will protect us. Me? I'm plenty scared of 'em." Eli reached into his back pocket and pulled out a sling made from a piece of leather attached to a rope. "But I got me a weapon. I just put a rock in here, twirl it around, and let go. You got a gun?"

"No, I don't. But I'm thinking I might need one."

The sun was straight overhead now, beaming down like a hot hickory fire upon the travelers. They moved slowly across the arid plains, which had only shadeless shrub trees and a smattering of thick, tall grass. Jacob tugged the old felt hat Rachel had given him lower over his eyes and looked down at his hands. He wore leather gloves that spoke of use, but it was not the kind of rough, hard work a trained hand or a driver might subject his gloves to. His boots were scuffed and worn, although still in good shape. But a gun? He had no recollection of owning one. Had he lived an easier life than some of the men on this trip?

Easier than Rachel's?

The wagon train had decided to travel slowly and eat on the move. Refilling their water kegs was becoming a concern, and the Green River was just ahead. Rachel had left biscuits and salt pork in a flour sack. Jacob shared the food with Eli, who sipped warm water from the keg to wash it down. The boy was so thin that he looked half starved.

Jacob was beginning to worry about Rachel, until he heard her singing. In the open spaces her pure and angel-like voice reached him long before he saw the line of horses that announced the return of Brother Joshua and his party.

The scout and Brother Joshua peeled off at the front of the train, leaving Jacob's wife to find her way to the back.

His wife? That was a thought he'd forced himself not to dwell on. They were married in the eyes of God, but until he knew who he was, it could be no more.

Still, he was aware of her quiet beauty, her kindness, the brightness in her eyes, and her optimism. He couldn't imagine what she must have been through with a husband who was sick. Jacob suspected he used that sickness to avoid work. A healthy man might go out west on his own or with his family, seeking a better future, but Jacob couldn't understand a crippled man forcing a tiny woman to endure such risks and unknown hardships.

As Rachel approached the wagon, her gaze caught Jacob's, and for a moment he felt a connection. He knew she felt something, too.

As if she'd revealed too much, she dropped her chin and slid off Eli's horse. Her dusty travel dress caught for a moment on the stirrups and exposed trim, shapely legs that sent a spasm of desire up Jacob's spine.

Rachel removed her packages and carryall and handed Eli the reins, along with a packet of folded brown paper. "This is for you, Eli," she said. "It's rock candy, for a fine young boy, the kind I wanted to have."

The boy's eyes lit up. "Candy? For me?" He glanced around, fearful that someone would take his prize, then crammed it into his pocket.

"Thank'ee, ma'am," he said, taking the horse's reins from her and leading the animal down the train at a trot.

"That was a nice thing you did, Rachel," Jacob said.

"He's a nice boy. And I don't think he gets much loving attention. His mother's ill. And the father, well, I don't think saving souls in Oregon is where he belongs. God must have easier work somewhere for a man like him."

Jacob climbed down, leaving the oxen to plod along behind the wagons in front. He placed Rachel's packages in the back of the wagon. When he reached for the carryall, Rachel shook her head and scrambled up to the wagon seat, where she placed the carrying case beneath her feet.

"You must be tired," she said. "I'll drive for awhile if you want to stretch your legs."

There was something odd about Rachel's gesture. He stood for a minute, puzzled, as she gave the reins a snap and the wagon moved forward. "Rachel. What did you learn? Is there word about a missing man? What's wrong?"

"I'm sorry, Jacob. I wish—" She shook her head and finished. "Nothing's wrong. The Green River is at least another day ahead. Once we cross it, we'll head south. My land isn't more than thirty miles downriver."

Part of him had hoped she'd learn something— anything—even if it was bad. But the other part was almost happy to keep going. "Your land is that close?"

"Yes." She hesitated for a minute and added, "Once I leave the wagon train, I'll find myself a man who'll work for room and board. I have no right to keep you with me. I know you need to find out who you really are, and I've held you up long enough. So if you need to leave, I'll understand."

"I do need to know who I am, Rachel. I won't rest until I do. But I can't go off and leave you out here alone. Suppose you don't find someone to help you? God would strike me dead if I did such a thing."

She let out a deep sigh of relief. "I know it's selfish of me, but I thank you, Jacob Christopher, for worrying about me."

Jacob climbed back up to the seat. Rachel had already started to hum when he heard another sound, a low whimper, coming from beneath Rachel's feet. "What's that, wife?"

"What? I don't hear anything," Rachel said playfully.

She couldn't help but smile. She wasn't sure if it was from the excitement she felt about her surprise or because Jacob called her *wife*.

He leaned down, lifting Rachel's skirts, and peered beneath her feet. "Your carrying case appears to be moving."

"You didn't think I'd bring Eli a treat and not bring one for you? You can stop looking at my legs, and see what's in the case."

"Well, if you give me the choice, I might just prefer looking at your legs."

At that moment a black shiny nose poked out of Rachel's carryall. The nose was followed by two sad black eyes, a pair of long ears, and a thin brown body. "A dog?"

"I thought we—you needed a companion. And he needed a home."

Jacob picked up the scrawny half-grown puppy and felt him snuggle close to his chest. "Do you take in every stray that crosses your path?"

"Just the ones who need help. He doesn't look as bad as you did, but he sure comes close. When we make camp for the night I suppose I'll have to cook for three now instead of two. What are you going to call him?"

"I don't know. I never had a dog before." As the words came out, he knew they were true.

Jacob closed Rachel's carrying case, his efforts resulting in a crinkling sound. He started to reopen the strings. "I think I may have crumpled something."

"No!" Rachel grabbed the case and shoved it back beneath the seat. "I mean, it was just my list of supplies. It isn't important now."

The sun was slipping over the mountains in the distance. Rachel glanced at the darkening horizon, hoping that the inky blur didn't signify an approaching storm.

She'd heard enough about what a storm meant out here. A shallow river could turn into a raging torrent.

She was afraid that Brother Joshua's God would send a rainstorm to punish her for her dishonesty about Jacob's identity. He still could. She'd prayed that God would send her a man like Jacob, but now she'd committed a sin by lying to him.

She could show him the paper. It would tell Jacob who he was and give him a name—Ben Callahan.

But that paper could also take him away.

"So, report," Perryman demanded, leaning back in his chair and puffing on his cigar.

Jerome smiled. "They got Callahan in jail."

"I know that. The sheriff sent for me last night to make certain nothing was missing. What about the girl? She's the one who can ruin my plans."

"She's at the hotel with her ma and pa. They come in on the morning stage."

"Dan Miller is here, in Sharpsburg? Why wasn't I told?"

"I'm telling you now. I just got back from town. He made a deposit at the bank too. Seven thousand dollars. Reckon she was serious about paying for them cows and them mortgage payments too."

"He brought the money. Damn! They might not have believed the girl, but Dan Miller, that's another story. And you haven't found any trace of the other brother?"

"Not a trace. There's been talk that a missionary wagon train picked him up. I put the word out that there's a reward for his return. Wouldn't hurt to have a little help running young Ben down. We could still—"

"Too late," Perryman said. "It's become much too

public. All on account of that Josie Miller. I'm thinking she started it, maybe I'll just let her finish it. Send somebody to watch her. I want to know every move she makes. Why don't you put a little scare into her?"

"How little?"

"Did I say little? Let's make sure she understands how serious I am."

Jerome smiled.

Callahan paced the small room where he'd been locked, growing angrier with each minute. He'd never felt so helpless, even when he'd been in the Kansas prison. At least then he'd had nothing at stake. Now he had Ben, the ranch, and—Josie.

He drew in a sharp breath. For most of last night he'd relived the day they'd spent together—at a time when he should have had Ben foremost in his mind. He remembered how she smelled, her touch on his bare skin, the way she'd responded to his kisses. His gut clenched at the way she'd let him love her, at her wild and free response. But all that was physical. That was all they shared, all they *could* share. She was the most aggravating, stubborn woman he'd ever encountered. Nothing he said made any difference to her.

What she'd done last night to save his life was beyond justification. What gave her the right to promise those ranchers that she'd repay the money they'd lost? It was his problem. He and Ben were responsible, and he and Ben would find the answer. The truth was, he felt as if she'd taken off his trousers, and it was time he put them back on. If he could just get out of this room.

A knock on the door shattered the silence.

"I'd let you in, but the door appears to be locked," he snapped.

There was a smattering of smothered conversation. "Mr. Callahan, we're Josie's grandfathers. I'm Teddy Miller."

"And I'm Roylston Sinclair," a more somber voice added. "We'd like a word with you."

"You can have several. But you'll have to yell for me to hear you through this door."

More muted words. Then, "Josie seems to be smitten with you. How do you feel about her?"

"That's private!" he roared.

"He's in love," Teddy Miller said confidently, then added, "She says you're innocent of the charges."

"I am."

"If Josie says you're innocent, that's all we need," Sinclair added. "Shall we break you out?"

Teddy snorted. "And how are we going to do that, Sinclair? We don't even have an ax. And if we had one I doubt either of us could chop down a door."

"You're right, Miller. Mr. Callahan, perhaps we'd better find help."

Callahan groaned. It was clear that Josie had not learned her expertise from her adoptive grandparents. "Just send Josie over here. Tell her I want to see her— now!"

"Oh, I don't think we can," Mr. Sinclair said. "I never thought she was anything like my wife, but in the middle of all this trouble, Josie's shopping."

"Shopping? Josie? What's she buying, cattle?"

Teddy Miller let out a deep laugh. "Nope, she's buying a ball gown, if they even have one in this one-horse town."

A ball gown? Perryman's party. "When is the ball?"

"I believe it's tomorrow night," Teddy answered.

She'd told him she was going, but Callahan couldn't

believe what he was hearing. He was in jail, still charged with stealing the ranchers' money, and his attorney, the woman he'd taken into his heart—then changed it to his bed—was going to a ball being hosted by the mastermind of the crime of which he was being accused. He didn't know what she was going to do, but it had to involve the jewelry. And it had to be dangerous.

And Callahan didn't believe for one minute that she was taking him along.

If Josie went through with her plan to repay the ranchers' money and advance them funds for their mortgages, Perryman wouldn't be able to foreclose on the ranchers. He stood to lose a lot of money. Worse, if she found any trace of the jewelry, he'd go to jail. Josie held all the cards. She could ruin Perryman.

Callahan knew that Perryman would have to get rid of Josie.

"Mr. Sinclair, Mr. Miller, I know I'm a stranger to you, but you have to listen to me. Josie could be in danger."

"Danger?" they both repeated at the same time.

"Perryman will find a way to stop her from making good on the ranchers' loans. You have to get me out of here."

"Maybe we'd better tell the sheriff," Miller said.

"Damn it, man, he can't stop Perryman by himself. He'll be outnumbered. There were at least five men in the gang that held us up."

"And there's four of us, counting Teddy, Dan, the sheriff, and me," Sinclair said confidently.

Callahan could just imagine how much help the grandfathers would be. "Just get Dan Miller and Will Spencer over here!" Callahan shouted. "Get them all over here, including Josie."

The grandfathers agreed and left the stable.

Callahan considered their options. He hoped Sheriff Spencer and Dan Miller could be convinced of the danger. Even so, the chances of two men taking Perryman weren't good. He had to get out. If the sheriff wouldn't release him, then the grandfathers would have to do it.

An hour later, he was still wondering where the hell Josie was.

Josie stared at the only dress left in the general store. "What am I going to do, Ellie? There isn't a ball gown in the store."

Ellie studied the garments hanging on the rack. "You're right. They'll send you to the servants' entrance. Unless . . ." She pulled a blue embroidered shawl from the shelf and held it against a blue and white striped walking dress which was several sizes too small for Josie. "I can take the bodice off, and I believe there's enough material in this skirt to let the waist out. If I can find needles and thread and some ribbon, I think I can make it fit."

"I'm not sure even you can stretch that into a ball gown that will fit me. Why didn't I bring more clothes?"

Ellie grinned. "I think it's because you had your mind somewhere else."

Her friend was right. She had barely thought of anything but Callahan since that first afternoon when she undressed him and treated his wounds. Even now she blushed, remembering the man—not just his body, though that was something to remember. "He is hard to forget," she admitted.

"A real scandal," Ellie said. "Josie Miller's fallen for an outlaw."

"What am I going to do, Ellie?"

"About Callahan? Prove his innocence and marry him."

"About a dress, I mean," Josie said. "Besides, Callahan isn't interested in marriage."

Ellie laughed. "Don't be too sure about that. I have an idea where we might find a dress. There's a saloon at the edge of town. Maybe that's the answer."

Josie frowned. "I want a dress, not a drink."

"Exactly. Let me pay a little visit to the girls there. I'll bet we can come up with something."

Josie turned around. "Fine, let's go."

Ellie followed her outside. "Not you, Josie," she said firmly. "You don't belong in a place like that."

"Neither do they," Josie said, "but they're there."

Before Josie could argue, the grandfathers were bearing down on them like a runaway train.

"Where are you going?" Grandfather Sinclair asked.

"To the saloon," Josie answered without slowing her pace.

Trying to keep up, Papa Miller stumbled, dropped his cigar, then picked it up and stuck it in his pocket. "Callahan thinks you're getting him out. He wants to see you. We've come to take you to him."

Josie was stunned by the announcement, but she was resolute. "Not now."

"But he thinks you're in danger," Teddy said.

That stopped her. "Why?"

The two old men came up beside Josie. Each held her arm while they caught their breath. Finally, Grandfather Sinclair spoke.

"Callahan believes that Perryman will stop you from making good on your offer to pay the mortgage payments.

He thinks you're in danger. But don't worry. We'll protect you."

"Thank you," Josie said, thinking furiously about
Callahan's wild idea. He could be right. Perryman knew
she was in the bank with Callahan. He probably knew she'd
helped him break out of jail, and he certainly knew that
she'd announced their impending marriage and the formation of the cattleman's association.

At the same time, she reasoned, if something happened
to her, Perryman had to know that he'd be in trouble. Dr.
Annie and Dan wouldn't stop until they got to the truth.
And the truth was exactly where she was headed—at a
fancy ball.

"We've bought firearms," Papa Miller added confidently.

She managed not to laugh at that idea. "Tell Callahan
I'm working on the problem. Right now, I'm going to
visit some ladies of the night."

The saloon was almost empty. Two cowboys were leaning against the bar, talking to one of the women. When
Ellie and Josie walked inside, the girl looked up, her eyes
wide in surprise.

"If you'll take me to your room," Josie told the scantily
clad bar girl, "I'll make you an offer you can't refuse."

"Lord have mercy," one of the drinkers said. "Did you
hear that? I don't know what this world is coming to.
Josie Miller in a place like this. First she's buying cows,
and now she's buying women."

17

The Green River was in the missionary train's sight when dark rain clouds appeared on the horizon. A brisk breeze came up, tossing the prairie grass first one way, then the other.

Eli was riding on the seat beside Jacob as he often did, asking questions, passing along information that Jacob's empty mind absorbed as it hungered for more. More and more, little scraps of memory returned. He could see rows of cotton growing in a field and could hear singing. But the singing blended in with the memory of Rachel's voice, and he couldn't be sure what was real and what was imagined.

He seemed to know how to ride a horse, but not drive a team of oxen. He could make biscuits, but he didn't know how to milk a cow. The most irritating thing of all was his total loss of memory about women. Surely he'd known a woman before. Every time he touched Rachel it set off a longing that seemed ongoing. He was certainly old enough to have married; he could have children, but nothing felt right about that supposition. And even though he and Rachel were strangers, everything about her did feel right.

The wind grew brisker. "Looks like it's gonna rain," Jacob said.

"Maybe," Eli said. "Maybe not. My pa says that lots of times it just spits lightning and thunder and sets the range on fire without giving us a drop of water to put it out."

Jacob frowned. A fire didn't sound good. As if they, too, were worried, the oxen began to pick up the pace. "I'm sure your mother will feel better after Rachel gives her some of her special tonic. It picked up the dog's appetite."

"Where is your dog?" Eli asked.

"He followed Rachel when she went down to check on your mama. He doesn't let her out of his sight. They ought to be back pretty soon," he added, as much to reassure himself as Eli.

"Pa says Ma don't need no tonic, she just needs to get over wanting to go back home."

More dark clouds slid across the sky. White and gray streaks stirred the cloud hanging between the distant mountains like a dingy fat hammock bulging with water.

Drops of moisture hit Jacob's upper lip. This time the storm was moving rapidly toward them. "Do we stop when it rains?" he asked.

"Not so long as nobody gets stuck," Eli answered.

"And do they often get stuck?"

"Not lately, but back in Missouri we lost a wagon in the river."

The wind picked up, throwing a fine, sharp mist across

his face. Jacob worried about Rachel. She was just down the train. She could take care of herself, probably better than he could—but he worried all the same.

The fine rain stung and slapped the nervous oxen, who seemed torn between fear and relishing the moisture. They stuck out their tongues to catch the water, lowing in pleasure.

Suddenly, the sky turned dark as night, and lightning zapped the ground like the pop of a bullwhip.

"Got any sacks?" Eli asked.

"Sacks? What for?"

"To beat out the fires."

Jacob would have answered the boy, but he didn't know.

Soon, younger boys appeared alongside the wagons, carrying feed sacks and strips of canvas. The trail quickly soaked up the water, dissolving the ruts and turning the trail into a quagmire.

As Eli predicted, one of the wagons at the front got stuck. The others pulled off the trail and into the thick grass, moving quickly toward the river ahead.

When Jacob came abreast of Eli's wagon he found Rachel on Eli's horse, a rope on the horse's saddle connected to the wagon. Eli's mother desperately whipped the team of mules, who pulled while Eli's small, bespectacled father leaned against the tailgate with his shoulder.

"Need some help?" Jacob called out, tying his reins as he slid down. "You stay put, Eli."

"Reckon not," Eli's father said.

"Well, I think I'll just change places with my . . . wife, anyway," Jacob said. "Rachel, get in the wagon with Eli!" he yelled over the pouring rain.

Before Rachel could respond, a bolt of lightning hit the ground near the lead ox's left haunch. The animal reared up and took off, dragging the rope from Rachel's hands.

A second bolt hit near her horse's rear. In seconds, Rachel and the horse disappeared into the storm, and the Oakes' family wagon crashed against Brother Joshua's conveyance.

Jacob climbed back into his wagon. "Untie the cow," he told Eli, "and go see about your folks. I've got to get to Rachel."

His heart in his throat, Jacob forced his reluctant team of oxen south alongside the river to find Rachel's runaway horse. The rain was coming down so heavy now that Jacob wasn't certain he'd even see Rachel if he drove by her. But he couldn't stop.

He whipped the frightened animals into a fast pace, fear welling up in him—fear that wasn't new. Suddenly, from behind him came the sound of hoofbeats. No, that was a memory. His head hurt as he remembered Callahan telling him to ride like hell. And he had, but his brother wasn't so lucky. He'd heard a gunshot and then—nothing. It hadn't been raining then. It had been hot and dry. The dribbling rocks lay across his path like marbles spilled from the carrying sack of a giant.

Terrifying pictures of his past flashed across his mind— the fear, his escape. Then his horse had stumbled. He'd fallen, hit the ground, and lay there stunned for a moment before he remembered the saddlebag of money Callahan had told him to protect. A few seconds was all he had to drop the bag behind a rock and turn around to face the five men who surrounded him.

"Where's the money?" one had asked.

"I don't know anything about any money," he'd answered.

The tall one, the one riding the dun-colored horse,

climbed down and hit him—hard—with his pistol. The others joined in, until he finally fell backwards and hit the rock, moving it and exposing the bag he'd been trying to hide.

Callahan. Jacob had a brother. And his own name wasn't Jacob.

The clear memories of his past were instantly replaced by those of Rachel astride a runaway horse.

An hour later it was pitch-dark, and he'd found no trace of the woman who was now his wife. Tearing around in the darkness was foolish and dangerous. He had to build a fire to warm himself and dry his clothes. And the oxen needed rest. He pulled up.

Wood. He needed to find dry wood, which would be next to impossible. He heard the sound of the river. There had been a thicket of cottonwoods alongside the water where they intended to cross. Cottonwoods meant underbrush. He made his way toward the sound of the water. Allowing his eyes to focus in the darkness, he leaned down to investigate the ground beneath the trees.

That's when he heard it—a noise.

Rising up, he listened, turning his head one way, then the other. There, it came again. Something or someone was crying. "Rachel?"

The sound of something scurrying through the brush drew him forward. The dog. He was yipping and running wildly about.

"Whoa, fella. I'm glad to see you, too."

He knew the dog had followed Rachel. Could he possibly have kept up with her when the horse bolted? "Rachel—do you know where she is, boy?"

The dog ran a few paces, stopped, and, as if answering, barked. He was waiting for Jacob to follow him.

The moon finally came out from behind the clouds and showered the area with silver light that pierced the stubby trees and gave Jacob hope. "Where is she, boy?"

The dog left the trees and ran into the grass, then stopped.

Jacob reached the spot and found her, lying on her stomach. She was still, too still.

"Sweet Jesus!" He knelt beside her, touching her neck beneath her ear. "Rachel, sweetheart. Are you all right?"

She didn't answer, but he felt her pulse beating beneath his fingertips. Alive. She was alive. Her hair and clothing were soaking wet, and she already felt like ice even though the night was just beginning to turn colder.

Finding no obvious broken bones, he carefully slid one arm underneath her neck and the other beneath her knees and lifted her. Jacob climbed into the rear of the wagon, unfolded the sleeping quilts, and laid them out as best he could. He quickly undressed Rachel, trying unsuccessfully not to feel the curves of her body as he laid her on the bed. The blankets and quilts were damp and cold, and building a fire would take too long. Tossing off any scruples, Jacob removed his own clothes and slid into the narrow space beside her.

Outside, he heard the dog whimpering.

Climbing back to his feet, Jacob reached out the opening of the canvas top. "Come on, Moses. You brought us through the wilderness, I guess you deserve to be warm, too." He'd unhitch the oxen later so they could graze. But for now, Rachel was his sole concern.

From the Green River, the storm rushed across the plains and hit Sharpsburg at dusk, whipping up such a frenzy that candles wouldn't stay lit and the lamp flames threatened to start a fire. The saloon women assured Josie that between Ellie and them they'd come up with something. It soon became clear that Josie was a fine attorney and doctor, but as a seamstress she was a failure. She was sent back to the hotel. At this point she would have worn a bedsheet if that's what it took to get her to Perryman's ball. Josie was ready to give up.

Someone was watching her. She shivered and hurried past the doorway of the general store. The watcher crossed the street and fell in behind Josie. Before she could get away, he caught her and pulled her into the narrow space between the general store and the livery stable. The darkness concealed his identity. He covered her mouth with his hand and held her so tightly that she couldn't get to the derringer hidden in her pocket.

"Listen to me," he said. "If you want Callahan to live, you'll forget about that cattleman's association and go back to Laramie. We've already killed the brother. It won't be no problem to kill him, too. You understand?"

Josie struggled furiously, then went limp, drew up one leg, and kicked her captor in the knees.

"Damn it to hell, you . . ." He turned her around, drew back, and punched her.

He hit me! she thought as she slid into darkness.

When she came to, the man was gone and she heard her mother's voice coming from inside the stable. She pulled herself up. She should have seen the attack coming. But it was Callahan whose life was in danger, not hers. Perryman was obviously desperate. Giving herself a few moments to gather her senses, she brushed off her travel dress and headed for the stable.

Will leaned against the doorway, his pistol in his hand. Callahan was lying on a cot and her mother was bending over him.

"You taught your daughter well," Callahan was saying. "She saved my life."

"Yes," Dr. Annie agreed. "And that worries me, Mr. Callahan. Josie, for all her worldliness, was an innocent young woman when I left."

Callahan waited a long time before answering. "I know."

"I guess my question is, can I say that about her now?"

"Whatever Josie is," Callahan finally said, "is what she wants to be. Neither you nor I can change that. Believe me, I've tried."

Dr. Annie sighed. "I know my daughter is headstrong, but breaking an outlaw out of jail isn't something I would have thought she'd do."

"She didn't break me out," Callahan said.

"Yes, I did," Josie said, standing in the doorway and taking in the rain-soaked room. "And I broke into Perryman's bank as well. Will ought to put me in here with Callahan."

Will blanched. "Now, Josie. I don't think that's a good idea."

"And for the record, my only relationship with Callahan is as his attorney," Josie stated.

"You mean other than as his future wife?" Dr. Annie asked as she closed her medical bag and stood up.

Josie frowned. "If you know about our 'marriage,' you know why I said it, Mama. I had to stop a lynching."

"There's not going to be a wedding," Callahan said, giving Josie an odd look. "You kept me from hanging. Send me a bill. It may take a while, but I'll pay it—with money. I'm not the marrying kind."

Josie crossed her arms over her chest and rippled her fingers against them. He thought he'd play the rough outlaw in front of her mother and use Dr. Annie's reaction to force Josie to back off. Well, that wasn't going to work. She was as tough as he was and he knew it.

"You're not the marrying kind?" Josie repeated. "Neither am I, Callahan. I'm thinking that when we catch the real thieves, maybe we'll just live in sin."

Dr. Annie pushed Josie out of the doorway. "I'm thinking that you might deserve each other," she said.

Will almost swallowed his chortle.

Josie didn't even attempt to swallow hers.

At that moment a wave of dizziness swept over Josie and she stumbled across the stable, whacking her forehead against the corner stall with a bang. Callahan sprang to his feet. Before either Will or Dr. Annie could stop him, he picked up Josie and ran across the street to the hotel.

"Stop where you are," Will shouted, in hot pursuit.

"Your stitches," Dr. Annie said.

Callahan covered the distance in long strides as if he'd never been hurt. "Get the door, Will," he snapped, then kicked it open and headed for the red serge couch inside, where he laid Josie down and came to his knees on the floor. "Josie?"

Moments later, Will, Annie, the grandfathers, and Dan were gathered around the sofa. Callahan placed his hands on either side of Josie's face.

"Josie? Please, sweetheart, I didn't mean for you to get hurt."

"Thanks," Josie whispered. "I knew you cared. I just wanted them to see."

"Damn it, Josie. I thought you were hurt."

"I was. You turned down my proposal."

"Your proposal wasn't honorable. I'd never agree to live in sin."

"You're an honorable man, Sims Callahan." She smiled, hoping the tingling feeling didn't mean she would have a black eye. At least she had an excuse. She could claim that it came from the accident in the stable, not from the stranger who'd socked her. All she needed was for Will and her father to learn about that. She'd be put under lock and key along with Callahan.

"Better let your mother take a look at you," Grandfather Sinclair said.

"Looks like you hit your head," Teddy said.

"My head is fine. I just hit it on the stall post. Please, Mother, Grandfather Sinclair, Papa Miller, I'd appreciate if you and Dan would let me have a moment with my fiancé."

Will scoffed. "And let him step out the door and be gone?"

"I didn't say you, Will. You can just turn your back. And Callahan won't try to get away, will you?"

"No promises, darlin'."

"Then I'll just have to use this to keep you here." Josie pulled her derringer from her pocket and pointed it at Callahan.

At Will's nod, the others filed out of the hotel lobby, chuckling or shaking their heads in dismay.

"Don't try anything, Callahan," Will warned. "You got two minutes."

"Will—"

"Shut up, Josie!" Callahan snapped. "You're wasting time. So listen good. I'm not going to marry you, but in spite of the fact that your hair could have crows nesting in it right now and the rest of you looks like something the cat dragged in, I am going to kiss you—one last time."

His lips touched her mouth at the same time his

words filtered through her mind. *Crows nesting in her hair. Cat dragged in?*

Josie jerked away. She was about to forget what she had planned. She must have been hit harder than she thought. "One last time? I don't think so," she whispered, and handed him the gun.

He drew back, puzzled.

"Now it's my turn to kiss you," she said in a loud voice. Then she gave him a shove and motioned toward the back door.

Will didn't even try to control his laughter as he turned around. "I don't think so. I'll take that gun, Callahan, and the next time you try a stunt like this, Josie Miller"—he tilted his head toward the reflective glass in the door—"don't do it in front of a mirror."

18

Jacob gathered Rachel into his arms and pulled up the covers. At least she had stopped shivering. Jacob had never felt so helpless, not even when he lost his memory. He simply lay, holding her, the horror of what had just happened to Rachel mixed with the memory of his own flight from harm. The woman who'd saved him was hurt, and it was up to him to keep her alive.

He could feel her breath on his chest, faint but present.

Warming her became his objective. Not knowing what else to do, he rubbed her arms. He threw his bare leg over hers and scrubbed it up and down her thighs and ankles. Over and over, he massaged her bare back, ranging lower, curving under her bottom and up her spine. She was a slim woman, firm from hard work, yet her skin was soft beneath his touch. He felt a responsibility for her, as a husband might feel for his wife, and that surprised him. It bothered him too. Why had he been running? Where had the money come from? What happened to it? What kind of man was he?

Rolling over, he covered her body with his own, giving her his warmth. Transferring his touch to her stomach, her chest, and finally her breast, he felt a stirring that he could not control.

She let out a tiny gasp and her breath feathered against his chin, then stopped. He thought she'd died. "Rachel." Without realizing what he was doing, he planted quick little kisses down her cheek. "Rachel, breathe."

"I would," she said, "if you weren't smothering me."

He leaned back, allowing a shaft of cold air inside the covers. Rachel pulled him down against her. "Maybe being smothered is better than freezing."

Jacob adjusted his weight onto one elbow, still holding her breast with his hand. "You were wet and cold. I didn't know what else to do. I'll move."

"Don't move, Jacob," she said shyly. "Every night I've waited for you to come to me, and you didn't. Now something has forced you into my bed. You're going to stay right here, where you belong, with your wife. Please?"

His heart rolled over in his chest. "I'm not your husband, Rachel, not really. I'm starting to remember."

She stopped moving. "You remember?"

"Not everything. Not yet, but soon."

The dog moved. "Be still, Moses," he said, grateful for the distraction.

Rachel touched his face with her fingertips. "Moses?"

"He led his people through the wilderness, didn't he? Well, our Moses led me to you. He earned his name."

"I'm thinking that somebody else had the idea of sending you to me first." She put her hand on the back of his neck, fingering his hair and the muscles that tightened beneath her touch. "Are you going to be my husband tonight?"

He caught his breath. "I want to kiss you, Rachel, in the worst way. But I'm not certain I can stop with a kiss. What if tomorrow we find out who I am? I might not be able to stay with you."

Rachel winced. She already knew who he was, and the truth was burning a hole in her heart. Come tomorrow, she'd show him the flyer, and after that he could be gone. Tonight might be all she would ever have.

Sucking in her breath, she pulled his face down to meet hers. The heat she'd felt while he rubbed her was a faint glow compared to the fire that let loose in her as his lips captured hers.

He stretched, rubbing his lower body against hers, making his need obvious. He tasted, planting little kisses along her nose and upper lip, whispering as he discovered her. "I want to touch you here and . . ." He moved his hand lower.

Her belly churned beneath his touch and she squirmed against him, trying desperately to contain the feelings she'd never imagined.

"And here," he said, his fingers ranging lower still. His kiss mirrored the rhythm of his lower body, and she felt herself turning to reach that which brushed urgently against her.

Then his fingers were inside her most private parts, and she gave up trying to be still.

Jacob pulled back. "Rachel, you'd better stop me." His voice was breathless and she could feel the tension in his restraint.

"Don't you want me?"

"Of course I want you. I'm dying with want," he muttered hoarsely, and took her breast inside his mouth.

She cried out and twisted toward him. He moved over her and replaced his fingers with the part of him that belonged there.

Rachel had been married so she was no stranger to a man's desire. She expected he'd give two or three thrusts and then collapse on top of her. But it wasn't happening like that. The urgency was still there, but Jacob curbed his movement while he kissed her again and again, moving so slowly that she thought she would die from this feeling she'd never known. Over and over again he built the rhythm to the breaking point, then stopped to kiss her body, always holding her beneath him.

"Oh, Rachel," he whispered. "My Rachel."

"Jacob, please. Please. I want . . ."

She couldn't continue. Something was gathering inside her that could not be stopped, and she rose against him as the explosion inside her let go. When he plunged into her, she welcomed him and the shudder of his release that followed. For a long time they didn't move. They simply lay in each other's arms.

"I didn't know," she said softly. "I was married, but I never knew what it was like to have my husband love me."

"Well, you know now," Jacob said. "And I intend to love you again and again—once I get Moses off my feet and unhitch the oxen."

As Jacob left the wagon, Rachel opened the trunk, unfolded a cloth, and called out, "Moses? Here, come sleep in this nice dry bed."

The dog, who'd followed Jacob out of the wagon, climbed inside and gave a shake. By the time Jacob returned, he'd settled himself for the rest of the night.

"Now then, Jacob, you're wet and cold. It's my turn to warm you."

As the pearl-gray dawn crept over the eastern mountains, Rachel and Jacob ate the peaches she'd bought at the trading post, feeding each other with their fingers and licking the sweetness they spilled. Finally they slept, each protecting a secret: Jacob, the return of his memory, and Rachel, the hiding of the truth.

In Sharpsburg, Callahan paced his cell. It wasn't just the confinement that was driving him crazy; it was Josie, missing Josie. He'd cursed her, railed at her for taking charge of his life, made love to her, and tried to send her away. But no matter how he felt about her interference, the memory of their time together fueled the desperate measures he was about to take to prevent her from attending Perryman's ball. The time had come to force Perryman's hand, and he had to do it, not Josie. He couldn't let her get hurt. He went back to digging at the wall.

Callahan couldn't wait any longer to find Ben.

Tomorrow would seal their future, Callahan thought. Then he'd find Ben.

Across the prairie, on the opposite side of the Green river, a black-and-white stallion approached the mare Rachel had been riding. The mare nickered softly, glanced toward the wagon, then followed the stallion into the shadows.

This was no ghost horse, as Lubina had feared when she first saw him in the storm. This night the two horses would join in order to bring about new life.

Tonight, across the plains, turmoil stirred the lives of Sims Callahan and Josie Miller. But here in the prairie there was harmony, and Rachel and Jacob were at peace.

———

The next morning Will met Ellie as she was headed out of the hotel.

"Where are you going?"

"To the saloon."

His surprised look cut through her. "Don't worry, Will, I'm not reporting to work. The girls and I are fashioning a ball gown for Josie."

"Oh." He looked confused, then guilty. "I'm sorry, Ellie, I didn't mean that. I thought—"

"But you did think that, didn't you?" They'd reached the last building and were headed across the muddy expanse of land between the town and the saloon. "Go back, Will. You don't want to be seen with me."

"Stop that!" he snapped. "Stop jumping to conclusions. I just thought if you needed money or something, I would make you an offer."

Ellie stopped. Horror closed off her throat. "You were going to offer to buy my services? Oh, Will."

He caught her arms angrily. "Of course not, Ellie. I mean I—I don't know what I mean. Ever since you sat with me, let me put my arms around you, I've seen you in a different way. All I can think about is—"

He pulled her close and kissed her, thoroughly, completely.

At first she went still for a long minute, then, clumsily, she returned his kiss.

Finally, she pulled away and stared at him in wonder. "The men I knew weren't much for kissing. Did I do it wrong?"

"You did it very right, Ellie Allgood. At least as far as I'm concerned. What'd you think?"

She gazed at him with an impish grin. "I think if I'd done this for pay, I'd have owned Two Rails and a Mirror instead of being a bar girl."

"That's what you want?"

"No, what I want is a ball gown for me, too. I want to waltz with my fella and practice kissing some more."

"You'd better get busy then," Will said. "I understand the musicians are already out at Perryman's, practicing to play the waltz."

"And what are you going to do?"

"Me? I'm going to find me somebody to teach me how to dance."

Josie tried to avoid the dinner table at the hotel, but Dr. Annie and the grandfathers wouldn't hear of it.

"When do you intend to settle up with the ranchers, Josie?" Dan asked.

"I was hoping you'd do that for me," she answered. "I think they'd accept my loan for their mortgages better if the money came from you."

Dan took a long drink of his coffee and met Josie's glance with a nod of agreement. "I will, but this doesn't sound like you. Usually you want to do everything yourself."

"And she could, if she wanted to, son," Teddy Miller said. "Josie's never been scared of anything in her life."

Grandfather Sinclair took a long look at Josie and shook his head. "I'm thinking that she's pretty scared now. What's wrong, Josie?"

"It's Callahan, isn't it?" Dr. Annie said softly.

Josie finally nodded. "He's innocent of the theft, and I'll prove it, tonight. But I don't know what to do about . . . him."

"You're in love with him, aren't you?" Dan asked.

"I think so, but that doesn't mean anything. There's no future for us. His brother comes first. As soon as he's free he's going after Ben, and I can't—no I won't—stop him. I'd do the same thing if it were me."

Annie reached out and took Josie's hand. "Then you have to go with him."

Josie fought the moisture gathering in her eyes. "He's not the marrying kind, Mama."

"You going to let that stop you?"

"But what about being a lady? What about my law practice? What about my hope of showing women that any one of them can be somebody? Lubina was right. Sims Callahan is a devil. I should never have let him—"

Annie folded her hands across her lap. "Josie, fourteen years ago I came out here with a dream. I wanted a place where I could be accepted for what I was, a woman doctor. I wanted no part of your father. He was an annoyance that I wanted to avoid. I was wrong. He became my strength. But the west gave me a chance, a promise that I could be whatever I wanted to be. The west hasn't changed."

Dan smiled. "Annie just set the example for you, Josie. Nobody asked you to be a lady. We only forced you to open your mind to your potential. You were the one who chose to practice law. Once you clear Callahan of the charges, you can marry him and hunt gold in Alaska if you want. Don't you understand? I hope that no matter what we've taught you, you've learned that a woman can be whatever she chooses, if she wants to work hard enough to accomplish it. You just have to decide what you want and what you'll pay to get it." He stood. "Now, let's get organized here. We need to load up and move out to the Perryman ranch for the ball. I expect Judge McSparren is already there. I want to have a little talk with him. I'll spread the word that the men should gather at the bank tomorrow at one o'clock to pick up their funds, and I'll ask the judge to join us. That will put pressure on Perryman to give up foreclosure for now."

"Thank you," Josie said. "Ellie and I haven't finished our dresses. We'll come out later."

"All right," Annie agreed, and hugged her daughter. "Just know that we'll support you in whatever you decide to do. And please make sure there are no more jailbreaks," she added. "Judge McSparren isn't likely to be sympathetic."

"No, he isn't," Josie agreed. *And he won't go easy on a burglar if I get caught breaking into Perryman's safe.*

It was only later when she looked into her mirror and saw that there was no darkening of the skin around her eye. She was doubly grateful that she hadn't mentioned the threat on her life. She touched the derringer in her pocket and sighed. Nobody was going to stop her. She'd find proof. No matter what.

Across the prairie, the late morning sun cut through the canvas of the wagon and fell across Rachel's face. She watched Jacob dress, still dazed and filled with awe at what they'd shared. "You're getting up?"

"It's late. Peaches only go so far. I think we're both in need of real food." He blushed. Surely he'd spent time with a woman before. Why was he feeling so foolish now?

"Yes, food," she said, and rimmed her lips with her tongue.

Jacob swallowed his breath and opened the canvas drawstrings at the front of the wagon. It took every ounce of control he possessed to climb down and leave Rachel lying there.

He found that everything was still soaked. After checking on the oxen, he headed for the river and the stand of cottonwoods that bordered it. They'd lost Rosie the cow, but he found the saddle near the place where Rachel had fallen. He took it to the wagon, then headed back to the cottonwoods in search of dry underbrush.

When he arrived back at the wagon, he could hear Rachel talking to the dog.

"Now, just because I let you sleep in my hope chest last night doesn't mean it's your bed, Moses. You've got to get up and go help your papa. I'm just going to move these linens and get my good dress. This old one is wet; it'll have to dry and I want my *husband* to see me looking nice. Don't moon at me with such a long face, little one. I'll find you another bed."

Jacob smiled. Rachel would make a good mother. Too bad she didn't have children. *Children.* The thought hit him in the gut like a bullet. He'd spent most of the night making love to her. Suppose he'd given her a child?

Savagely, he ripped a dry blanket into strips and dipped them into the grease he used to keep the wagon wheels lubricated. Then he piled twigs and dead limbs in a triangle.

Inside the wagon, the trunk slammed shut, drawing Jacob's attention. He gazed at Rachel in a chemise and petticoat. Looking up, she saw him watching, blushed, and turned away, uncertain now that it was daylight. They'd become two separate people again.

Jacob shook himself. *You have to make a new plan, one that lets her know you aren't going to leave her.* The oxen appeared to be in good shape, and they had supplies. Farming might not be what he'd done in the past, but for Rachel, he could learn. *Fire, get the fire going and some coffee made, and then you'll talk.*

But first, he needed one of Rachel's matches.

Jacob reached under the wagon seat and pulled out the carrying case she'd hidden Moses in. Somewhere inside was her packet of matches. Rummaging through the bag, he came across a rumpled paper.

He smoothed it out and read the words once, then again.

WANTED FOR ROBBERY
SIMS AND BEN CALLAHAN
BROTHERS FROM SHARPSBURG
REWARD
Telegraph Sheriff Will Spencer
Laramie, Wyoming
ARMED AND DANGEROUS

It was him. It had to be. Rachel had said he'd called out Sims or something like that. And he knew he had a brother. But robbery? Armed and dangerous?

Jacob—no, Ben. Ben Callahan. Suddenly the strange fragments of dreams made sense. He'd been carrying the money bag at the time he was being chased. He was caught, beaten, and left for dead.

What had happened to his brother?

And why hadn't Rachel told him?

He was still staring at the flyer when she pushed through the canvas covering. "Jacob?"

He lifted his gaze, catching her stricken one. "You knew? All this time, you knew?"

"Only since I went to the trading post."

"And you didn't tell me?"

She shook her head. "I'm so sorry, Jacob. I was going to, but I was afraid you'd leave me."

Jacob glanced around. "I'll find someone to take you to your land, Rachel. Then I have to go. I have to find my brother."

"But you'll be arrested, Jacob. There's a reward."

She looked beautiful, wearing a soft green dress with lace around the neck. Her hair hung loose, falling to her shoulders, the color of new honey. The kisses they'd shared last night had left her lips swollen, her cheeks pink. She was the prettiest thing he'd ever seen and, even if she had lied to him, she was his.

At least she had been, when he was Jacob Christopher, the answer to her prayers.

But he wasn't that man any longer. The part of him that he'd filled with a new life of loving Rachel was gone, and the hole it left was cold and deep.

"I knew you'd go when you saw the flyer. I won't try to stop you. Leave now, I'll get to my land alone. And Ben—that sounds wrong somehow, but I know that's you—Ben, I wouldn't change what happened. I was married for eight years, but last night was the only time I ever felt loved. If your life doesn't turn out to be what you want, come back to me. I'll be waiting."

As if she'd been called, the mare, still wearing her bridle, trotted slowly out of the woods, came to the wagon, and stopped.

"Go on, Ben," Rachel said. "Go home."

But it wasn't easy. He saddled the mare, mounted her, and said, "Rachel Christopher, you did a wrong thing, but what I did might be worse."

She looked puzzled.

"I made love to you when I didn't have a right. And I'd do it again. Christ, I'm riding away when I may have given you a child."

"No, Ben," she said stoically. "I won't let you carry that on your conscience. I'm barren. That's one of my sorrows, but it's true. So you go back to your past and know that these days we've been together have been the happiest times of my life."

"I can't let you go on alone, Rachel. I give you my word. I'll find the wagon train and somebody to take you to your land. I'll send money so you'll be able to hire a farmhand."

Then he thought about the money he'd been carrying, stolen money, according to the flyer. If he was a thief, he'd stolen at least once. To help Rachel, he'd steal again—if he had to.

Unless . . .

The flyer. There was a reward on his head. With the reward money Rachel could hire help. She could survive.

He was wanted by a Sheriff Will Spencer in Laramie. Ben wasn't certain where Laramie was, or how he'd get there. Then it came to him. The fort. Rachel had gone to the trading post to avoid exposing him to the army at Fort Bridger. There would surely be a telegraph line and payroll money at the fort. He made up his mind. "Get ready, Rachel," he said decisively. "We're heading for the fort."

Being chased was his last memory of his past. All he could hope for now was that Sims could clear up the past, that Ben Callahan wasn't a thief, that Will Spencer was a fair man, and that tomorrow would not be the disaster he seemed to be heading for.

If he could only remember.

19

—⁂—

Rachel protested all the way to the fort. "I can't do this, Ben. I can't hand you over to be arrested. You're no thief."

"I never thought so, but obviously we're both wrong, Rachel." He hadn't told her that he remembered carrying a money pouch, that he'd been chased by men he didn't recognize.

"I won't do it."

"Then I'll turn myself in."

She caught his arm and forced him to look at her. "No matter what you say, you'll always be my husband, and I want a future with you. If it means giving up that land, so be it. I won't miss what I never had. We'll keep heading west until we find a place where nobody will ever find us."

"There is no such place," he said softly, wishing he could take away the turmoil in her eyes. Life had worn her out, but she still had bright dreams. He'd miss that optimism, but the truth was more important.

"Of course there is," she argued softly.

"Even if there was, I couldn't make a life with you without knowing the truth, not now."

"Then I'll just wait at the fort until we know."

He took her hand and held it. "No, that might be months. You need to get to your land so that you can get ready for winter. I meant to go with you, but now . . . I can't. I don't know what will happen, but when it's settled, if I can, I'll come and find you."

"And how long do I wait?" she asked, with a rare touch of bitterness in her voice. "A month? A year? Five years?"

She was right. He could go to jail. He was being selfish by asking her to wait. "I'm sorry," he said. "You have to get on with your life. If you find someone—forget about me. That's the best idea."

Rachel didn't argue any further. And for the first time, she didn't sing.

That afternoon they reached the fort. He stopped the wagon at the gate and gave her one last look. He wanted to tell her that he'd fallen in love with her, but he didn't. Their life together was over. He'd ask the commanding officer to recommend someone who could escort her to her land, perhaps stay on through the winter. The reward money would pay for that.

"Rachel," he said softly. "Thank you. Whatever happens, I will never forget that you gave a future to a man who had no past. I'm almost sorry that I have it back." He thought about Brother Joshua and repeated his words: "Perhaps it's God's will."

Rachel pulled her hat from her head and rubbed her arm against her forehead. She looked tired. "You forget, Jacob—I'm a heathen."

————————

Back in his stable prison cell, Callahan pressed his eye to the crack in the wall, straining to see a coach drawn by two gray horses rattle down the street and stop in front of the hotel.

It was picking up two women. Ellie wore a soft blue dress trimmed in lace and ribbons and—he almost didn't recognize Josie, who was wearing a scandalously low-cut dress with a pale pink satin bodice. A velvet flower of the same color was placed at the waist, a similar flower curling up and over the shoulder. The skirt had a kind of apron in a darker shade of pink and fit her like a glove. He smiled as he watched her adjusting her steps to the tightness of the garment. He realized that he'd never seen her as the lady she was tonight, and he'd never seen her so uncomfortable. It made him smile.

The carriage driver assisted Ellie inside. He turned back to Josie, who struggled for a moment, then hiked up her dress and climbed in without any help. She hadn't looked across the street, but Callahan knew she was watching now. Why hadn't she come to talk to him about her plans? Why hadn't she broken him out?

Dr. Annie, Dan Miller, and a young girl who had to be Josie's little sister had left at noon. He didn't know where the grandfathers were, but they weren't acting as Ellie and Josie's escorts, and neither was Will. Callahan bristled. Surely these two women weren't going alone. He'd warned Will and the Millers that Josie might be in danger. Why wasn't she being protected?

Fear feeding his anger, Callahan slammed the iron cot against the wall over and over until he ripped off one leg. He'd use that to work on the chink in the wall. Nobody else understood the danger Josie was in, but he did, and he refused to let anything happen to the woman he loved.

"Be still, Josie. This road is bad enough, and you know that dress is held together with pins and prayers. I've decided that we ought to go into the dressmaking business instead of opening a restaurant."

"Fine. If that's what you want."

"It is. I sew better than I cook. But if you don't stop fidgeting, you're going to tear your gown apart before we get to the ball," Ellie snapped. "What's wrong with you?"

"I'm worried, Ellie. I should have sent you on with Dr. Annie and Dan."

"Why?"

"Last evening someone was . . . outside the saloon when I left, and all day I've felt like I was being watched. Now you've got me in a dress that's so tight I can't move. I feel like I'm caught between two hard rocks. Couldn't you find a corset that was made for a woman instead of a child?"

"Not if you wanted to get into Darla Mae's dress. She's at least a size smaller than you, and I couldn't make any more room in the bodice than I did, at least not in time for—" Ellie stopped short. "What do you mean *outside* the saloon?"

Telling Ellie would scare her to death, but not telling her could put her in danger. "A man stopped me," she finally explained, "and warned me not to replace the money."

"Did you tell Will?"

"No. I should have, but I didn't see who he was. But don't worry, the driver won't let anything happen to us, and the only thing that could possibly do me harm is this corset. What in the world is it made out of?"

"Whalebone and steel. The girls like them because they make their waists small and their . . . their bosoms bigger. Stop trying to switch the subject, Josie. You can't fool me," Ellie said knowingly. "Exactly what is it you're planning for tonight?"

"Planning? I'm not planning anything, Ellie. I'm just going to have a look around. That stolen jewelry has to be somewhere. If can find it, I can prove to Judge McSparren that Callahan didn't steal the money."

Josie glanced out the carriage window at the moon, almost half full now. There wasn't a cloud in the sky. It would have helped if there had been clouds. Or if her dress had been darker. Moving in and out of the shadows would have been easier that way.

Ellie was right. She was up to something, and the guilt she felt was beginning to overwhelm her. Most of the illegal things she'd done in her early life had revolved around herself—her survival. But this time, she was breaking the law not for herself, but for an outlaw.

She wanted to curse, but she didn't have enough breath to get the words out. Maybe she'd feel better if she'd been able to talk it over with Callahan, if he'd come with her. But she couldn't take a chance on bringing him along; he'd have found a way to stop her.

She had to find that jewelry.

Find the money.

Get Callahan out of jail so that . . . so that what? All her life she'd sworn she'd never lie with a man, never care about one, never marry.

Well, her plan to remain unmarried didn't look as if it was going to change. No matter what Callahan felt—and she was sure he cared about her—he'd made his position clear. No wedding. She stretched and her dress dipped lower. The stitching at the top of the neckline grated on her nipple, and a shiver of pleasure ran through her.

Callahan.

The carriage came to a stop. "Well, we're here, Josie, safe and sound."

Josie tugged at her bodice and opened the door before the driver could get to it. "Let's go."

Hiking up her dress once more, she put her feet on the ground, then rearranged her skirt. Thank goodness Darla Mae was tall. They'd still had to stitch two lengths of wide ribbon around the bottom of the skirt to hide her riding boots. She had to make certain she didn't dance.

Perryman himself greeted her and Ellie at the door. "Good evening, ladies. I was about to give up on you."

"So were we," Dr. Annie said, giving Josie's ball dress a jaundiced eye.

"Mama, look at Josie's dress," Laura whispered. "She's falling out of it."

Annie nodded. "That is an interesting gown. I wouldn't have thought the general store would carry something so . . . so . . ."

"Lovely? They didn't, Mother," Josie said, studying the large room filled with people. The walls were lined with chairs and benches, leaving the center open for the dancers. "It's borrowed. Ellie was able to alter it. Good evening, Mr. Perryman. Your party has turned into quite an event."

"Yes, indeed. And I'd like to say, Miss Miller, that I'm willing to forget about what happened in the bank. I know you were forced to take part."

"I was—"

"Where are your grandfathers?" Dr. Annie interrupted, cutting off Josie before she could deny Mr. Perryman's statement.

"Aren't they here?" Josie asked. "Are you certain they aren't playing poker somewhere? I'll look around."

At that moment, the music started up.

"They're probably in my game room trying out my new billiards table. In the meantime, may I have the honor?" Perryman asked, offering Josie his arm.

Short of making a scene, she couldn't refuse. He led her into the center of the room and started a gentle sweep around the floor.

So much for worrying about the shoes, Josie thought, and tossed back her head. Dipping and swaying, she studied all the women seated along the wall and dancing about her. Not a woman wore a cameo brooch that she could see.

"I understand that you're defending Mr. Callahan," Perryman said. "Are you sure that's wise? I mean, given your parents' position in the community. Your father is heavily involved in the future of Wyoming. You wouldn't want to cast doubts on his future. And your mother, she's made great strides on behalf of women."

"Is this a threat, Mr. Perryman?"

"Just a warning, my dear. Sometimes we have to be careful who we do business with, else their reputations rub off on us."

Josie didn't like the way Perryman's conversation was going. To divert him, she said, "An attorney is sworn to defend those who seek her services. By the way, where is Mrs. Perryman? I want to tell her how lovely her home is."

The music ended. Perryman gave Josie a little bow and, still holding her hand, said, "I'd like you to meet her, but she isn't well. She'll join us a little later for refreshments." With his lips curved into a smile, he pulled her close, tightening his hold on her hand. "In the meantime, you little thief, be warned. Nobody gets in my way."

Shocked, Josie tried to pull away, but he held her with a steel grip.

"I don't believe for one minute that you were kidnapped by Callahan. You broke into my bank, and I don't take kindly to that. If you don't stay out of this, you'll be sorry."

"And what are you going to do if I don't?"

"When I'm governor, your father and your mother will pay for your loyalties—one way or the other."

He gave her another bow, twisted her fingers cruelly, and turned her back toward her parents. "Dr. Annie, Dan? Will you excuse me for a moment? I need to check on my wife. She isn't feeling well."

"Would you like me to examine her?" Dr. Annie inquired.

"No, it's just one of her headaches. I'm sure she'll be fine."

Dan frowned. "What was that all about, Josie? It looked like he was threatening you."

"It was nothing," Josie said quickly. If she told her father what had just happened, he'd want her to leave. Another glance about the room made it abundantly clear that Perryman needed a large income to support the lifestyle he was already enjoying, and Josie intended to prove tonight how he'd acquired that income. Perryman didn't know that a real leader set an example by honor, not wealth.

Josie tightened her resolve. She began by speaking with every woman around the dance floor. When she finished, she'd still seen no sign of the cameo. It was time to look for the cash. Perryman wouldn't have kept the money in his bank; his teller might have seen it. If it wasn't there, it had to be in his office here at home—if he had one. She'd have to search for it. To do that, she needed help.

She needed Ellie.

Callahan had made a hole almost big enough to escape through when he heard a man yell. He looked through the peephole to get a good look.

Someone had left the stage office and was running toward the hotel. "Sheriff Spencer! Sheriff Spencer!"

Will Spencer strode out of the hotel, where he must have been waiting just inside the doorway. *Watching me,* Callahan thought, *waiting for me to break out.* Will had to know that's what he was planning to do when everyone left Sharpsburg to attend Perryman's party. That's why he hadn't gone with Ellie and Josie.

The sheriff looked at the paper he'd been handed and frowned. He tapped it against the palm of his hand for a long moment, then headed across the street and into the livery stable. Moments later Callahan heard the board being lifted from its brackets, and the door opened.

Will Spencer walked in, surveyed the damage Callahan had done, and shook his head. "You wouldn't have gotten away. I was watching you. I have some news, Callahan."

"What news?"

"Your brother's been found."

Callahan let out a long, tight breath. Finally. "Is he . . . all right?"

"The captain didn't say."

"What captain? Where is he?"

"Fort Bridger. Seems a woman turned him in. She's asking for the reward."

Callahan looked surprised. "Reward?"

"Well, I thought it was a good idea. The telegraph operator is sending authorization to the army to pay it."

"Well, I'm sure my new fiancée will oblige you with a loan for the reward," Callahan snapped. "That is, if she doesn't get killed first. Why'd you let her go to that party alone?"

"I'm having a hard time believing that anybody is going to harm Josie Miller. The money is already in the bank for the bail-out."

"Perryman wants the cattle and our land. He's gone to great lengths to get them. He'll blame the holdup on me. Then he'll get rid of Josie before she proves that he's behind it all. You've allowed her to ride straight into danger."

"Perryman might be guilty of having high ambitions, but with Judge McSparren and Dan at the party and me here, he won't take a chance on being blamed for anything."

"Hell, Spencer. Are you slow or just plain stupid? Are you willing to take the chance that she won't be harmed? And if Josie's in trouble, Ellie is, too. I'm willing to make you a deal to prove it. Take me with you to Perryman's ranch. I won't escape. I give you my word."

"That's good enough for us." Roylston Sinclair stood in the doorway, a rifle tucked in the crook of his arm. "Let's go."

"And if you don't want to go with us, Sheriff, well, I guess we'll have to do this alone. Brought you a weapon, son," Teddy Miller said, handing Callahan a pistol and gun belt.

"You two old fools know what you're doing?" Spencer asked.

Roylston Sinclair was all business now. "We do, and we may be old, but we didn't get where we are by being fools. Sometimes it just pays to look like one. Callahan, we have horses saddled behind the stable. Spencer, make up your mind. Are you with us?"

With a quick nod of his head, Will pushed through the grandfathers and out the front. "Let's go," he said sharply, moving toward his own horse tied to the rail in front of the hotel, while the other three men scrambled onto the horses in the back.

With Will leading the way, they tore out of Sharpsburg in a cloud of dust.

Long before they reached Perryman's place they saw the lights and heard music. A waltz, Will thought ruefully.

"Where did so many people come from?" Sinclair asked.

"Everywhere," Spencer answered. "There are ranches scattered from here to Cheyenne and south into Colorado. Perryman is becoming a powerful man."

"What's our plan?" Teddy asked.

Roylston Sinclair reined in his horse and held up his hand. "Teddy and I will go in and check out the situation. You two look around. Make sure there's no army of hoodlums hidden behind all these buggies and flowerpots. Teddy, I believe you're looking for a poker game. You get Perryman involved in one, and I'll come back and give Will and Callahan a report."

Once the two grandfathers were inside, Will gave Callahan a long, hard look. "You're still charged with robbery. The only reason you're here is that I'm more concerned about Ellie and Josie than I am about you. And if you make one attempt to get away, I'll shoot you."

"I give you my word of honor, Spencer. Besides"—he

grinned—"I expect to be released. I have the best attorney in Wyoming."

"Maybe. I'm thinking someday Josie is going to be just as good a judge."

Judge Miller. Callahan shook his head. Josie would always get what she wanted. She'd already told the world that they were to be married. He'd told her that he wouldn't be bought, but since then he hadn't been able to banish the fantasy of changing Josie Miller's name to Josie Callahan. Now Callahan had to put that out of his mind and move on to his next step. She hadn't told him her plan, but he guessed her intentions were to open Perryman's safe. And he had to stop her from being hurt, even if it meant serving a few more years for breaking out of jail again.

20

—⚶—

Banker Perryman held up his hand, asking for silence. A tiny brown-haired woman dressed in an almond-colored gown was standing on the staircase. She smiled wanly and waited for Perryman to mount the stairs and stand beside her.

"Honored guests, my wife, Mabel. Please join us for refreshments."

On his command, the doors to the veranda were opened to reveal several candlelit tables covered with crisp white linen and mountains of food. Servants hovered beyond, ready to assist the guests who bore down on the abundant fare.

Josie stared, mesmerized, as the Perrymans walked toward her—for there, pinned on a strip of ribbon tied around Mabel Perryman's neck, was the cameo. She knew without a doubt that she had just found her evidence. The money must be nearby.

"What is it?" Ellie asked. "You look like a dying woman who's just spotted heaven's gate."

"I have. Come with me."

"Now? I'm hungry."

"And I'm about to get ambushed by the grandfathers. Hurry!"

Ellie saw them, too, and she allowed Josie to pull her behind the drapes beside the doors leading to the veranda. "I know you're going to do something you shouldn't, Josie, and I promised your grandfathers I'd keep you out of trouble."

Josie laughed. "I think you might need to protect someone else tonight. Unless I'm mistaken, Papa Miller is wearing a pistol and Grandfather Sinclair is hiding a shotgun in the flowerpot. What or who do you think they're hunting?"

"That's not hard to answer—you."

"Well, they're are not going to find me. Be still and let them pass." Moments later she whispered, "Now, come with me."

Ellie groaned. "I wish Will were here."

"And I wish Callahan were here. But they aren't, and we are. So come on."

Josie took Ellie's arm and pulled her down the corridor to the opposite wing of the house. "We're looking for Perryman's office," she said. "We have to get inside."

"I don't!" Ellie said.

"Then you'll keep watch for me. Just stand here in the hallway and let me know if anyone comes. Can you whistle?"

"I used to."

"Then if anyone comes, whistle and run."

"What should I whistle?" she asked sharply.

"I don't know—'The Battle Hymn of the Republic'!" Josie snapped, and opened the first door.

She backed away. "This looks like Mabel's sitting room," she said, and moved to the next door. "No, this isn't it either. Where is it? I know this monstrosity of a house has an office the size of Perryman's ego."

"There's a room at the other end of the corridor," Ellie said.

Josie pulled at the neckline of her dress and headed down the dark hallway. The location made sense. He'd deliberately left that part of the hallway dark so no one would notice it.

The door was locked. Josie pulled a hairpin from her hair and went to work.

"Josie, don't you dare open that door. Your mother and father are right out there. Suppose—"

"Shush! Don't talk, Ellie. Just whistle, if you need to."

"Where in tarnation is she, Sinclair?"

Roylston Sinclair stood on the third stair step and studied the veranda, where the guests had taken seats at small tables. "I don't see her anywhere. Here comes Dan. Maybe he knows."

"Mr. Sinclair," Dan said, then nodded to his father. "I thought you two had decided not to come."

"Don't be foolish, son, of course we've come. Where's Josie? Have you seen her?"

Dan frowned. "She's around here somewhere. She was dancing with Perryman earlier."

Sinclair gave Teddy a questioning look, to which Teddy nodded.

Dan sensed that they were worried and frowned. "Well, let's split up and look for her. Mr. Sinclair, you check the upstairs."

"I'll look around in here," Teddy volunteered.

Dan nodded. "Then I'll go outside and mingle with the guests."

Roylston watched Dan speak to Annie out on the veranda, but any mingling on his part was thwarted by Perryman, whose hardy voice carried inside the house to where the two grandfathers were standing.

"Dan, come and try Mabel's iced dessert. I had the ice brought down from Canada."

"Maybe later," Dan said, trying to escape his host. "Have you seen Josie?"

"Not since she honored me with a dance." Perryman frowned. "Maybe she's in the garden. It's a bit stuffy in here."

Dan hesitated, then made his way off the veranda and into the rose garden beyond. Josie had never been one to admire flowers, but she could have other reasons for leaving the house.

"Look," Teddy said, "Perryman is coming this way. Quick, up the stairs."

Scampering out of sight, they waited, watching as Perryman headed purposefully into the other wing of the house.

"After him," Sinclair said. "I don't know where he's going, but I'll bet he leads us right to Josie."

Will moved through the garden toward the house. Perryman's carriage was there. The driver had confirmed bringing Josie and Ellie to the party, but said he hadn't seen them since.

At the sound of footsteps, Will paused. Someone was walking furtively toward him. He pulled out his revolver and waited until the shadow of a man came near.

"Hold it," Will said.

"Will?"

"Dan? What are you doing out here?"

"Looking for Josie. She's not with the other guests. What are you doing?"

"Trying to keep her from getting killed. Let's go the other way. Maybe Callahan's seen her."

"Callahan's out of jail? How?"

"I let him out. I'm beginning to think that Josie is right. He didn't steal that money. But she's got some wild idea that she has to prove it tonight. Callahan's worried."

"So am I. What could she be looking for? Of course . . . Perryman's safe," Dan said. "Let's go."

Callahan made his way around the other side of the house, looking for an open door and a room that wasn't lit up like a Fourth of July fireworks display. He had to get inside unnoticed. Finally, he spotted a darkened room with French doors.

He reached for the doorknob and saw the reflection of a dim light through the glass, then movement. Someone was there. He paused, waiting for the person to be revealed.

It was Josie. She lifted a candle and held it close to the wall, at the open door of a safe. Reaching inside, she pulled out a leather bag. Callahan opened the door and stepped inside. "Josie, what in hell are you doing?"

"Callahan, you almost scared me to death! Come look at this. I think I found the saddlebag with the money."

Suddenly the shrill sound of a whistle pierced the silence.

"Damn!" he said, stumbling over the corner of a chair. It skidded toward the desk.

Josie blew out the candle.

The whistling grew louder. The study door opened

and Ellie dashed inside. "Didn't you hear me, Josie? Perryman's coming. You have to run."

"Ellie, find Will." Callahan grabbed Ellie and shoved her out the veranda door. "Let's get out of here, Josie."

"No. You don't understand. I've got it, Callahan, the saddlebag. There's money in here," she said, rifling through it. "And I feel at least one strand of pearls and a ring. I think we have all the evidence you need."

Perryman burst into the room, holding a lamp in one hand and a pistol in the other. He aimed it straight at Callahan. "Well, well. What have we here? I think you'd better give that bag to me, Miss Miller, unless you'd like me to shoot your fiancé." He set the lamp on a table and held out his hand.

"Forget it, Perryman. It's all over," Callahan said. "Ben's been found. We have the money, and he didn't take it. There are too many people who know the truth now."

Josie gasped. "Ben's been found?"

"I don't think that's going to matter," Perryman said as he gripped the gun desperately. "I own this town and everybody in it. They know which side their bread is buttered on. The only thing they know is that Josie Miller fell in love with an outlaw and that the two of them were caught red-handed trying to rob my bank. Now she's broken into my personal safe."

"Put the gun down," Callahan said, working his way across the room toward Josie. "We've seen the saddlebag. You'll have to kill us both. By the time you get off the second shot, Will Spencer will be in here."

"I don't think so. The bag will be gone and I'll regret that you and Miss Miller were killed, but it was dark and I was unable to see who the intruders were."

"Mr. Perryman," Josie said softly, "so far you're guilty

only of larcenous intent. A good lawyer will be able to get you off with nothing more than assault charges if you return the money and forgive the ranchers' loans as a show of good faith. But if you use that gun, you'll spend some time in the new prison they're building over in Rawlings. I don't think you'll like that."

There was a sound in the hallway. "Mr. Perryman? What are you doing in here?" Mabel Perryman wandered into the room, carrying a lamp.

"Go back to the party, Mabel," Perryman snapped.

Josie turned to Callahan. "Mrs. Perryman is wearing a very unusual cameo tonight."

"She certainly is," Callahan added. "I'll bet your husband gave it to you, didn't he?"

She seemed pleased. "Why, yes."

"I'll bet you've already told everyone here what a generous man he is for having done so, haven't you?" Josie asked.

Perryman moved slowly forward, set his own lamp on the table, and waved his pistol between the two captives. "You can't prove anything," he said.

"Mr. Perryman, is that a gun?" Mabel asked in astonishment.

"So it is, my dear." He held out his hand to Josie. "Give me the saddlebag, please. Or Callahan is a dead man."

"Of course." Josie feigned defeat, but then she startled Perryman by swinging the saddlebag toward him. A shot rang out. It went wide, missing Callahan's head and breaking a pane in the French doors.

Mabel screamed.

The bag landed in a clatter at Perryman's feet.

A few seconds later the music stopped.

"Give me the gun, Perryman," Callahan said. "It's over. Everyone heard the gunshot."

Perryman drew back the hammer again. Another shot rang out, then another as Josie dove toward Callahan, knocked him down, and fell on top of him.

Teddy Miller and Roylston Sinclair appeared in the doorway, stumbling over each other to come to the rescue. Will, followed by Ellie, charged in from the veranda and grabbed the banker.

Callahan lay on the floor, holding Josie against his chest, his hand cradling the back of her head.

"How'd you get out of jail?" Josie asked, touching his ear and cheek with her fingers.

"Your grandfathers broke me out."

Josie gazed at the face of the man she loved, and she smiled. "Aren't they something? Guess we're really a couple of outlaws now."

"Not this time," Judge McSparren said, stepping in from the veranda. "I came up just as you pitched Miss Ellie out the door. Started to help, but decided you were doing fine. I saw the whole thing. Is everybody all right?"

"I don't think so," Josie said, her voice fading. "I think you'd better call my mama. I've been shot."

"Dr. Annie!" Callahan let out a roar. He looked down at his bloody hand. "Josie's wounded."

Moments later the study was cleared of everyone but Josie, Dr. Annie, and Callahan, who refused to budge. Will reassured Ellie and the grandfathers, who'd been sent to the library, where they morosely shared a bottle of whiskey with the judge.

"All right, Callahan, let me have a look at her."

Callahan let go of Josie and moved behind the sofa.

Annie felt Josie's head, parting her hair to examine the wound. It was only a surface abrasion, as if the bullet had creased her and moved on—bloody, but not fatal.

"She's only fainted. Open your eyes, Josie!" Dr. Annie ordered. "Now!"

As if she were lifting a heavy curtain, Josie slowly opened her lids. "Mother, stop giving me orders."

"I heard three shots. Were you hurt anywhere else?"

Josie put her hand on her back. "The first shot missed. The second one hit my head, and the third one got me back here, I think."

Josie was rolled forward so that her nose was pressed against Annie's shoulder. She ran her fingers across Josie's back, then she started to laugh. "What on earth are you wearing, a suit of armor?"

"A corset. I had to. There was no other way. I couldn't fit into this dress."

"What's it made of?"

"Ellie said it's made of whalebone and steel."

"Well, the bullet must have hit the bone and bounced off. The only reason you fainted is because your corset's too tight. It saved your life—and probably this big outlaw's life as well."

"I think we're lucky that Perryman is the worst shot in Wyoming," Callahan said.

"Callahan?" Josie shoved her mother aside and sat up. "Are you all right?" She reached for his hand and pulled him down beside her.

"Thanks to you taking charge of the situation, as usual. What were you doing, diving in front of me? Do you realize that the bullet you took was meant for me? I should be dead."

"You should have been dead the last time you got shot. I saved you then, too."

"Just how many times do you think I'm going to let you do that?"

"I'm your attorney; it's my job. I'll save you any way I can."

"I told you, you're fired."

"Callahan, shut up and kiss me."

"Yes, ma'am," he said, and did. Not once, but twice. When Annie backed out of Perryman's office, Callahan was still kissing Josie. "I don't want her moved tonight, Callahan, but I want someone to stay with her," Annie said.

"I'll look after her," he said. "I promise."

Annie smiled and closed the door. All in all, she was satisfied that Josie had found as good a man as she had— a little rough around the edges, perhaps, but strong enough to handle a stubborn woman. Annie glanced at Laura, who waited quietly in the corridor. If Laura could grow up to be half the woman Josie had become, she and Dan Miller would be very lucky. And so would Wyoming.

21

Two days later, the Miller entourage, which now included Callahan, was back in Laramie. They left Perryman occupying the stable, while Will waited for instructions from the governor about where the trial would be held. Josie had made it plain that she wouldn't be representing the ruined banker. Before she boarded the Union Pacific headed back to Chicago to stay with her father, Mabel returned the cameo to Callahan. Ellie was already making plans to move into a house in Laramie where she would start a dressmaking business.

Callahan wired the fort, saying that he would come for Ben as soon as he made arrangements to drive the cattle from Laramie to Sharpsburg.

"What puzzles me," Josie said to Callahan as they sat in the courtyard under Lubina's watchful eye, "is the woman who claimed the reward money. Who is she?"

"That puzzles me, too. Ben was never a fighter, but he

must be in bad shape for a woman to hog-tie him and take him prisoner."

Josie stood and walked across the courtyard and into the trees. The river gurgled in the distance. She'd always found peace here, but tonight she felt as if she were standing in a bog of boiling mud searching for solid land. "Isn't that about what I did to you—take you prisoner?"

Callahan stood and followed her. He'd known this would be a hard good-bye. He'd been right. "Only because I was wounded," he said.

"Miss Josie," Lubina called out, "the *señora* won't like es for you two to be out there by yourselves. When she and Mr. Dan left, they said I was to stay with you."

Josie stopped and drew in a deep breath. "Lubina, do you remember the night Callahan came? You saw the black-and-white stallion on the ridge. You thought it meant that someone would be taken away."

"Es what that Indian say."

"Well, Bear Claw was right. And if I were you, I wouldn't push my luck. He could still come back."

Lubina left her bench in the corner of the garden and headed toward the house. "Es time for prayers," she said, and disappeared through the archway.

"You know, I like Lubina," Callahan said with a chuckle. "She's a woman who knows when to give up."

Josie walked deeper into the trees. For once in her life she didn't know what to do. She was head-over-her-whalebone-corset in love with Callahan, and he was going to leave her, unless she could find a way to stop him. "When are you going?"

"Tomorrow. I'm catching the morning train. I don't know what kind of shape Ben is in, so I wired the fort commander to hold onto him until I get there."

"You're not leaving me behind. I've decided to go with you."

"Josie. I've spent some hard hours thinking about what you were going to say when I left. You're an attorney, an educated woman who has a real future in the Wyoming Territory. I'll always be an outlaw with a criminal record. Those two things don't match."

"Says who?"

Callahan turned her to him, his eyes dark and threatening. "Don't do this, Josie. I have nothing to offer you. I don't intend to let you pay our mortgage, and I refuse to bury you on a ranch with a passel of children. You're meant for better things. When I get back with Ben, we'll go straight to the ranch."

He meant it. He was going without her. There was no place in his life for her when Ben got home. She wanted to hurt him, to make him feel what she was feeling. Callahan wasn't the only one who'd changed. She'd fallen in love. Tears brimmed her eyes. She was an attorney, yes, perhaps even a better doctor than most of the sawbones in the west, but she was a woman too, a woman in love. And the thing Dr. Annie had taught her was that a woman could have it all.

"Like you said, I'm a stubborn woman, Sims Callahan. There's no reason I can't be an attorney—even a judge—and still be your wife. But if I have to choose, I'll give up the law. Either you let me go with you, or I follow you. It's your choice."

The night air was thick and hot. He wanted to kiss her good-bye; the want thrummed in his veins, but she'd stated her case and rendered the verdict.

"Josie, don't do this," he pleaded.

She didn't answer. She simply turned and walked away.

His inability to resist following her frightened him. "Damn it, Josie. Use your head."

She turned and took in a quick breath. Then he heard the rustle of clothing. "I'd rather use my heart." She reached out, took his hand, and pulled him close.

She was wearing a dressing gown over her nightdress. The fabric was so sheer that she might have been nude. He could feel her hard nipples and her heartbeat. His mind was saying no, while his head was drifting down.

"Josie . . ." His voice was strangled so tightly that he almost couldn't speak.

"I love you, Sims Callahan, and before you leave here tonight I want to hear you say that you love me, too."

"I . . . I don't know, Josie."

"Yes, you do. You're not a liar, Callahan. I'm asking you. Tell me the truth."

"All right, Josie. Words don't come easy to me. So listen good. I may never say this again. I love you. You may already be with child, and the city of Laramie—not to mention Dan and Dr. Annie—won't take kindly to my having dishonored you. I know what it means to be threatened by a lynch mob."

"Lynch mobs are puppy play compared to what I'm going to do to you if you don't marry me," she said. "It's quite simply a case of *in pari delicto*. That means the fault is equal. And that, in plain English, means if you don't marry me and make me an honest woman, I'll sue you."

"You wouldn't."

"Oh, but I would. And when I'm through, the state of Wyoming won't be big enough to hold you. Believe me, Callahan, I'm good at lawyering. I can do it. Now, kiss me before I use my derringer to become an outlaw bride."

And he was kissing her, just as she'd wanted him to do.

For he'd taught her another thing: He'd taught her about "womanly ways." He was loving her as though hers was the only mouth in the world and he would die of wanting it.

As the faint rays of the sun began to line the early morning sky, he knew he was committed. Hell, he'd been committed since that first night when he'd opened his eyes to see this angel looking down at him. He gave up resisting.

"All right, Josie, I'll go for Ben. While I'm away, you plan the wedding. I don't know what kind of future we'll have or how we'll work out the details, but I think I'm the only man in the west who can put up with you."

"Put up with me?" She sighed, wrapping her arms around his neck. "That's called love, Callahan. It's a simple matter of *quid pro quo*. In legal terms that means I need you and you need me. The rest, we'll figure out as we go."

After giving her a kiss that made her melt, he said, "Right now, I have to figure out how to get out of here without running into your folks. I have to catch the noon train heading west, and I don't need to do any more explaining than I already have."

"Don't worry," she said, "I'll head my folks off. You just get to the barn and get the horses ready."

Callahan watched her go back inside the house, fighting every instinct that told him to go after her. What had he done? He'd asked her to marry him. Well, actually he hadn't. She'd told him he was going to be her husband. Ben was going to twist a gut laughing at this turn of events. Callahan smiled. Maybe it would work out. Ben could always teach Josie how to cook.

By sunup, Rachel had hitched a ride to the rail line on a supply wagon, hoping she wasn't making a mistake.

Federal Judge McSparren had sent a wire to the fort dismissing the charges against the Callahan brothers. They were free men. Ben had arranged for a man to take her to her land, but Rachel wasn't ready to go. Ben had a head start; he was already on his way to catch the morning train to Laramie to meet his brother, Sims—and so was she.

Rachel feared that Ben would make her stay behind if he knew she was following him. She waited until he'd picked a seat toward the front of the train and then climbed into the last car. Rachel held Moses close. He didn't think much of train travel. The other passengers glared at the dog, but something in Rachel's expression warned them not to complain.

She touched the bodice of her good dress and was reassured by the crackle of the reward money given to her by the captain. For a small fee, he had agreed to keep her oxen, wagon, and other goods for a month. If at the end of that time she hadn't returned, he'd sell them and wire her the money.

The towns raced by—Rock Springs, Thayer, Hallville, and Tipton. She began to relax, and by noon they were coming into Laramie.

Closing her eyes, she said a little prayer. Being a heathen was one of the things she'd left behind. If God had sent Jacob—Ben—to her, she intended to give Him the credit He deserved. She hoped Ben would just give her another shot at being his wife.

As the train came to a stop, Moses began to dance around, tugging on his rope. It was apparent by his excited yelps that he was ready to get off.

A crowd was gathered at the Laramie depot when Callahan arrived. They watched as Will turned Perryman over to a federal marshal who was to escort him to Rawlings, where he'd be tried for a number of crimes.

It was ironic. After all that had happened, Callahan the outlaw and Perryman the banker had reversed what they thought was their destiny. Callahan had served his time, and Perryman was about to find out what it meant to go to prison.

In the confusion of people departing and boarding, Wash, the Miller stablehand, drove up in the buggy with Josie and her traveling cases in tow.

"You're not going with me, Josie," Callahan said firmly.

"Of course not. I'm going by myself. Judge McSparren has been raving about the plans for the proposed new prison in Rawlings. I've decided I ought to see them myself."

"You know that Perryman is on the train," Callahan said. "You might not be safe. Who knows what he has planned? There could be an attempt to break him out."

"Don't worry," she said sweetly, "I can take care of myself. I have my derringer."

Callahan rolled his eyes.

"Shush, Moses!" Rachel said firmly as they left the train. But this time, there was no restraining the little dog. As soon as they stepped onto the wooden platform, he jerked free and took off down the train, his long tail waving like a broken clothesline in the wind. He darted across the tracks toward the westbound train and was gone.

The reality of what had just happened swept over her, and for the first time since all this had begun, Rachel began to cry. This was an omen. What on earth had made her think that Ben Callahan would want her? She'd been a fool. Chasing after a man who clearly didn't want her as a wife, and now she'd lost Moses. What had she been thinking?

She sat down on a trunk, sniffing. A beautiful golden-haired woman followed by a big, dark-eyed man came down the platform. "Is there something wrong?" the woman asked. "Are you in need of help?"

"Everything's wrong," she said as the tears rolled silently down her face. "But there's nothing you can do to help."

"Don't bet on that," the man said. "You might as well tell her. She won't stop until you do."

"Well, I'd appreciate it if you'd help me find my dog. He got away when I stepped off the railcar. Once I find him, I'm buying myself a ticket back the way I came."

"Well, of course," Josie said. "If you're sure that's what you want."

"I'm sure. I've got me a piece of land in the Oregon Territory and I mean to farm it, even if—if Ben would rather have his old life and his brother here in Laramie than me."

"If who?" The man frowned.

"My husband, Ben—no, my husband's name was Jacob Christopher, not Ben Callahan. You see, he lost his memory, and when it came back he was somebody else. I'd be much appreciative if you'd help me find Moses so we can get on that train, Mr . . . ?" She looked up at Callahan and Josie. "I'm sorry," she said softly. "I don't know your name."

"I think you do. I'm Sims Callahan. I'm Ben's brother."

Rachel's eyes widened. She was struck speechless. "You're Sims Callahan?"

"I am."

"Quit frowning, Callahan. You'll scare her to death." Josie sat beside Rachel and smiled.

"Are you the woman who captured my brother, Ben?" Callahan questioned.

"I didn't capture him. It was more like I rescued him, or he rescued me. It wasn't his fault I fell in love with him. He never promised me anything, Mr. Callahan. I just wanted him so bad I tried to make him love me. I thought he did. But his need to get back to you was stronger."

"But he's supposed to be back at the fort. I sent a telegram to the fort commander to hold onto him until I could get there."

She looked puzzled. "No, he's here. He just doesn't know I am. I should be on my way to my land right now, but I just couldn't go without him. He's probably in the depot."

You couldn't leave him, Callahan thought. *You tried, but you turned your back on everything you ever wanted and came after Ben, just like Josie came after me.* How did the Callahan men deserve such strong women? Women who jumped in and made rights out of wrongs, women who knew how to love at the expense of everything they held dear.

An angry stationmaster appeared in the doorway, tugging a fractious animal who turned flips in the air and howled at the top of his lungs. "I've got you, you mangy critter. Who belongs to this dog?"

Ben Callahan had rounded the front of the train and started up the street toward the livery stable when the commotion started. He stopped, then cocked his head to listen. If he hadn't known better, he'd have said that was Moses. But it couldn't be.

Could it?

He turned and retraced his steps. "Moses?"

The sound of Ben's voice turned the dog into a tail-wagging, drooling mass of gangly flesh.

At the same time, a woman's voice came from the other side of the train heading east. "Moses! Come here, you bad boy."

Moses freed himself and took off around the engine. Ben followed in hot pursuit, and as he rounded the corner, a woman came barreling into him.

"Jacob—Ben?"

"Rachel! What are you doing here?"

She laughed and cried. "I was coming to you."

He opened his arms and she flew into them. After a few seconds, Ben lifted his head, meeting the astonished gaze of the man and woman watching. "Callahan?"

Rachel let Ben go and stood back as the two brothers embraced.

Callahan leaned back to study Ben. "You look like you've had a rough time of it."

"Yep. Lost my memory and got married. But I'm fine, thanks to Rachel," Ben answered, reaching back to put his arm around her. "How'd you know I'd be on this train?" he asked Callahan.

"I didn't. I was coming after you. Didn't you get my wire to wait for me?"

"No. I left without any questions the minute the captain said I'd been cleared. What happened?"

"It was Perryman's thugs who held us up and hurt you. Josie and I caught him red-handed. He's been arrested. We're free men."

Ben looked puzzled. "Josie?"

Callahan held out his hand to Josie and drew her close. "Ben, this is Josie, my future wife."

Callahan had been right about Ben's reaction. He burst out laughing. "You're getting married?"

"I know, it's hard to believe. But it's true. You're looking at a man in love. Josie, this is my little brother, Ben."

"Thank you, Josie," Ben said. "Not just for getting us out of this mess, but for falling for this big galoot. I was beginning to think I'd have to spend the rest of my life looking after him. And this is Rachel, my wife—well, I guess I'd better say my future wife. Because I'm not certain we're really married."

The eastbound train heading for Cheyenne built up steam and began to roll out of the station. Moments later, the westbound train carrying Perryman began to move.

"I guess we'd better start thinking about adding a wing to our house, Ben."

Ben looked at Callahan. "I don't think so, big brother. Rachel and I have a piece of land in Oregon. She thinks she wants to make a farmer out of me."

This time it was Callahan's turn to laugh. "You, a farmer?"

"Who knows? I'm thinking of giving it a try. But, you've still got the ranch. You interested in running it by yourself?"

"Don't worry," Callahan said with a smile. "The way I see it, you've got Rachel and Moses, I've got Josie and a bulldog named Lubina. And you still own half of our cattle. Let's have the first double wedding in Laramie. Then we'll figure it all out."

Callahan was wrong again, a practice he was becoming used to. Instead of the first double wedding in

Laramie, it was a triple joining—in Dan and Annie's courtyard. The entire town turned out, along with some of the ranchers from Sharpsburg.

When the minister asked, "Do you, Sims Callahan, *and* Ben Callahan, *and* Will Spencer, take these women, Josie Miller, *and* Rachel Warren, *and* Eleanor Allgood, to be your wedded wives?" Callahan didn't hesitate to say, "I do." He'd already felt the weight of Josie's derringer in her pocket as she'd joined him at the altar. And he'd grinned all the way through the ceremony as he remembered that first night he'd loved Josie on the veranda.

Will's "You betcha" drew glances of envy from the men. And Ben's "Oh, yes" made the women smile.

The brides, all dressed in new gowns stitched by Ellie herself, answered the same question in unison with a resounding, "Yes, sir."

The minister responded with his own smile and said, "I now pronounce you man and wife. Man and wife. Man and wife. You may kiss your brides."

Will and Ellie's kiss was serious. Ben and Rachel's was gentle. Callahan lifted Josie off the ground, kissed her soundly, and whispered, "Can we get out of here now? I want to take you back to the hotel and ravish you."

Josie caught her breath and shook her head. "*Sine qua non.*"

"I'm afraid to ask what that means."

"It means you have to get through the reception before you get to the bed."

As it turned out, after making a quick appearance with their guests and sampling Lubina's wedding cake, all three couples decided the reception would proceed very well without the brides and grooms.

Later that night, a wide-awake guest pounded on his

hotel room wall and threatened to call the sheriff if the occupants didn't quiet down.

Will Spencer yelled out, "I *am* the sheriff."

Ben Callahan said, "We've got God on our side."

And Sims Callahan roared, "So sue us!" and kissed Josie again.

EPILOGUE

Cheyenne, Wyoming—July 1890

Callahan followed Josie down the aisle of the elaborate Cheyenne Opera House, where the Wyoming statehood celebration was taking place. His hand rested possessively on her back. She still stirred him, this woman he'd married eight years ago. Tonight her hair was carefully styled in a mess of curls on the back of her head. The chandelier overhead caught the diamonds Lubina had threaded through them and turned them into a crown of starlight. She was wearing a silk dress with some kind of flowing cape that concealed her advanced state of pregnancy—the latest creation by the designer simply known as *Ellie*.

Ellie was extremely satisfied that she'd finished the gown with so little time on her hands. After all, little Will was only three weeks old.

Nodding at the dignitaries and politicians, Josie took her seat at the end of a long row reserved for the Millers.

Now silver-haired, Dan had earned that distinction due to his ongoing negotiations with the Indians and later his efforts to have Wyoming declared a state. He'd been offered a distinguished job in Washington, but he wouldn't leave Dr. Annie, and Wyoming needed her.

Ben and Rachel had come from their ranch in Oregon. They'd brought Eli, the boy they adopted when his parents were killed by a flood, and their daughter, a dark-haired little beauty who had come as a surprise to a woman who'd thought she was barren. They'd also brought a gift to Josie—a young black-and-white filly who was a descendant of the black-and-white stallion who appeared whenever something special occurred in the lives of the Callahan women.

Josie and Callahan had left six-year-old Ted, named for his Papa Teddy, and four-year-old Clair, more formally known as Sinclair, at the hotel with Lubina. Exposing two impressionable boys to the grandfathers was a risk that Josie limited. She wasn't ready for Clair to adopt the first half of his name or for Ted to learn to play poker. Josie was already suspicious of her sister Laura's relationship with the two old rascals. Laura had been with the grandfathers for almost a year while she attended finishing school, and she was up to something, Josie could tell.

"Too bad it's not Lily Langtry or Buffalo Bill Cody we've come to see," Callahan said under his breath.

"Stop scowling, outlaw," she whispered lovingly.

"I'm not scowling. I'm practicing my husband-of-the-most-famous-judge-in-the-new-state-of-Wyoming look."

"Oh, I thought it was your President-of-the-Wyoming-Cattleman's-Association look."

Callahan grinned, then turned serious. "How long is this ceremony going to last? You know Annie said this baby could come any time. We're too far from the ranch to suit me."

"With Mama here, you don't have to worry. But I've had two children. I'm an old hand at this. Believe me, she won't arrive before next week," Josie said confidently.

Callahan didn't argue. He'd stopped arguing with his take-charge wife long ago. If she said the baby would arrive next week, she would. Then he realized exactly what Josie had said and smiled. "She? After two sons, we're going to have a girl? How do you know?"

"Lubina said so, and you know I never contradict Lubina."

"You always contradict Lubina. You just don't let her hear you do it." He put his arm across the back of Josie's seat. He was never comfortable unless he was touching her. When his fingertips cupped her shoulder, she glanced at him with the stormy look he'd come to love.

"When does this shindig get started? I want to get you back to our room and . . . Ah, hell! When can we—?"

"Any minute now the celebration will begin," she said, deliberately ignoring his question. She remembered the first time he'd "loved" her, and she shivered. That had never changed. "There'll be speeches. Governor Warren will raise the state flag. But first Laura is going to sing that patriotic song Francis Scott Key wrote."

Callahan grinned. "I know. I know. We have to wait. Look," he said, giving her a pained smile. "They've raised the curtain. There's Laura."

"I told you the dress would be perfect, Sinclair," Teddy Miller said in his normal P.T. Barnum voice.

Sinclair shook his head in disagreement. "I still think all those stars and stripes are gaudy. Statehood for Wyoming is a serious affair. She should be wearing something more . . . more stately. Next time we'll hire the best fashion consultants in New York for our Laura."

"Hush," Dr. Annie said. "I knew better than to turn her over to the two of you. Now she wants to study opera. That is not what I have in mind for my youngest daughter."

Teddy cleared his throat. "But she's not—"

"Quiet, Miller," Roylston Sinclair said with a scowl. "They'll find out soon enough she's going on the stage."

"Ladies and gentlemen," the elderly Judge McSparren said. "Please rise as we hear our national anthem being sung by our very own Laura Miller."

Annie caught her husband's hand and squeezed it. "How are we going to stop her, Dan? A performer? I wanted so much more for her."

"She's our daughter, Annie. She'll be the kind of woman she chooses to be."

On the stage, Laura Miller looked at the grandfathers, gave them a big wink, and started to sing.

At the end of the row, Josie felt a stirring, almost as if the child inside her was impatient, knowing she was about to become another independent woman of Wyoming. "Callahan," Josie whispered, "maybe I was wrong about coming here tonight."

"Judge Josie Callahan, wrong? That must be a first. Darlin', you want to skip all this and get back to the hotel? We don't need to see Wyoming celebrate becoming a state; we've lived it."

Josie laid her head on her husband's shoulder and touched her stomach with her hand. "Yes, we have."

About the Author

With more than forty books in print, award-winning author Sandra Chastain still considers herself a storyteller rather than a writer, and feels extraordinarily lucky that readers and reviewers have liked her work. She has been nominated for a Rita by Romance Writers of America and for a Career Achievement Award from *Romantic Times* magazine. *The Redhead and the Preacher* was named one of the five favorite books of the year by the members of RWA. Among her other honors, she has been awarded a Maggie by Georgia Romance Writers, a Silver Pen Award, and named Favorite Author of the Year by *Affair de Coeur,* Best Romance Love and Laughter by *Romantic Times*, and nominated as Georgia Author of the Year. Her last two books have been Featured Alternate Selections of the Doubleday Book-of-the-Month Club.

She enjoys hearing from her readers.
Her address is P.O. Box 67, Smyrna, GA 30081
or www.romancejournal.com